paging
the dead

paging the dead

A FAMILY HISTORY MYSTERY

brynn bonner

GALLERY BOOKS

NEW YORK LONDON TORONTO SYDNEY NEW DELHI

G

Gallery Books
A Division of Simon & Schuster, Inc.
1230 Avenue of the Americas
New York, NY 10020

First Gallery Books trade paperback edition March 2013

GALLERY BOOKS and colophon are registered trademarks of Simon & Schuster, Inc.

For information about special discounts for bulk purchases, please contact Simon & Schuster Special Sales at 1-866-506-1949 or business@simonandschuster.com

The Simon & Schuster Speakers Bureau can bring authors to your live event. For more information or to book an event contact the Simon & Schuster Speakers Bureau at 1-866-248-3049 or visit our website at www.simonspeakers.com.

Designed by Akasha Archer

Manufactured in the United States of America

10 9 8 7 6 5 4 3 2 1

Library of Congress Cataloging-in-Publication Data

Bonner, Brynn
    Paging the dead: a family history mystery : a novel / by Brynn Bonner.—
First Gallery Books trade paperback edition.
    pages cm
    Summary: "When a professional genealogist who teaches classes in family history scrapbooking is implicated in the murder of her client, she starts her own investigation to clear her name—and avoid jail!"—Provided by publisher. 1. Women genealogists—Fiction. 2. Women mediums—Fiction. 3. Scrapbooking—Fiction. I. Title.
PS3608.A7828P34 2013
813'.6—dc23
                                                    2012042150

ISBN 978-1-4516-6186-6
ISBN 978-1-4516-6188-0 (ebook)

For Brenda Upchurch Smart,
a fine writer and a fine friend.
Gone too soon.

acknowledgments

With heartfelt thanks to my six sages and paladins: Margaret Maron, Sarah Shaber, Diane Chamberlain, Kathy Trocheck (aka Mary Kay Andrews), Katy Munger and Alex Sokoloff for your counsel, support and friendship. I'm privileged to be one of the Weymouth Seven. 'Tis a wondrous gift! Thanks also to the members of the Cary Writers' Group for early reading and input. Many thanks to my agent, Cynthia Manson, for her steadfastness and tenaciousness and to my editor, Micki Nuding, for her invaluable guidance. Most of all, thanks to my family for supporting me, always, as we make our own family history.

paging
the dead

one

Every family has secrets. Skeletons in the closet, a rotten apple dangling from a blighted limb on the family tree, the crazy aunt hidden away in the attic. And while the families who hire me to trace their family lineage pay me handsomely to haul their secrets into the light, usually they don't thank me for it in the end. Such is the genealogist's lot.

Today was an exception. The client sitting across from me was about to be thrilled. Dorothy Pritchett Porter spread her bejeweled fingers on her chest and looked to me expectantly. Milking the drama, I held out my fist and opened my fingers like a flower blossoming. All I needed was a hallelujah choir and a shaft of light streaming down on my palm, which held a ruby and diamond ring that could have choked a moose.

I congratulated myself as the woman's jowly jaw dropped. I had definitely flabbered her gast, smacked her gob. If I'd had a feather handy I could have knocked her over with it. I, Sophreena Angelica McClure, have done it again. I have dazzled a client. With some unconventional help to be sure, but I couldn't let on about that.

I only wished all the effort could have been for a client I liked more. Dorothy Porter is what my mother would've called a woman of breeding. I thought maybe there'd been some over-breeding somewhere along the line. Still, I was thrilled with the way her flinty blue eyes lit up at the sight of this long lost bauble and gladder still to see a smile overtake her inner sourpuss. I got a whiff of a bonus in the offing.

"I've been searching for this for years, how in the world did you ever find it?" Dorothy asked breathlessly, reaching out to pluck the ring from my hand. "*Where* did you find it?"

"Oh, I can't give away my secret methods," I said, my voice sing-songy. "Let's just say I am very, very good at what I do."

My business partner, Esme Sabatier, was seated next to me on the *divan*, as Dorothy insisted on calling the molting velvet monstrosity that occupied half her sitting room. Esme made a sound halfway between a *harumph* and a swear word in French. I covered with a cough and Dorothy went right on admiring the way the light caught those diamonds while I gave Esme my sternest look.

Alas, Esme is immune. She rolled her eyes, looking around for an escape route. Esme hates dealing with clients, Dorothy in particular. But she'd had to cart me out here since my car was in the shop and I can't drive her hulking SUV because it's a stick, not to mention I can't see over the steering wheel.

I gave Dorothy a smile. "Actually, what I did was put together everything I'd learned about your grandmother to get to know the kind of person she was and when I saw that box among her things in the attic I knew at once it was a puzzle box with a secret compartment. I've seen them before. I thought there was a good chance that's where she would have hidden the ring for safekeeping. Here, let me show you how it works."

I took the box from the side table and demonstrated the various sliding, pulling and pushing manipulations required to open the secret compartment.

"And to think," Dorothy said, her eyes wide. "I almost threw that box out when we moved my grandmother's things to the attic. You can't imagine what this means to me."

"Oh, Lorda mercy, she's gonna cry," Esme said, leaning toward me and whispering out of the side of her mouth. "Get me outta here, quick."

Just at that moment little Cassidy Garrison, Dorothy's great-niece, came literally skipping into the room, ending Esme's mutterings. Esme does not brook foolishness from adults, but she's got a big ol' mushy spot for kids.

Cassidy perched like a little bird on the arm of Dorothy's chair and I marveled at the transformation in the woman. She beamed as she slid an arm around the child. Cassidy was six years old but small for her age. She had the blond hair and clear blue eyes that ran through the Pritchett line.

"Say hello," Dorothy instructed, hugging Cassidy in tight.

Cassidy gave us a shy wave, then the ring caught her eye. "Ooh, that's pretty, Auntie Dot," she cooed, fingering the stones.

"It's more than pretty," Dorothy said. "This is the Pritchett family ring. It's belonged to our ancestors for generations. It's an heirloom from an illustrious family—our family. Remember, I told you I hired these two ladies to research our

Pritchett family tree so you'd know where you came from. That's important."

"Oh," Cassidy said, clearly underwhelmed. She tangled her fingers in the triple ropes of pearls draping Dorothy's neck. That necklace was also a family heirloom and I couldn't believe the officious Dorothy was allowing Cassidy to play with the pearls and muss her perfectly coiffed hair, but she made no attempt to stay the child's busy hands.

"I'm glad you're pleased, Mrs. Porter. You have our report and of course we'll be working diligently on your family heritage scrapbooks over the next couple of weeks. You have a fine family, lots of truly accomplished people," I said, remembering how I'd struggled to shear a couple of black sheep in one branch without compromising my genealogist's integrity. "I'm going to leave a couple of our business cards here with you," I plowed on, placing them on the marble-topped coffee table. "We'd appreciate it if you'd recommend us to your friends."

"Yes, of course," Dorothy said, still mesmerized by the ring. Then she seemed to snap out of it. "But now, don't forget." She held up a finger and actually wagged it at me like a school marm. "You absolutely must have the scrapbooks finished for my Founders' Day open house on the Friday before the Honeysuckle Festival. I'll have important guests and I want those books on display. That is specifically stipulated in our contract." She eyed us as if we were trying to put one over on her. "You do not get your final payment if you don't deliver."

"Of course," I said, "you'll have them in ample time." I felt the divan vibrate as Esme's aggravation grew.

We exited quickly once we'd stood to go. The sight of Esme and me side-by-side makes people want to snicker. Some try to hide it and nearly bust a gut holding it in while others just let go and laugh right in our faces.

I know we make a funny-looking pair. I'm short. So short I sometimes don't make the cut at the amusement park attractions where signs decree YOU MUST BE THIS TALL TO RIDE. If I wear heels, don't slouch and pouf my hair up I can do five feet even. I'm thirty-one years old and part Asian—maybe, that's a whole 'nother story—and part some pale Celtic tribe. My eyes are brown and my hair borrowed from both sides of my heritage and settled at a light auburn that can't decide if it wants to be straight or curly. Sometimes I wear contacts, but most of the time I wear glasses in a style once worn only by the hopelessly nerdy. Now the hipster crowd has adopted the look and made me fashionable. I look small and meek. I am not meek.

Esme is six foot two in her stocking feet and doesn't cotton to flat shoes. She's descended from sturdy Creole stock and is the color of a mocha latte. She's fifty-two years old and the way she sees it she's earned a pass on pulling her punches. Esme's got both altitude *and* attitude. She looks regal and mellow. Esme is not mellow.

We've been partners in our family history research business for five years. Since I'm accustomed to looking at life across multiple generations, five years should seem like the blink of an eye, but I can hardly remember what my life was like before Esme and can't imagine life without her, despite how she likes to needle me.

"Wait 'til I tell the others about this one," she said, chuckling as she climbed behind the wheel. " 'I'm very, very good at what I do,'" she mimicked my voice, which is small like the rest of me.

Now it was my turn for an eye roll. "What did you expect me to say? *'Well, Mrs. Porter, we use rather unusual research methods. My sidekick here has the gift and your dearly departed Granny told her where she put that ring. Anything else you want to ask while we've got her on the line?'"*

"I'll not be asking the poor woman anything else. Let her rest in peace. I got the feeling she had a troublesome life. Anyway, you know very well I don't appreciate being called on to do family therapy from the great beyond. If they didn't get their stuff together here on earth they got all eternity to work on their issues. And honest to Pete, sometimes I don't think even that'll be long enough."

Esme gunned out onto Larkwood Drive, which would take us down out of the rarefied air of Crescent Hill and back into Morningside Village where the normal people live, and continued her rant. "All I want to know from the departed is where did they put the will, the cash bonds, the jewelry. Did he or didn't he father that child? Who is that standing beside them in the photo? That kind of thing usually comes through pretty clear but the other stuff is just gobbledygook. I can't make heads nor tails out of it most of the time."

I'd heard this speech from Esme many times so I made some agreement noises as I gazed out the window at the green lawns, a luxury only those in this part of town could afford what with the relentless North Carolina sun intent on parching every sprig. It had been a dry June and people in our middle-class neighborhood had made their peace with some browning of the turf, but the rich continued to sprinkle with abandon.

Not that I have anything against rich people. After all, only the well heeled can afford to hire us. But I don't envy them either. After working closely with so many rich families I've seen the truth in that old saw about money not buying happiness.

We don't get much work from regular families. Most make do with their own DIY genealogists—the great-aunt who spends vacations visiting courthouses and graveyards, or the kid who's assigned a school project and gets hooked on filling out the family tree.

My mother had set the hook for me. She was adopted and all her life longed to know about her origins. For her it hadn't been a hobby, it had been her personal Moby Dick. And now that she's gone I continue the hunt for her.

I meant it when I told Dorothy I'm good at what I do. I studied hard and I work hard. But Esme's unorthodox contribution to our success is a secret we guard closely. First off, it sounds flaky when you say it out loud, and in the genealogy world where everything is predicated on hard facts and documentation this could quickly get me a reputation as a kook. Secondly, Esme's gift is vague and maddeningly temperamental.

I was a total skeptic in the beginning, but I've seen it work too many times now to have doubts.

I glanced at my watch, nearly three. "We're going to have to hurry along with our errands. The others will be waiting."

"Marydale will get everything ready if we run late."

The *others* are our four closest friends. We get together

weekly to work on our family history projects. At least that's how the friendships started.

Marydale Thompson, the mother hen of the group, owns a papercraft shop in downtown Morningside called Keepsake Corner. She'd invited me—hounded me, actually—to teach a class on family heritage scrapbooking a few years ago. I'd resisted. I didn't think we'd get much interest. Shows how much I know. The class filled immediately and we'd started a waiting list. The others had all been in that first class. It was the perfect storm of personalities, interests and unidentifiable chemistry and we'd bonded. When the class was over we didn't want to give up one another's company so we kept going as sort of an informal club.

Esme hummed a song her choir was learning as we drove out to the big box store to buy plastic bins for Dorothy's family memorabilia. On principle I don't like giving the chain stores business, but it's the only place I can find uncoated pure polyethylene boxes. For full-service customers like Dorothy we organize and store the family history artifacts in archival-quality materials and containers. Although we charge a hefty fee—one that sometimes makes the client's eyes bug out—we earn every penny. It's tedious work. For Dorothy we were not only doing that, we were actually constructing her scrapbooks for her. Heaven forbid she should have to learn to operate a glue stick.

Our next stop was the garden nursery to pick up drought-resistant plants for our patio. As we were cruising along in the greenhouse I almost ran my sled into a man who was bent over checking out the Japanese boxwoods.

As he turned in response to my apology I realized it was Jeremy Garrison, Cassidy's father. From his suit and tie I gathered he'd probably come straight from the bank where he worked as some kind of manager.

"Hi, there," I said. "We just saw your daughter over at your Aunt Dorothy's house."

"Oh, hey, Sophreena," he said, stumbling a little over my name as people often do. My grandmothers' names were Sophie and Doreen and my parents didn't want to play favorites.

"Yeah, her day camp was closed today," he said, "and she decided she'd rather go to Dorothy's than to work with her grandmother or me. Course, why wouldn't she? Dorothy spoils her rotten."

I'd noticed that Jeremy always skipped the *aunt* honorific, but given his frosty relationship with Dorothy I figured he didn't feel inclined to honor a kinship he didn't feel.

"You two about done with the illustrious Pritchett family?" he asked. His tone was light, but I heard an edge. Whereas Dorothy had used the word *illustrious* reverently, Jeremy packed it with sarcasm.

"Wrapping it up," I said, resisting the urge to crow about finding the ring. There's an understanding between genealogist and client that their family business will be held in confidence. And even though Jeremy was a family member, his aunt Dorothy alternately tried to pull him into the family fold one minute and push him out the next.

"It's weird," Jeremy said, frowning, "you two probably know more about my family than I do."

"The scrapbooks will be done for your aunt's open house. They'll document your family line back through several generations. Maybe those will help."

I thought Jeremy smirked, but maybe it was a smile. "I'll have to study up, I guess."

Esme made a show of checking her watch and I got the message. I said a quick goodbye and we hustled to the checkout. But I was thinking about Jeremy and Dorothy as we loaded everything into the back of the SUV, and still pondering as Esme pulled into the gas station a few minutes later and got out to fill the ever-thirsty tank. I noticed one of the plants had fallen over and went around to open the hatch and right it.

"That is one family dynamic I just can't figure," I said to Esme as she watched the price ticker fly by on the pump. "It's clear Jeremy has no real affection for his aunt Dorothy, yet he visits her regularly and he lets Cassidy spend time with her, too. What's the deal?"

"A deal is exactly what it is," Esme said. "Dorothy's got money and no heirs. Jeremy may not like Dorothy but I imagine he's got admiration aplenty for her money. Cassidy's the trump card. She's crazy about that kid." Then her expression softened. "And why wouldn't she be? She *is* cute as a button, and smart, too."

She snatched her receipt from the pump and glared at it and I went around to begin the climb up into the passenger side of the SUV. Where are ropes and pulleys when you need them?

"Considering how Dorothy and her sister fight, wouldn't you think Jeremy's kissing up to Dorothy might seem like disloyalty to his mother?" I asked.

"Well, if I were Ingrid I'd sure think so, but maybe she's a bigger person than I am." Esme swiveled her head and shot me a warning look over her sunglasses. "And no smart remarks about my size, girly. You know what I mean." She blew out a breath. "All I've got to say is this job is nearly over and I'll be glad to be done with Dorothy Pritchett Porter *forever*."

two

As Esme predicted by the time we got back to our place Marydale had the food set out and everyone had taken up their customary spots in our living room.

Marydale Thompson had been widowed very young and raised a son and a daughter on her own. She and my mother had been good friends and I'd grown up with Marydale's kids as the cousins I never had. They both live in California now and don't get back to see her as much as any of them would like, so we're the beneficiaries of Marydale's pent-up need to mother.

"There you two are," she said, hooking a strand of salt and pepper hair behind her ear. "I was beginning to think we should send out the hounds."

Esme sniffed. "If by *hounds* you mean your two yappy Westies, we'd be lost forever. Their short legs don't cover much territory." She bent to give Gadget a scratch behind his ears to show she meant no offense and Sprocket came skittering over to horn in on the action.

"They make up in tenacity what they lack in size," Winston

Lovett said. He dangled his big hand over the edge of the couch cushion and snapped his fingers. Gadget came running and Winston scooped him up and cradled him in his lap. The little dog looked mighty pleased.

At sixty-five, Winston is the elder of our tribe. He's lived in Morningside all his life, knows practically everyone in town and is privy to all the peccadilloes and backroom deals that go on among Morningside's citizenry. Up until two years ago he'd owned and operated Sugar Magnolias, the best bakery for miles around. Now that he's retired he no longer has to get up before the roosters every day, but he still loves to bake and we benefit from that, too.

It usually takes us a while to get down to any actual business. We like to gab and eat first and since Esme and I had skipped lunch we set in on the food with enthusiasm.

Jackson Ford had taken his usual seat, a straight-backed chair at the end of the coffee table. He was dressed in his typical jeans and work boots. He's a landscape architect and at only thirty-two he already owns a thriving business. His progress on his family history has been stalled for a while now but he still hangs out with us.

Jack is my best male friend. I've never had a close guy friend, not one like him, anyway, and it's confusing sometimes.

"You two give your report to the duchess?" Winston asked, dropping crumbs as he bit into one of the croissants he'd brought to share. Gadget's tiny tongue shot out to capture the unexpected treat and I could have sworn the little mutt smiled.

"Oh, yes, we did," Esme said, chuckling. "Wait'll y'all hear how that went."

As I said, there's a sort of code among genealogists that we keep confidences, but we do consult amongst ourselves. And in the "ancient history club," as Winston's wife, Patsy, disparagingly calls us, we all consider ourselves genealogists so we feel free to share. Not once had a confidence ever left this room—at least not that I'd gotten wind of. And since Morningside's a small town, I would've definitely caught the scent.

"Well, come on, dish!" said Colette Newsome, the amulets on her bracelet jangling as she gestured encouragement to Esme.

Colette, Coco to all of us, is in her mid-forties and is what might be called a "seeker." She's always having her chakras adjusted, her auras read or her head bumps interpreted. She's dabbled in numerology, palmistry, aromatherapy and reflexology. She's a talented potter and makes a good living at it. Tourists snap up her wares by the armload from the Morningside Craft Co-op and she gets lots of commissions.

Esme grabbed another ham biscuit from the tray Marydale had brought and launched into the story of how we'd restored Grandma Pritchett's bling to its rightful owner. There was no need to be coy about how we found it with this group. They know all about Esme's being a large medium—my joke, which Esme doesn't appreciate.

She was just getting to the good part—the part where she got to mock me—when my cell phone rang. I didn't recognize the number and thought it might be a potential client so I stepped into the kitchen to answer.

When I came back to the living room a few minutes later the others looked my way and the laughter and chatter stopped cold. I struggled to find words, gulping like an air-drowning fish.

"Sophreena, what's wrong?" Esme asked.

"It's Dorothy. Mrs. Pritchett. I mean Mrs. Porter. Mrs. Pritchett Porter," I sputtered, then forced myself to stop and draw a breath. "Esme, she's dead. Dorothy's dead. She's been murdered."

three

BY THE TIME THE POLICE ARRIVED TO QUESTION US I'D stopped shaking and willed myself into a state of calm. Esme, on the other hand, was all het up and taking it very personally that Dorothy had managed to get herself dead and had somehow involved us in it.

Not that Esme's callous. Just the opposite—she cares so deeply that if she doesn't get mad, sadness overcomes her. When something bad happens she needs to find someone to pin it on so she can channel it all out.

The only question I'd thought to ask while I was on the phone with the detective was about Cassidy. He'd assured me the girl was okay and that whatever had happened to Dorothy, it had happened after Cassidy left.

Our card had been found at the scene and they'd learned we'd been at Dorothy's earlier in the day. The detective told me they'd very much like to have a chat while things were still fresh in our minds. His tone was pleasant, but he made it clear it wasn't optional.

Even in my stupor, when I opened the door to the

detectives I had to suppress a snicker. Either their com-
manding officer had a sense of humor or one of them had
ticked somebody off. The male detective identified himself
as Denton Carlson. He was about fifty, black, burly and
at least six foot five. His partner, Jennifer Jeffers, wasn't
much taller than me. She must've barely made the height
requirement for the force. She was a green-eyed strawberry
blonde and her freckled skin was pale against the dark
business suit she'd adopted to cadge whatever authority
she could get.

She looked up at Esme then caught my eye and an understanding passed between us. Shorty Solidarity.

As I motioned for the detectives to sit at the kitchen table
I could hear the others out in the living room whispering.
They were clustered around the door and I only hoped they
wouldn't lean on it and fall into a pile on the kitchen floor
like some Three Stooges skit.

"Could I offer you some coffee or tea?" I asked, my mother's hospitality training kicking in despite the circumstances.

"Coffee would be great," Detective Carlson said and
Jeffers nodded. I caught Carlson checking out the dinette
chairs as if wondering whether they'd support him. I considered telling him they'd been Esme-tested, but thought better
of it since she was in a mood.

She went to the cupboard and retrieved four mugs while I
launched a brew in the Mr. Coffee. She was humming softly,
but it wasn't a contented hum, it was more like a thrum or a
drone. As she leaned in to set the mugs down she muttered,
"Denny and Jenny? Seriously?"

The names hadn't registered on me and I had to choke down an unseemly giggle. Our client had been murdered. That was about as serious as things get. But dark humor is another way Esme copes and sometimes she sucks me right in.

Jeffers began the questioning. I admired her methodical approach and tried to match it as I detailed our dealings with Dorothy up to and including that afternoon's meeting. "She'd expressed a particular interest in anything we might learn that would help her locate an heirloom piece of jewelry, a ring that had been in the family for many generations."

Jeffers seemed unfamiliar with the whole concept of genealogy and couldn't wrap her mind around the fact that this was how Esme and I earn a living.

"So, she hired you to find a ring?" she asked.

"Not directly," I said. "She hired us to trace her family lineage. Which we did, back to the British Isles. The family name is occupational. It comes from a word meaning 'maker of pointy weapons,'" I said, then realized I was babbling. "Anyway, finding the ring was just a lucky bonus."

"And you told me on the phone earlier," Denton Carlson interjected, "that you did locate the ring and that you handed it over to Mrs. Porter earlier today?"

"Yes," I said, "she put it on her finger. You didn't see it?"

Jeffers ignored the question. "Could you describe this ring?" she asked. She might as well have said, *Could you describe this unicorn?* She eyed me suspiciously. So much for our moment of solidarity.

I tried not to be insulted. These two didn't know us and they were simply doing their jobs. I closed my eyes and pictured the ring. "A center ruby, quite large, and faceted. I'm not a gem expert, but I think they call it a brilliant cut. There were rows of diamonds surrounding it, two rows, maybe three."

"How large would you say the ruby was?" Jeffers asked, holding her thumb and forefinger to form a circle.

"Big enough to be considered a weapon in some states," Esme cut in, clearly growing impatient with both the pace and the focus of the interview.

Detective Carlson either registered a fleeting smile or he had a facial tic, I couldn't tell which. He turned his attention to Esme and took the lead in the interview. Jeffers didn't seem to mind that he'd hijacked the conversation and I figured this must be their regular routine. Esme and I do that sometimes when interviewing clients. It helps keep things moving.

"So you two spent a lot of time with Mrs. Porter?" Carlson asked, pulling a small notebook from his pocket and clicking a ballpoint pen as if it were a starter's pistol.

"Too much," Esme said, with characteristic, if ill-advised, candor. "Not to speak ill of the dead, but a little bit of the woman went a long way."

"You didn't get on well with her?" Carlson asked, staring at his little pad.

"Oh, we got on fine," Esme said. "I get along with every-body. It's just she was a rich woman with a rich woman's ex-pectations. Used to calling the shots." Esme drew in a sharp breath. "Oh, dear Lord, that was a bad choice of words. Was she shot? Is that how she died?"

"We'll get to that," Carlson said, his eyes glued on Esme. "Now, is there anyone you can think of who might have a grudge against Mrs. Porter? Any bad blood in this family you investigated?"

"Oh, honey," Esme said, turning sideways to put her arm along the back of her chair, "you're gonna need a bigger notebook." She wiggled her finger at his small tablet.

"Yeah?" he said. "Tell me about it."

"Where do we start?" Esme said. "First there's her nephew, Jeremy Garrison. He talked her into some investments a few months back and they tanked. He's been in the doghouse ever since, probably even before that just on general principle. And believe me, she got off on making him lick her boots."

Jeffers showed Carlson something in her own notepad. "Her sister's son, she's trying to reach him."

"Uh-huh," Esme said. "And there's you another one." She motioned for Carlson to write. "Her sister, Ingrid. She and Dorothy were always gettin' into it. I never heard such caterwaulin'. "

I was growing increasingly uncomfortable with how free Esme was being with both information and her opinions.

"Mrs. Porter and her sister had a strained relationship," I cut in, trying to tamp down the tone. "Ingrid only recently moved back here after years away. There were some hard feelings over the distribution of their parents' estate. But Mrs. Porter told us she was eager to heal those old wounds. She and her sister were trying to work things out."

"It was a workout, all right," Esme mumbled.

"Anybody else we might want to talk with?" Carlson asked, turning back to Esme, who was obviously a more interesting interview subject than me.

"Let me see," Esme said, staring up at the ceiling. "I guess you'll want to speak with her soon-would've-been-ex-husband. Isn't that the first person you people suspect?"

Carlson ignored the question. "Anyone else who should be on our radar?" he asked and this time he made no attempt to hide a wry smile.

Esme sighed. I could tell she'd about spent her anger. "Well, I understand she was tough on all her service people: handymen, gardeners, like that. And I happen to know she blackballed a couple trying to get into the country club and they were pretty cheesed off at her; you might want to check that out."

I heard rumblings from the living room and knew Marydale was taking credit for having brought us that tidbit of gossip.

Carlson heard it too, and raised an eyebrow.

"It's our genealogy group," I explained. "We have a regular Tuesday meeting. They're waiting for us."

"Well, I guess we need to wrap this up, then," Carlson said, giving me a tight smile. It was quite unlike the one he'd bestowed on Esme. "Just a couple more questions. You're absolutely certain Mrs. Porter had this ring in her possession when you left her this afternoon?"

"Right there," Esme said, holding up her right hand and pointing to her ring finger. "She had it in her possession, all right, and if it's gone you can be sure somebody had to fight her to get it." Esme stopped again and her eyes widened. "Did they? Did they beat on her? Oh, Lord in heaven, nobody deserves that! How *did* she die?"

"I'm sorry," Carlson said. "I can't release that information."

Esme muttered under her breath and I didn't need a good grasp of French to get her meaning.

"And how did you ladies pass the rest of the afternoon?" Carlson asked casually, leaning back in his chair and making a ceremony of putting his notebook into his inside jacket pocket and clicking his ballpoint before he put it away.

He didn't say, *Can you account for your whereabouts*, but that's what I heard. It was only then that I realized he might consider us actual suspects in Dorothy's murder.

It must have occurred to Esme as well. When I looked over she was pulling her arm off the back of the chair and leaning forward, her eyes narrowed.

I piped up before she could speak and gave the man our itinerary for the afternoon, doing mental inventory about how we might prove it. We had time-stamped receipts from the big box store and from the plant nursery. And *maybe* Esme had the one from the service station. She's careless about receipts. Out of sheer habit I began to figure a timeline, then realized I had no idea what time Dorothy died, or how she died—or why. I felt tears welling up and was surprised. How was it that I cared more for Dorothy in death than I had in life? I pictured her radiant smile when she'd first seen the ring and remembered how tender she was with Cassidy. Who could have known those would be among the last moments of her life? And now who would mourn her? Who would miss her?

Losing my parents was horrific and it had left a big hole in my heart. I still miss them every day. My mother died a wasting death over many months. It was awful, but at least we'd had the chance to say everything we wanted to say to each other. My dad died three years later in a car wreck. When last I'd seen him we'd tossed off a casual "See you later," as if we had all the time in the world stretching out before us.

But we didn't.

"We may need to talk with you again," Carlson was saying, and I realized they had stood to leave. "Will you be in town for the next few days?"

"We'll be right here, Detective Carlson," I said, this time holding out a hand to quell Esme. "And we'll do anything we can to help."

four

"DID YOU HEAR HIM?" ESME ASKED THE OTHERS INDIGNANTLY after the detectives had gone and we'd all gathered back in the living room. "He told us not to leave town, just like in the cop shows."

"Now, Esme," Marydale said soothingly, "he didn't say that."

"He might as well have," Esme insisted. "I didn't like his attitude."

"Esme," I said, "you can bluster all you want; Dorothy Porter is still going to be dead. It's a terrible thing, but it's happened."

Her face twisted into a pained expression and she sat down hard on the loveseat. "I know," she said at last. "I'm sorry. This is no way to act. I don't handle bad news well. Plus I'm feeling guilty because I had so little patience with Dorothy Porter and now the poor woman's dead. I mean, she wasn't a *bad* woman."

"That would be a sad thing to have on your tombstone, wouldn't it?" Coco said with a sigh. " 'She wasn't a bad woman.' "

A silence fell over the room, the festive camaraderie of an hour ago smothered by a gloomy pall.

"Dorothy wasn't always like that, you know," Winston said, a rueful smile on his rugged face. "I've known her all my life. When Dorothy was a girl she could charm the birds out of the trees. She was pretty and *so* cheerful. Had a laugh like a silver bell and lots of friends. All that despite growing up without a mama and with a daddy mean as a snake with a belly rash."

"I can't even imagine her like that," Marydale said. "Don't get me wrong, she was never unpleasant to me, but she wasn't what you'd call friendly, either. And it seemed like she crossed swords with a lot of people around town."

"Well, she did," Winston allowed, "but some of that was for causes worth battling about. Thirty years ago this was a dying southern town, just like lots of other little burgs that dotted the railroad lines back in the day. Our little downtown was nothing but a cluster of rundown buildings. Lots has changed since those days thanks to Dorothy Porter. Without her, Morningside wouldn't be Morningside."

"And the town wouldn't be here in the first place if it weren't for her grandfather starting up his company here," I said.

"What was that company anyway?" Coco asked. "That was before my time."

"It all started before any of our times, even mine," Winston said. "Harrison Pritchett, Dorothy's grandfather, came here when this was nearly 'bout wilderness. He set up a saw-mill down by the river that feeds our lake. Then he found out the lumber he was milling was good for tool handles and he decided rather than becoming a supplier he'd manufacture them himself. He was successful in that and kept branching out. But the real money came when he started building comfort stations for construction sites."

"Comfort stations? What's that?" Coco asked.

"You might know them better as port-a-johns," I said. "Dorothy preferred we play down that particular detail of how the family empire was built."

"I'm sure she did," Winston said. "She got teased about it when we were kids in school."

The silence fell again, all of us lost in our own thoughts, until Marydale spoke up. "Sophreena, do you and Esme want to skip tonight? Would you like us to clear out?"

"No, please, don't go," I said. "I think we'd both welcome some distraction."

"We're good at distraction," Coco said. "But before we leave the subject, Esme, have you, you know, *heard* anything from Mrs. Porter?"

Esme, her ire exhausted, was patient in her answer. "It doesn't work that way, Coco, at least not for me. I hardly ever get anything from people who've died recently. Maybe it takes a while for them to process out or something. I don't think time works the same in that dimension. Maybe there's something they have to do before their spirits join the transcendence or whatever. But, in any case, I don't think Dorothy Porter would pick me as her tether to the temporal world."

"Probably just as well," Coco said. "I mean, even if she did tell you something that'd help with her case, how would you explain how you knew?"

"Good point," Jack said, fiddling with his phone. "Listen, I've got a reporter friend over in Raleigh. We've been texting back and forth while you were talking with the cops. I wanted to see if I could find out anything."

"And did you?" I asked.

Jack continued to stare at his phone's screen. "Apparently the cause of death was strangulation," he said. "That's all for now."

"Please, tell him if he finds out anything more to let us know," Esme said.

"Her," Jack said, and put his thumbs to work.

I felt a pang. What was it? Jealousy? I certainly had no right to feel that. Jack and I are just friends, pals, amigos. And while there's a part of me deep down that might like that to change, it never will. I care too much about the friendship to risk it. And anyway, he doesn't think of me that way.

"Okay, now," Coco announced, uncurling from her end of the couch and starting to clear away the food. "We said we were going to move on to more pleasant things. Let's get this cleared and go to the shop to work." She slipped on her sandals and headed for the kitchen, her bracelets and the tiny bells on her anklets tinkling like wind chimes for leprechauns. It was a happy sound.

We headed out our front door into the hot, muggy dusk for the four-block walk to Keepsake Corner. I hoped Marydale's niece, Roxie Mimms, who watches the shop for her a few hours a week, had remembered to leave the air-conditioning on this time. Last week we'd been miserable for the first half hour as we worked in the small back room where motors from the dehumidifiers had pushed the temps into sauna range.

Morningside is a beautiful town. Except for my college and post-grad years this has been my home. I've traveled a lot for someone my age, but I'm always happy to come back again. I can't remember the dying town Winston described.

Morningside is technically an incorporated town. We have a council government, several churches and a compact commercial district. But during the revitalization campaign the town elders had taken to calling it Morningside Village and made sure all the literature and signage reflected that designation. It sounded quaint, though Morningside had long ago outgrown village status.

Winston dropped back to walk alongside me, pointing to one of the wrought-iron lamp stanchions bordering the sidewalk. "That was Dorothy's handiwork. That was the opening salvo in her war on shabbiness."

The stanchions held old-fashioned globed streetlights, and on lower arms hanging baskets of greenery and colorful perennials gave the commercial district a charming, vibrant look.

"Dorothy gave those to the town?" I asked.

"Well, no," Winston said. "It wasn't like that. If you saw old pictures of this strip here you wouldn't recognize it. The shops were all rundown with peeling paint and dirty windows. The sidewalks were cracked and the gutters littered. No such thing as landscaping. People just let things grow as they might, weeds and all. It wasn't pretty."

"What happened to turn it around?" Jack asked.

"Dorothy and her family pride," Winston said. "She was not going to have the place her grandfather founded go to shambles. Dorothy had a pet word she used: *tacky*. Couldn't abide anything she found tacky. She made a fiery speech to her garden club on the sorry state of affairs and got those women stirred up enough to go to the historical commission to rabble rouse. When they didn't get action there they marched on the town council, which in those days met conveniently around the supper hour at the old Bar-B-Que Hut out on Orchard Road."

"And the council came up with a plan?" Jack asked.

"Not really," Winston said. "The town fathers—and it was all men back then—allowed as how, yes, things were looking a little downtrodden and could use some sprucing up. But they never did anything about it."

"Well, clearly, *someone* did," I said, gesturing toward the row of shops with their faux Old World facades, tasteful signs, immaculate landscaping and sparkling panes of glass. The rest of the group had keyed in on Winston's story and he held court as we strolled, more comfortable now that the sun was setting.

"Dorothy went commando on 'em." Winston said. "She said if they weren't going to do anything she would. She and her garden clubbers started staging unsanctioned beautification projects. They had bake sales and quilt raffles and all such as that and raised a good bit of money, plus they put their backs into the actual physical work. Big planter pots like those," he pointed to an urn overrun with brightly colored petunias, coleus and trailing honeysuckle vines, "just showed up along the sidewalks and Dorothy and her posse of women—and it was mostly women—started having come-to-Jesus talks with the shop owners about taking pride in the appearance of their places. I know 'cause I was one of those owners." He nodded toward Sugar Magnolias Bakery on the opposite side of the street.

We'd arrived at Keepsake Corner and Marydale was, as usual, having difficulty with the lock. She wiggled the key and jiggled the knob as she spoke. "Your shop was beautiful, Win. And the new owners are keeping it up nicely."

As Winston turned his back to the bakery I thought I detected a wistful expression. "You're being generous, Marydale," he said. "But I'll be honest, back in those days I was as guilty as anybody around about letting things fall into disrepair. I kept it clean and sanitary inside, but I was so focused on getting bread and pastries into my ovens I didn't give much thought to how the place looked outside."

"Enter Dorothy?" Esme asked.

"Enter Dorothy," Winston confirmed as Marydale finally freed the door and we all caught a blessed waft of cool air. "But she didn't just yammer at us about it. She actually drew up sketches and plans and helped us figure out what we could accomplish with the meager spare dollars any of us had back then."

"So this showcase town came about because of a grass-roots movement?" Jack asked. "That is so cool."

"That's how it *started*," Winston said. "And it was pretty cool in the beginning. Course, like it happens with lots of great ideas, this one got hijacked by politicians. Dorothy got active in local politics and staged a coup at the next election. She and her cohorts took over the town council and all her gentle encouragement hardened into regulations, codes and ordinances. She got a little power drunk and they started pushing stuff through that put a real hardship on some of the shop owners. Put some people out of business. I nearly went under myself, but I managed to hold on through a couple of lean years. That's one thing about being a baker; you'll always have bread so you won't starve." He took off his Panama hat and set it on the counter. "Now we said we were going to talk about something more cheerful; sorry I got off on all this." He went to the shelves to pull out his scrapbooking box.

"Just one more question," I said, pulling out my own over-flowing container. "I take it Dorothy may have earned herself some bad feelings after she took over the council?"

"That's putting it mildly," Winston said. "She was widely and deeply hated there for a while. And while Morningside is made up of mostly kind and gentle people, there are some folks around who *really* know how to hold on to a grudge."

five

Once we'd settled at the long work table Esme called the meeting to order by asking, "Okay, y'all, what's up?"

This was about as formal as we get.

"I'll go first," Marydale said. She flipped open her scrapbook to a copy of the daguerreotype she'd scanned and painstakingly repaired with computer software. "I've found out who this woman is. I emailed a copy to everybody in the family and a cousin sent me tons of info on her. She's my great-great-aunt. I'm going to make a page for her tonight and write in everything I've learned about her life."

Jack was next. "Nothing to report," he said. "No time. With the Honeysuckle Festival coming up everybody wants their places looking good. We're working from dawn to dusk, or as the old folks say, 'from *can see* to *cain't see.*'"

Jack's family lore has it that he's descended from Robert Ford, the man who shot and killed infamous outlaw Jesse James back in the Wild West days. Though he'd hit a brick wall in his research he was still plugging away on what he'd gathered so far for his scrapbooks.

Coco had brought along an envelope full of old family photos her mother had found. Her task for the evening was to organize them and start to document what she knew about the people, locations and dates.

Then it was Winston's turn. He'd made more progress than any of us on his family research. There'd always been whispered rumors in his family about a liaison between one of his direct ancestors and a slave woman. Winston had set out to get the whole story and he wanted to know everything regardless of how his ancestor's reputation fared. Winston subscribes to the warts-and-all school of genealogy and I heartily approve. Otherwise it's just an exercise in vanity.

"I'm getting somewhere finally," he said. "I got those papers I sent off for months ago. Remember? From that historical society down in South Carolina?"

We all nodded.

"About Bonaventure plantation?" I asked.

"Yeah, Bonaventure," Winston said, crooking his head to one side, "though I don't rightly know if it was much of a plantation by the time my—let me see, it would be my great-great-grandfather—by the time he came to own it."

"Let's use the ahnentafel chart to avoid confusion, Winston," I said. "Horace Lovett would be your number twelve, four generations back from you."

Esme rolled her eyes. She and I have an ongoing argument about how to reference ancestors and it perfectly illustrates the differences in our approach to our work. Esme is unbothered by the monotonous repetition of a confusing string of "greats" to signify generations. I, on the other hand, prefer the Teutonic orderliness of the ahnentafel, the family table, which handily supplies each relation a number.

"Okay," Winston said. "So my twelve bought the plantation lock, stock and barrel, including the slaves. Got it at a fire-sale price and looks like maybe there was a good reason for that. It was pitifully rundown by then."

"Did you find anything about what you *really* want to know?" Coco asked.

"Nothing that'll stand up to Sophreena's standards," he said. "But there's a list of all the assets that came with the plantation, and, just alongside where they'd put down a plow and a rocking chair, there's a woman named Delsie." He shook his head. "Awful. A human being, just another thing in the inventory."

"Is that her?" Coco pressed. "Is that the one you think might be your—okay let's see, what would that be? Your thirteen?"

"I don't know if it's her," Winston said. "I thought the name I'd heard whispered about in the family was Della, but maybe Delsie is a nickname." He hunched a shoulder. "Or maybe I'm remembering wrong, could be it's a different person altogether. But this is a start anyway."

Winston hadn't understood what the family secret was about when he was a child, but he'd known it was something shameful. When he was in his forties a great-aunt decided she was tired of carrying the secret and told him all she knew. That her grandfather had been the master of a plantation and he'd had children with a slave woman and that she was descended from that union. Winston tried to ask his family about it, but was told never to speak of it again. Now

Winston had grandchildren of his own and he wanted his family history to be honest and complete.

This was the purest of reasons for documenting family history, to leave for subsequent generations the legacy of really knowing their people. Winston's wife, Patsy, felt otherwise; she hated that he was "dredging up all that old stuff." But his children and his grandchildren were into it. They trailed along with him when he hit the libraries, courthouses and graveyards searching for information.

Winston's scrapbooks weren't beautiful. He didn't have an eye for layout or embellishment and his craft was a bit sloppy, but they were genuine and personal.

I couldn't help but contrast them to the vanity books we'd be constructing for Dorothy. Then it hit me. *Would* we be making the Pritchett books? The woman was dead; she'd have no use for them now. Then the second thought hit and I felt at once panicked and ashamed. We hadn't been paid. Thinking of money at a time like this was crass but we'd already put in hours of work and our bottom line for next month was going to look positively anemic without that final payment.

"Sophreena?" Esme said and her tone let me know she'd already asked me once. "Are you with us?"

"Sorry. Tonight I actually have something for my scrapbook," I said, tapping a small packet of photos, scanned and printed from the originals. "I got these in the mail this week from a distant cousin of my mother's I'd contacted years ago. Course, you all know Mom was adopted so they weren't blood relations. And since my mother grew up in Kansas and this cousin grew up in Minnesota they hardly ever saw each other. But she recently ran across these pictures and thank goodness she remembered me and still had my address. This one's Mom," I said, pointing to a little girl on a tricycle. "She'd have been about four then."

"About four? That's not very precise, Sophreena," Coco teased, turning my own words back on me.

"I know," I sighed. "But with Mom's adoption being so murky I have to resort to best guesses about a lot of things."

"Have you found out any more about the adoption?" Marydale asked.

"I wrote more letters last week trying to locate people who might have known my grandparents around the time they adopted Mom, and I've got more requests in for public records, but no breakthrough yet."

"Your mom would be proud you're continuing her quest," Marydale said, patting my hand. "It was very important to her."

I nodded, afraid to say more on that subject since my emotions were already raw. "Okay, Esme," I said, "your turn."

"Tonight I'm working on July, 1952," she said. "It was a busy time in Louisiana. I may have several pages."

Esme had enough photographs and memorabilia from her mother to fill many scrapbooks. Clementine Sabatier had been a sentimental woman, a saver and an avid photo buff. Plus she'd kept a regular diary for years.

We worked companionably for the next couple of hours, with one or the other of us occasionally wandering into the shop to fetch supplies which we added to our tabs.

Coco whooped as she held up a picture. The hand-tinted photograph depicted a woman dressed in an exotic outfit and holding two giant fans festooned with feathers. She was smiling seductively, one foot drawn up to rest her pointed toe on the humped back of an old steamer trunk.

"It's my great-aunt, Colette," Coco said, showing the photo around. "She was a fan dancer back in the 1930s in New York. She was no Sally Rand, but she was pretty well known. She's our family scandal but my mother adored her. She named me after her, much to the rest of the family's dismay. They were afraid it might influence the way I'd turn out. Imagine that." She jangled her bracelets and laughed.

Going about our normal routines was like a balm after the shock of Dorothy's death and being questioned by the police, and we stayed later than usual. Coco, Winston and Marydale had all left their cars in the Keepsake Corner parking lot, but Jack had come directly to our house as usual. He always insists on walking Esme and me home, though until today there'd been little serious crime in Morningside. And anyway, Esme was better bodyguard material. Jack wouldn't exactly strike fear in the heart of an assailant. Topping out at about five foot eight, he was slight of build, though well muscled—I couldn't help but notice that. And handsome, which has nothing to do with safety, but is definitely worth noting.

On the short walk we talked of happy things, mostly to do with the upcoming Honeysuckle Festival.

"Did you hear there's going to be music all day long on both Saturday *and* Sunday on the town square," Jack said, "and fireworks out over the lake on Sunday night? First time for that."

The festival was the highlight of the summer in our little

corner of the world. It had started about ten years back as an attempt to entertain visitors who came for a seniors' golf tournament. The geezer tourney, as Jack called it, was still a highlight of the weekend so once again we'd be inundated with men in plaid pants and women in support hose and culottes. But the festival was growing every year.

When we got to the house Esme went on inside but Jack put a hand on my shoulder and pulled me back.

"Wait up, Soph. You okay? You want to talk about anything?"

"I'm okay," I said. "Not my best day, but I'm hanging in."

"Good," he said, putting his arms around me. It was a good hug. A really. Good. Hug. I felt myself melting a little, but then there it was, the brotherly *pat, pat, pat* on my back.

Jack's phone buzzed and I was irked when he dug it out of his pocket. Dissing people for a ringtone is a pet peeve of mine and he knows it.

"Sorry," he said. "But I need to take this. It's a text from my reporter friend, Julie. Let me see what she's found out."

I waited while he read the message from *Julie*. Of course she had to have one of those perky, girly names. I wondered if he ever called her "Jule" like he calls me "Soph." I didn't like Julie. I'd never met her, but I didn't like the idea of her.

"That's crazy," Jack said, looking up at me. His eyes were wide and though they are a clear Carolina blue in the light of day, they shone like dark pools in the faint glow from the porch light.

"What is it?"

"She says the cops have got viable suspects in the murder of Dorothy Porter."

"Well, great, that was quick," I said. "Who? Who do they think did it?"

"They aren't giving out names," he said, still reading off the phone's screen, "but the scuttlebutt around the station is that two women—investigators Mrs. Porter hired to dig up dirt on her family—were at the house earlier in the day. They're the prime suspects."

"That's us! We weren't hired to dig up dirt on her family, for pity sake, we were hired to trace her family roots. That's crazy!"

"I know, that's what I said." Jack pushed his hands down in a settling motion.

Only then did I realize I'd been flailing my arms and yelling.

"It's just a ridiculous rumor," Jack said. "And even if there's any truth to it you'll get it all straightened out when you talk with the detectives again."

"You're right," I said. "We'll get it cleared up first thing tomorrow. We will." I tried to force confidence into my voice, but my legs had turned to jelly.

six

I AWAKENED THE NEXT MORNING TO CLANKING AND BANGING noises coming from the kitchen and the mingled aromas of what Esme calls *big breakfast*. That's when I got *really* worried. When things are going badly Esme cooks. She believes in deep-fried comfort food therapy. During these cooking episodes it's as if she's exorcizing demons. She slams the pots and pans around and wields wooden spoons like weapons. She doesn't blend ingredients, she punishes them.

"Everything's ready," she said as I came into the kitchen. "Sit down."

I did as I was told. I knew Esme would tell me what was on her mind when she was good and ready and there was no use asking 'til that time came.

I'd told her last night what Jack's reporter friend had texted about us being suspects and she was surprisingly blasé about it. No hissy fit, no threats of bodily harm. She'd simply said, "Detective Carlson will be hearing from me first thing tomorrow morning. I will not have people talking this kind of nonsense." Then she'd dismissed the whole thing with a flap of her hand and gone off to bed. But she must have mulled it over in the night and now she was ticked off big time.

She set a plate full of food in front of me that could've fed a small family—bacon, eggs, cheese grits, homemade biscuits, fresh fruit; and a totally unnecessary softball-sized blueberry muffin balanced on the side of the plate.

"Uh-oh, things must be worse than I thought."

"Stop mumbling and eat," Esme said. "Things always look better after a hearty breakfast."

I took a sip of juice then searched for a spot to attack my plate. I wondered how much of our weekly food budget was on the table, which brought me back to the question that had occurred to me last night.

"Esme," I said, "you know, now that Dorothy is gone—"

"Yeah, I've been wondering about that, too," she cut in, picking at her food. "And no, you're not a terrible person because you're thinking about money at a time like this."

"How do you *do* that?" I asked.

"Child, you are as transparent as Saran Wrap. And besides, I had the same thought last night and I felt guilty about it, too—but only for a second and a half."

"I don't know if we should even start the scrapbooks. I know how much Dorothy wanted them done, especially for Cassidy, and it would be a shame not to see the project through. But it's a *ton* of work and if we're not going to collect the rest of the fee maybe we should just return the stuff to somebody, I don't even know who, and cut our losses."

"But it seems disrespectful, doesn't it? You know I didn't have much love for the woman, but I do want her to rest peaceful."

The doorbell rang and Esme looked over at the clock. "Who in the world comes calling at seven-thirty in the morning?"

We gave each other the once over. I was barefoot and wearing the yoga pants and threadbare Weezer T-shirt I'd slept in; Esme had her hair tied up and was in a nightgown, bed jacket and pink fluffy slippers. I was elected to go to the door.

My heart started beating fast as I went into the front hall. Could it be the police here to arrest us? Who else would be coming around at this hour? I told myself I was being absurd, but I wasn't terribly persuasive.

I mounted the stepstool I have to use to see through the peephole and let out a puff of relief when I saw Ingrid Garrison standing there with Cassidy. Then relief gave over to confusion. Why would they be here?

"Well, you won't know until you open the door and talk to them," I muttered to myself, as I thumbed the lock and wrested the door open.

Ingrid had obviously had a *very* bad night. She was a younger, prettier and warmer version of Dorothy with wide-set blue eyes and a ready smile. Her blond hair was shot through with gray and worn in a pixie cut. She was trim and fit and exuded an earthiness that was appealing. But today her eyes were swollen and her whole body seemed to sag.

"Sophreena, I am so sorry to bother you at this hour of the morning, but Cassidy really wanted to speak with you and Esme." She gave the child a quick glance and me a beseeching look. "I'm sure you've heard what's happened with Dorothy," she said, "I've got to meet Joe to make the arrangements in a few minutes and this is the only time I could bring her."

Her euphemism lingered in my ear: not what had happened *to* Dorothy, but what had happened *with* her. Cassidy was clutching a small cloth bag to her chest, her little face a mask of misery and confusion.

"No, it's fine," I said, motioning them inside. "You caught us at breakfast. Want to join us? There's plenty."

"A cup of coffee would be a godsend," Ingrid said, settling on the couch and covertly checking her watch.

"How about you, Cassidy? Would you like a glass of juice or a muffin?"

"No, thank you," Cassidy said. "Is Miss Esme here? I need both of you."

I fetched Esme and the coffee and Cassidy got right to her agenda.

"Could you and Miss Esme find out who hurt my Auntie Dot? She said you and Miss Esme were smart people. She said if you two couldn't find something it could never be found. I heard her tell her friend Miss Vivian that."

Ingrid cringed. Clearly she hadn't known what Cassidy had on her mind. Now what? Did I placate the girl by making a false promise that we'd find Dorothy's killer? Or did I tell her flat out that wasn't our job? One thing that seemed unwise to lay on her was that we were suspects.

"Please," Cassidy added, her lower lip trembling and tears splashing over onto her pale cheeks.

"Cassidy," Esme said, leaning forward and touching the girl's cheek, "your Aunt Dot was very kind to say that about us. And we do know how to find out things, but mostly things that are written down somewhere. This isn't like that. But do you know who is really, *really* good at finding out about who does something bad to another person, like who hurt your Aunt Dot?"

"Who?" Cassidy asked, worrying the little cloth bag's handles.

"Detectives," Esme said. "Police detectives. I'm going to see the detective today and I'll make sure he knows how important it is that they find the bad person who did this so no one else gets hurt."

"But my daddy says they're local yokels. He says they couldn't find their heinies with both hands, except he didn't say heinies, but I'm not supposed to say *asses*." She whispered the last word, wiping the tears away with the flat of her palm.

I didn't dare look at Esme, for fear I'd lose it.

Ingrid's eyes widened and her mouth formed a perfect O. "Little pitchers, big ears," she said. "Cassidy, Daddy didn't mean that. He was just frustrated."

"I tell you what," Esme said. "Sophreena and I will try to help the police. How would that be?"

"Good," Cassidy said with a nod. She rose as if to signal her business here was done, still clutching the bag.

"That's a cute bag, Cassidy," I said, for lack of anything else to say. "I like the heart design on it."

"Thank you," Cassidy said, on automatic manners. "I have all my special things in here," she said, digging inside the bag. "Like my books, my special stuffed dog, and this box Auntie Dot gave me. I'm going to solve it." She brought out a familiar wooden box.

"That's the puzzle box we—" Esme started, then caught herself, "that belonged to your great-great-grandmother."

Cassidy shrugged. "I guess. Auntie Dot gave it to me yesterday. I was supposed to leave it at her house and play with it there, but I wanted to bring it home so I put it in my bag. Auntie Dot said if I can solve the puzzle my dreams will come true."

"Would you like a little hint?" I asked Cassidy.

"No!" Cassidy pulled the box to her chest. "That would be cheating. I have to do it myself or else it won't work."

"What are your dreams?" Esme asked.

Cassidy didn't hesitate. "I want to be a doctor when I grow up. And I want to have a husband who likes me and maybe he'll be my nurse. And I want four kids—two girls and two boys, and I want a dog and a cat, maybe two cats. And a horse. Oh, and a blue house, sort of a purplish blue."

"Wow, you've given this some thought, haven't you?" I said.

"She's a planner," Ingrid said. "Speaking of which, we'd better get going, I'm supposed to meet Joe in a few minutes to sort out the arrangements for Dorothy. Thank you so much, and again I'm sorry we came so early, and so unannounced."

When we reached the front door, Ingrid said, "Cassidy, you can go on to the car, honey. I need to speak with Sophreena and Esme about some adult things."

Cassidy made her way in slow steady steps to the car. No skipping today. She held on tight to the bag that held the key to all her dreams.

"I am so sorry I put you on the spot like that," Ingrid said once the girl was out of earshot. "I had no idea why she was hell bent on talking to you. She was so torn up last night

I didn't know what to do and all she kept saying was she needed to talk to you two."

"It's okay. Really," I said, then steeled myself for an awkward moment and plowed on. "Listen, I *know* this isn't the right time to bring this up with everyone still in shock, but I think I have to ask. Esme and I were wondering if we should go ahead with the family history scrapbooks."

"Well, I'm not sure," Ingrid said. "Speaking for myself I'd still like them done for Cassidy, but I'm not sure it's up to me. Honestly, I haven't even thought about stuff like that yet. I guess you should talk with Joe about it. He and Dorothy were still legally married and he'll be handling all her outstanding business."

"Okay, I'll ask him in a few days," I said. "And I am so sorry about your sister."

"I'm sorry, too," Ingrid said, her eyes focusing on the lone cloud intruding on the Carolina blue sky. "I'm sorry about a whole lot of things when it comes to my sister."

I had no appetite now for the remainder of my big breakfast. I couldn't get Cassidy's face out of my mind. For that child to love Dorothy with that kind of devotion she must have known a side of the woman Esme and I seldom saw.

Family means everything to me, maybe because I no longer have one. I *had* a great family. When I was young and brought home those little trophies from the Secret Santa shop at school that said WORLD'S BEST MOM or WORLD'S BEST DAD I really thought they'd made them just for my parents.

I was older than Cassidy when I lost my folks but I felt no

less confused than Cassidy seemed about them being here one moment and gone the next. Gone *where*? I couldn't get my mind around that, not then and not now. And Esme was no help. Her spirits have a strict don't-call-us-we'll-call-you policy.

Both my parents were only children so what few relatives I have left are distant, in both consanguinity and geography. I long for family and envy people from big garrulous families that hold noisy family reunions and squabble over a deceased loved one's soup tureen or the Postage Stamp quilt Aunt Lulu made when she was a bride. Those things matter enough to fight over because they're the artifacts that help us identify with our tribe—that let us know we belong.

"Best run up and get dressed," Esme said as she came down the stairs from the mother-in-law suite that's her part of the house. My dad had added the space when his mother's health started to fail, intending to have her come live with us, but she hadn't lived to occupy it. I'd offered it to Esme when she came here five years ago, just until she could find a place of her own. She'd been in no hurry to apartment hunt and had insisted on paying me rent. I quickly got used to having her here and now it seemed like the most natural ar-rangement in the world.

"Do we have somewhere we need to be?" I asked. Esme is always careful with her appearance, but she looked espe-cially well put together today.

"No, but that Detective Carlson is coming over to talk with us and I want us looking like a couple of respectable professionals."

"So you think he's going to suspect us less if we're well dressed?" I asked.

"Just go get ready," she said, picking up a dishtowel and giving it a half-hearted snap in my direction.

I donned the black slacks and tailored blouse I usually wear to meet with clients instead of my work-at-home uniform of jeans and T-shirt. The issue of Dorothy's scrapbooks was weighing on me. If we got the go-ahead with the original deadline, we'd be hard pressed to make it if we lost two or three working days. I debated calling Joe Porter later in the day but decided it really would be gauche to ask him right now.

As it turned out I could have saved myself the worry. While I was slipping on my sandals my cell phone rang. I was surprised to discover Joe Porter on the other end. He accepted my condolences, then asked if I would come over to his service station that afternoon to discuss some things.

I said I could, but it made me uneasy. Why couldn't he just state his business on the phone? I had a sinking feeling our project was about to get the ax.

I didn't have time to stew about it though. I'd just gotten my hair tamed into a ponytail when the doorbell rang. Had to be the detective. I couldn't decide whether to be relieved or scared. Surely we'd get this all straightened out, but what if we didn't?

Detective Carlson was alone this time and he and Esme were already settled into opposing armchairs when I came into the living room. The detective started to stand but I motioned for him to stay seated, amused that being a cop hadn't strained the southern gentleman out of him. I sat on the middle cushion of the sofa in case I needed to referee and placed my time-stamped receipts from yesterday on the coffee table. I like to be prepared.

"Thank you for coming by, Detective Carlson," Esme said. She was cordial, but I knew it was killing her to hold in what she was really feeling. "Sophreena and I are concerned that there seems to be a rumor going around that we are suspects in the death of Mrs. Porter. We would like these rumors nipped in the bud. We'd like to clear up any questions you have right now."

The last two words came out a little harsh. I gave her a warning glance, but Carlson didn't seem ruffled.

"Where did you hear such a rumor?" he asked.

"That's not important," Esme said. "We just want it to stop."

"Look, we aren't in charge of the town's rumor mill," he said, spreading his hand, palm up. "And the truth is, you are suspects."

I held my breath, expecting Esme to erupt, but she kept her cool—in fact she was downright frosty. "Pardon me?" she asked.

"Everyone who had contact with Dorothy Porter yesterday is a suspect," Carlson said, "until they're ruled out. Doesn't mean I think you killed the woman, but it does mean we're going to investigate. I wouldn't be doing my job otherwise."

"We understand that," I said. " That's why we contacted you. Once we're cleared you won't have to waste any more time and energy on us and you can get on with finding the person who did it." I picked up the receipts and handed them over. "These will prove our whereabouts yesterday afternoon and I'm sure there are store cameras if you can't accept these."

Carlson studied them for a moment, then took out his

little notebook and scribbled in it. "Thanks," he said, handing back the receipts. "Could you tell me where you were later in the afternoon?"

"Here," Esme said. "We got here about six, or six-fifteen maybe. Our friends were here waiting for us. Oh, and we stopped for gas at the service station over on Carver Street before that. I'm sure they have cameras, too. Fact, I know they do. I was there when they were installing them a few months ago. Guy that runs the place told me he was having trouble with drive-offs since the price of gas got so high and he'd finally decided to pony up for cameras."

"Unfortunately, Miss Sabatier," Carlson said, lifting an eyebrow, "he put in dummy cams; as effective a deterrent as real cameras but at a fraction of the cost. Course, I probably shouldn't let that cat out of the bag; let's keep that just between us." He gave her a smile, but she wasn't having any of it.

She crossed her arms. Never a good sign.

"I'm sure we have the receipt somewhere," I said quickly, "or that the clerk will remember. Her name's Cindy, she knows me, I used to babysit her. She was looking out the window and I waved to her."

"That's fine," Carlson said.

"Other people saw Dorothy after we left," Esme said, getting snippy now. "Doesn't that clear us?"

"Not really," Carlson said, putting his notebook away. "You could have come back. But I'll follow up," he said, pointing to my receipts. "And I appreciate you ladies being so helpful. I apologize if the rumors are distressing you, but as I say, we don't have any control over that. If you think of anything else, please don't hesitate to call." He pulled out a card, then wrote on the back and handed it to Esme, even though I was standing closer. "Day or night. That's my personal cell on the back."

"One more thing," Esme said, taking the card and tossing it onto the side table. "Mrs. Porter's great-niece, Cassidy, came to see us this morning. She and her grandmother Ingrid, Dorothy's sister. That little girl is just purely heartbroken about Mrs. Porter's death. I gave her a promise you'd find who did this. Are you going to make a liar out of me?"

"No, ma'am," Carlson said. "I intend to track this person down and see they get what's coming to them, no matter who the culprit turns out to be," he added, his voice grave. He gave her a long, penetrating look, but Esme's gaze didn't waver.

The soundtrack from a gunfight scene in a spaghetti western started playing in my head.

seven

Esme dropped me by the dealership to pick up my car, then she was off to her gig as a volunteer in a summer tutoring program at her church. I was on my own for the meeting with Joe Porter. Just as well. I love Esme dearly, but she can be a loose cannon when dealing with clients. Once she forms an opinion sometimes she can't help but say it out loud.

I had nearly an hour to kill so I stopped by Keepsake Corner to leave a book I'd promised to loan Marydale. She was doing brisk business for a weekday morning. I tried not to groan when I saw a young woman checking out a stack of decorative stickers and factory-made embellishments. I appreciate an attractive scrapbook page as much as the next person, but this trend of using embellishments at the expense of documentation makes me sad. Fifty years from now those pretty stickers won't mean a thing, and family members will be left pining for more information about the photos. What was the occasion? When was it? Who are those people? What happened that day?

But whenever I preach the importance of journaling in

scrapbooking workshops people claim they can't think of what to say or their handwriting isn't pretty or some other lame excuse not to document. To which I say *Pfft!*

I browsed while I waited for Marydale to get a free moment. She'd gotten in some beautiful handmade papers that would be perfect for Dorothy's heritage scrapbooks *if* we got to do them.

Two older women were perusing the stationery section. They were relative newcomers to Morningside and I recognized them as garden club ladies.

"I was scared half to death to stay by myself last night. I checked the locks three times," one of them said.

"I heard they're looking at the nephew," the other said. "I hate to say it but I hope it does turn out to be a family thing and not some psychopath going around breaking in at random and killing people."

"I heard that about the nephew, too," the first woman said, "but I also heard they suspect those two—" At that point she looked up and saw me and became flummoxed. "Never mind," she said.

They both seemed to come to the sudden realization they didn't need any stationery after all and hustled out of the store.

"Pay no attention," Marydale said, coming up behind me and putting her arm around my shoulders. "People like to gossip."

"But I *have* to pay attention, Marydale," I said. "This could hurt our business, not to mention it's humiliating to have people looking at me like that."

"It'll soon pass and they'll realize what ninnies they've been," she assured me.

I told her what Jack had found out from his reporter friend, then filled her in on our visit with Ingrid and Cassidy and our talk with Detective Carlson.

"My, you've had a busy morning," she said.

"You should have seen Cassidy," I said. "Do you know anything about her mother, by the way? I never asked when we were doing the research since we were tracing backward."

"From what I understand her mother took off for parts unknown when Cassidy was an infant. Ingrid was divorced by then, so she left San Francisco and moved down to where Jeremy lived—Sacramento, I think it was—so she could help out with the baby. Then when Cassidy was school age they decided to move back here. Ingrid got a job as a receptionist for Dr. Warren and Jeremy got on at the bank. They moved into one of those little duplexes down on River Road so Cassidy could go back and forth easily between them. It's a far cry from Dorothy's life up on the hill."

"Why would Ingrid want to come back here, do you suppose? Seems like there's so many bad memories for her here."

"She's getting older," Marydale said, "maybe she thought it was time to heal old wounds."

Or settle old scores, I thought, but did not say aloud. "Did you know Ingrid when you were growing up?" I asked, only now realizing she and Marydale must be around the same age.

"I did." Marydale nodded. "I mean, we weren't good

friends or anything, but we were schoolmates when we were little. She left home young, and I mean really young, like in her early teens. At first the story was that she was sent away to boarding school, but she never came home on school breaks or summers. There was even a rumor for a while that she was dead. But a couple of the girls at school had some contact with her. A few postcards and a phone call or two. Turns out she'd just had enough of the Pritchett family—her father, in particular—and ran away. It was the sixties"— Marydale shrugged—"so of course she struck out for San Francisco."

"It's hard to believe she and Dorothy were even sisters. Dorothy was so proper and Ingrid's more the free spirit type."

"True," Marydale allowed, "but they were very close at one time. Their mother died when Ingrid was small. Dorothy looked after her like a fierce little mama lion. But Ingrid was strong willed and the relationship got more complicated as they got older."

"I'll say. It seems like every time we saw them together they were having words—loud, angry words."

"Not every family's the Waltons," Marydale said. "Doesn't mean they didn't love one another deep down."

"You're right," I said. "Sometimes people are like porcupines. The more they try to get close, the more they hurt one another."

I still had a half hour so I stopped by The Morningside Apothecary, which most of the locals still call Stanton's Drugs. I slowed my pace to admire the front window display of antique apothecary bottles, old measuring implements and vintage medicine boxes and tins. Uber quaint, though I knew once I got past the register I'd find the store stocked with the same assortment of health and beauty items as any chain, plus aisles full of things a person might not know he needed until they beckoned from the shelf. Chia Pets, battery-operated spaghetti twirler forks, T-shirts and all manner of plastic toys with a half-life of about three minutes once they'd been wrestled from the blister packaging.

I nodded hello to Mr. Stanton, who was tidying the magazine rack. He'd given over the pharmacy operation to his son about a year ago and now spent his days puttering around the store, slipping out to play golf whenever the urge struck him.

I followed the familiar path to where I knew I'd find my contact lens solution. One of the perks of small town shopping is that even blindfolded I could locate every item I needed from this store.

As I filled my basket I overheard two teenaged boys at the other end of the aisle. "I betcha it was the husband. It's always the husband."

"I thought the old woman was divorced. Wasn't she that rich old lady who married a grease monkey?"

"He's not a grease monkey, dude. He, like, owns a whole string of gas stations. And my mom says they weren't divorced yet, just heading for it. Maybe he offed her *before* she could divorce him to get all her money."

"Or maybe you watch too many cop shows, nimrod. My dad says it was probably a robbery gone bad. He says there's no telling what kind of stuff she had stashed up there in that big old house."

"My mom is freakin' out, man! She's all like, *Lock the doors! Lock the doors!* Like we got anything anybody'd wanna steal. And anyway, she heard it's got something to do with these two women, like private eyes or something the old lady hired to dig up dirt on somebody."

"That's kinda hot."

"You're sick, man."

"Not the murder, I mean women private eyes. Like Charlie's Angels, right?"

They started making some kind of teenage boy rutting noises. One of them punched the other on the arm and they guffawed some more. I had a fleeting fantasy about borrowing one of the hair dryers from a rack and blowing my hair back as I walked toward them in slow motion. *Here you are, boys, here's your Charlie's Angel.* But first off, with my short legs it would have taken me forever to get to their end of the aisle. And secondly, it was freaking me out that this bizarre rumor about Esme and me was spreading. To top it off, when I checked out I could have sworn I was getting the stink eye from the girl working the register, but it could have been my imagination.

As I pulled out on River Road and headed for Joe's service station I was filled with dread. I did some mental bookkeeping and saw lots of mac 'n' cheese dinners in our immediate future. It didn't seem fair. We'd already put in so much work on this project. I wondered if I could at least negotiate a kill fee.

"Note to self," I muttered. "Don't call it *that* when you make the pitch."

I knew Joe Porter, but only remotely. My father, who had

been particular about our vehicles, had always taken them to Porter's place for service. So I knew my dad must have trusted the man. On the other hand, Dorothy hadn't had much good to say about Joe. She'd made it clear she felt she'd married *well* beneath her station. Once she referred to her marriage as "an unfortunate lapse in judgment." Course, she and Porter had been married for twenty-five years, so it hardly seemed a *momentary* lapse.

I parked on the street alongside a row of crepe myrtle trees, hoping the meager shade would keep the car's interior from reaching broiling temps before I returned. I got out and headed across a parking lot shimmering from heat and gasoline fumes. This was no quickie-mart gas station. No stale snacks, sodas, tacky souvenirs or bad coffee inside. Customers looking to stave off starvation had to depend on the vending machine outside the door. And no self-service nonsense, this was a filling station of the old-fashioned variety. I heard a crisp double-ding as a car ran over the alert hose and pulled to the pump. This brought a young man trotting out to fill the tank. He set the nozzle then proceeded to wash the windshield while a man sat in the car talking on his cell. As I walked by the man grunted and pointed to a spot the young man had missed. You just can't do enough to please some people.

The two big bay doors were up and cars were on the lifts. One of the men looked up from where he was checking parts at a workbench. He wiped his hands on a dirty rag, then picked up a wrench and came in my direction. Something about the way he held that wrench looked menacing. Now I really *hoped* I was being paranoid.

"Excuse me," I said, trying to make myself heard over the air compressors and the clanging noises of the garage. "Could you tell me where I could find Mr. Porter?"

"Who wants to know?" the man asked, still holding the wrench as if it were a club. "You a reporter?"

"No, I'm Sophreena McClure. I'm not a reporter, I'm—" I stopped. This is a problem with introducing myself by my profession. Half the time people start asking about rock formations and I have to explain that no, I'm not a geologist. Sometimes people ask if I'm *some kinda doctor* and even the ones who know what it is can't understand how it translates into an actual job.

"Mr. Porter asked me to come," I said.

"Okay. Right back there on the left," the man said, pointing with the wrench.

Once I was seated in his small office Joe Porter didn't waste time. "Sophreena, thanks for coming. I'll make this quick. I'm sure you have things to do and I know I do." He was handsome in a rugged sort of way. I knew he was several years younger than Dorothy and he'd aged well. His hair was gray, but he still had plenty of it and he was lean and fit for his age and seemed comfortable in his own skin.

"I've talked to Ingrid and it's been decided we'll have a private funeral and burial for Dorothy tomorrow, family only," he said, staring down at the desk.

"I see," I said, though I had no idea why he'd summoned me here to tell me that.

"Tell me, what was your arrangement with Dorothy?" he asked, looking up.

"Arrangement?"

"I know she hired you to trace her family. You finished up with that?"

"Mostly," I said, seeing that final payment circling the drain.

"And you saw her yesterday? You were out at the house?"

"Yes," I said, slowly. "We saw her in the *early* afternoon. Others saw her after that." I felt compelled to add that last in case he was accusing me of something.

He stared out the window, though I didn't think he could see much with the glass panes covered in a thin film of oil and grime.

"You see anybody else when you were out there?" he asked, his eyes narrowed.

"Only Dorothy's housekeeper, Linda, and Cassidy," I said.

"Cassidy," he said with a sigh. "That poor kid." He dragged his hand down his face, forehead to chin, as if this could erase the fatigue. "So tell me, what do you mean when you say *mostly* finished? Ingrid said you had some questions."

"Yes, I do. I hope you'll forgive me, I know it's bad form to be asking about trivial things right now. We gave Mrs. Porter our report yesterday but she also hired us to archive the materials and construct heritage scrapbooks. She'd wanted them done before the Founders' Day open house she was planning to host just before the Honeysuckle Festival. Esme and I wondered if we should go ahead with the project?"

"Yes," Porter answered straight away. "Yes, she'd want that."

This cheered me, but I thought it inappropriate to whoop it up given the circumstances. Anyhow, next came the delicate part. "We'd be happy to," I said, "but we wondered if we were still looking at the same timeline for delivery and the same payment schedule?" My voice went up on the last words and Porter gave me a weary smile.

"It's okay, Sophreena. Money's not a taboo subject. Tell me specifics."

I'd brought along our contract and invoices just in case and I pulled them from my bag. He waved them away. "Just tell me how much Dorothy owed you."

"She didn't owe us anything until the heritage scrapbooks are done. The outstanding balance once we complete those will be thirty-two hundred dollars. It's a lot of work and that includes the supplies and—"

Porter held up a hand to cut me off. He reached into a desk drawer and brought out an oversized checkbook, the business kind with three checks on a page. I noticed his hands as he picked up a ballpoint pen. They'd definitely seen lots of manual labor in his lifetime and they looked strong and capable. *Capable of what?* I wondered.

He wrote out a check for the full amount, tore it from its moorings and handed it over. "There will be a memorial service for Dorothy up at the house on the day she'd planned that party. It would mean a lot to the family to have these things finished by then. Dorothy would've liked that. You can still have them done?"

"Yes, but our understanding with Mrs. Porter was that we weren't to receive payment until the job was finished."

I caught a brief sardonic smile. "I'm sure that was your arrangement with her," he said. "*Will* you have the scrapbooks done when you promised?"

"Yes, sir, we definitely will," I said, sitting up straight in the chair.

"Then we have a new understanding, you and me."

"Would you like to see them before the memorial?"

"I've got no use for the Pritchett family story," he said, making no attempt to hide his bitterness. "You can give them to Ingrid, though I don't know if she feels much different than I do about it. Meant something to Dorothy, though, and this is about her."

He pushed back from his desk and I took this as my dismissal. I quickly gathered my things and he walked me to the door. He grabbed the doorknob then hesitated. "Tell me, when you were at the house yesterday did Dorothy do or say anything out of the ordinary? Did she seem like she was okay? Happy?"

"She seemed very pleased with our report," I offered. I debated whether to tell him about the ring and how over-the-moon she'd been about that but decided I'd best keep that to myself for now. "She was happy to have Cassidy with her. And, now that you mention it she did seem like she was in an unusually good mood."

Porter nodded and pursed his lips. "Good. That's good, then."

He walked me all the way outside to the parking lot where we said our goodbyes. As I headed for my car I glanced back to see him talking with the mechanic who'd directed me to the office. The mechanic scowled in my direction and nodded.

I had the words of the kid from the drugstore echoing in

my head as I pulled back out onto River Road. "It's always the husband."

Something seemed off. I couldn't put my finger on it, but just *something*. Joe and Dorothy were in the midst of a split and from what I'd heard it hadn't been that most miraculous of wonders, an amicable divorce. But I was getting mixed signals.

The man had written me a very nice check, and he'd wanted Dorothy's wishes carried out. That was a caring gesture, wasn't it? But then again, maybe money was no object if he was set to inherit Dorothy's estate.

Dorothy's complaints about Joe had always been more about his shortcomings than his actions. He wasn't sophisticated enough. Not well traveled. Not cultured. But she'd never claimed he was unfaithful or abusive in any way. He simply hadn't been enough for her. I wasn't sure about all the legalities, but I knew in North Carolina couples have to live apart for a year before a no-fault divorce can be granted. And Joe Porter had vacated Dorothy's big house on the hill nearly a year ago, right about the time she hired us. I wondered if the two events were related in some way. Maybe after rejecting Joe, Dorothy was trying to renew her allegiance to her family of birth. She hadn't yet taken back her family name, but she'd intended to once the divorce became final.

I wondered what they'd put on her tombstone.

eight

"Sweet Lord. We're gonna need a whole lotta coffee," Esme said as we surveyed the workroom later that afternoon, "and a big ol' vat of midnight oil."

"The good news is I am fastidiously organized, as you well know," I said.

Esme gave me a look.

"Well, okay, in my work anyway. And yeah, there's tons of stuff in here, but it is all sorted and divided into job areas." I pointed to the table running along the far wall. "Since this is such a big job I moved the scanning station over to the long table. We've got huge stacks of photos and documents and other ephemera yet to scan and print."

"Bless your little cotton socks, Sophreena, you've been a busy gal. But oh, how I wish we could move that table over by the window so we could look out onto the backyard while we're working and remind ourselves there's a world out there? Watch the birds at the feeder? Maybe catch a cloud floating by."

"Me, too, but you know we can't," I said. "That flood of

sunlight may be good for our psyches, but those are death rays for old photographs. I'm afraid we're in for some long hours in that dark corner."

Esme let out a big sigh. "Yes, so here we go, to the bat-cave. Where do I start?"

"We need to prepare the boxes we'll store the archives in. They're still out in the garage. You get those and I'll warm up the scanners."

I turned on both flatbeds and placed a pair of thin white cotton gloves at Esme's place before pulling on my own pair. The natural oils on human fingers are another enemy of old photos so when we handle originals we take every precaution.

Esme brought the boxes in and kicked the door shut behind her. We keep this room closed up and a dehumidifier going twenty-four-seven to maintain climate control. In the rest of the house we're casual housekeepers, and a peek into my closet would let anyone know I'm not so organized in all areas of my life, but when it comes to this room I'm a card-carrying control freak.

As Esme settled in her chair she put her hand across her forehead and winced, a move she often makes when she's getting something from beyond—wherever that is.

"What is it?" I asked. "Something from Dorothy?"

Esme shook her head. "No, I told you, Dorothy Porter barely deigned to talk to me while she was alive, why would she get chatty with me now? But I am getting something from somebody. I don't know who and I don't know what it's supposed to mean. Just this awful heavy sense of shame and guilt."

"That's pretty vague," I said.

"That's the way it is sometimes, *too many* times," Esme said. "It's like they're timid or something. They sidle up on me, drop a cryptic hint—no pun intended—then scurry back behind the veil. I wish they'd just come on out with it." She sighed as she pulled on her gloves, then took a photo from the top of a tall stack sandwiched with rag paper. "Okay, what do we have here? Note says Dorothy and Ingrid, circa 1954. Ingrid was a cute little thing, and look at Dorothy. Winston's right; she was a pretty girl. You know, Cassidy favors Dorothy even more than she does Ingrid."

"Yeah, in those pictures of Dorothy as a child she could be Cassidy's twin."

Just at that moment the telephone rang and Ingrid Garrison was on the other end of the line, as if our speaking of her had prompted the call.

"I'm so sorry to bother you again, Sophreena," she said, her voice low and thready, "but I'm worried sick about Cassidy. Nothing I say seems to help—except when she heard Joe and me talking about the scrapbooks. That seemed to brighten her up for a bit. I understand Joe's given you the green light. Would it be okay if we dropped by so she can watch you work? Maybe she'd feel part of it somehow?"

"Sure, if you think it would help. But we've still got prep work to do. I'll call you tomorrow and let you know when we're ready to start."

Ingrid sighed audibly as if to say, *If that's the best you can do,* but she thanked me.

"Poor child," Esme said after I told her why Ingrid called.

"I hope this is the right thing," I said, staring down at the photo of the sisters Pritchett. "Maybe it's too soon for Cassidy to be looking at these pictures of Dorothy and all these dead ancestors. We deal in death a lot, don't we, Esme?"

"I prefer to think of it as dealing with lives fully lived. Anyway, we'll take our cues from Cassidy. At least somebody's paying attention to the child's needs. There's nothing that tugs at my heart like a motherless child."

"Me, too," I said, "and I suspect that's because we both had wonderful mothers. Cassidy's left when she was a baby. It's so sad to think of what she's missed out on. There's nothing like a mama's love."

I'd met Esme through her mother, Clementine, when I was on my first big genealogy gig. An old professor had recommended me for a primo job tracing the lineage of one of Louisiana's most prominent political families. The job had paid extremely well, and I'd gotten a crash course in white-glove diplomacy. Sometimes when well-known people want their family line traced it's not because they want to connect with the past; it's a bid for prestige and they insist on cherry-picking what's included in the record.

Clementine Sabatier had worked for years as a domestic in the household. Though she hadn't been treated very well she'd been loyal and discreet while she was in their employ, but by the time I interviewed her she was retired and inclined toward speaking the unvarnished truth. She wasn't mean-spirited, but she answered my questions straight out. "I was in charge of polishing their silver," she'd said, "but I'm not beholden to polish their image." I'd gotten a ton of tantalizing information from her—most of which I'd been prohibited to use.

I'd liked Clementine Sabatier immediately and grew to have a deep respect and fondness for her over the weeks I'd visited her. She was elderly and frail by then, but with a mind still agile and a tongue still quick.

Esme was another story. I hadn't known what to make of her in the beginning. When she shook my hand on our first meeting she said, "So this is how it's gonna be." I wasn't sure how I was supposed to respond to that greeting and I muttered something unintelligible and reclaimed my hand as quickly as possible. Esme told me later she'd gotten a strong feeling that day that we were destined to work together to somehow turn her gift toward something useful. It was the one and only time she'd ever gotten any kind of cosmic vibe from a living person. I still don't know how to feel about that.

I got to know Esme better over the course of the weeks I was coming by to interview Clementine. I came to appreciate her dry wit and her sharp observations and to discover what a big heart she has.

Clementine died a few months after my job in Louisiana was finished. Esme called to let me know and I went down for the funeral. The next thing I knew Esme had moved here and we were in business together.

I owe eternal thanks to whatever Fates conspired to make that happen, though I don't believe in stuff like the Fates. Or at least I didn't. I can't deny something happens with Esme, but I don't know what it is or how to characterize it. Which is okay, because neither does Esme. Is it really an extra-sensory gift or just heightened intuition? It's easiest just to adopt her it-is-what-it-is philosophy and accept whatever comes to her as deserving of consideration. She's gotten things she's never been able to figure out, but she's never gotten anything wrong.

We scanned for hours, carefully cataloguing the photos and other artifacts as we went along. We never use originals in the scrapbooks we create since most are too delicate to be handled on a regular basis. We'd be supplying high-resolution scans, indexing and storing the original materials and using prints for the scrapbooks.

Along about mid-afternoon I started wondering what we had in the fridge that could be thrown together for supper. I stood and stretched but before I could head to the kitchen to investigate the phone rang again. When I answered it I decided this must be my day to deal with women on the brink. Vivian Evans, Dorothy's best friend, sounded even more distraught than Ingrid had earlier.

"Joe told me that he's given you and Esme the go-ahead to finish the Pritchett scrapbooks."

"Yes," I said warily.

"This really meant a lot to Dorothy, just meant the world to her, really," Vivian said, alternating between sniffling and choking up. "It will be a gift to the whole community. I just wanted to let you know Joe and Ingrid have put me in charge of planning the memorial for Dorothy up at the house."

I'd never known anyone who'd engaged an event planner to handle a funeral, but I learned a long time ago that the wealthy do things differently.

"I see," I answered, which was politese for *So why are you telling me this?*

"I want to make sure you know how important it is the

scrapbooks be done and ready for display. And how absolutely critical it is that you do a *thorough* job with this. Harrison Pritchett was the town father, the founder. We need a *complete* history. So if you need to do more research you should definitely plan on that."

That last hit at my pride. "I'm not sure what you're trying to say," I said. "Mrs. Porter was very happy with our report."

"Yes, of course she was. I didn't mean anything," Vivian said, still sniffling, "I'm just so upset. Dorothy and I were such close friends. I just can't believe she's gone. I want to make sure her legacy, the Pritchett family legacy, lives on. I'm only saying if there's anything you might have missed, there's still time."

"Good to know," I said. "We'll certainly follow up if we find any loose ends."

"What was all that about?" Esme asked as I placed the receiver back in the cradle.

"Vivian Evans," I said, "urging us to be thorough."

"Are we ever anything else?" Esme said. "Those two seem like unlikely friends, don't they?" she mused. "I hear she's taking Dorothy's death harder than anybody, except little Cassidy maybe."

"I don't think you and I are in any position to talk about unlikely friendships. Look at the two of us."

We both cocked our heads as we heard a "Yoo-hoo" coming from the front hall. We have a liberal open door policy with our friends and we never lock our doors when we're home, though in light of what happened to Dorothy I was wondering if we needed to rethink things. I opened the door to the workroom and caught the multi-hued blur of a broomstick skirt as its wearer disappeared into the kitchen. I followed.

"Brought you tomatoes," Coco said, pulling things from the bag she'd set on the table. She lined up six of the gnarliest-looking tomatoes I'd ever seen on the counter. Then she saw my face.

"Yes, I know, sweetie, they look awful. They're heritage tomatoes so they haven't had symmetry and color bred into them, but on the other hand they haven't had the taste bred *out* of them. These are tomatoes as the Almighty intended. You'll see."

"Great timing, Coco," Esme said, coming up behind me. "We'll have BLTs for supper. You got time for a glass of tea with us?"

Coco consulted the little watch hanging from a long chain around her neck. "Sure thing," she said, "and BLTs sound luscious. Mind if I invite myself to supper?"

Esme went into kitchen-general mode and started issuing orders. "Coco, you toast the bread. Sophreena, you wash the lettuce and slice the tomatoes and I'll fry up the bacon."

"Okay, so I hear you two are to go ahead with the Pritchett family scrapbooks. How's that going?" Coco said as she rummaged in the bread drawer.

"How do you *know* this?" I asked. "We didn't even know it ourselves until a few hours ago."

"Small town, hon," Coco said, shrugging. "Vivian told me. She came by the studio wanting me to do an urn for Dorothy's remains, but I told her I'm not the potter for the job."

"You don't do urns?" I asked.

"Oh yes, I do them. I've done some lovely ones if I do say so myself. But always for people I knew and liked. If I'm honest I have to say I didn't particularly like Dorothy Porter. I didn't dislike her either, really. I just didn't know her. But the little contact I had with her left a negative vibe with me. And that sinks right into the clay when I'm working it. If the urn's to be her eternal resting place she should have good vibes around her, especially considering how she went."

"I hear you," Esme said, making a bacon colonnade in her trusty cast-iron skillet.

"I know you do, Esme," Coco said. "That's why I love you, darlin'. I feel so much less alone in my little strange world since you've come to us. Now, on a more earthly plane, I hear the police questioned that couple that moved down here last year from New Jersey about Dorothy's murder. The ones that bought the old McPherson house up on Crescent Hill."

"The Emersons," I said. "I know Audrey from the Friends of the Library group. Very nice lady. Why in the world are the police questioning them?"

"They're the ones Dorothy blackballed for country club membership. I don't know what she had against them, but apparently they got off on the wrong foot with her and she held the deciding vote on the membership committee. Allen Emerson made some unfortunate remarks in front of a bunch of people about wanting to"—Coco made two-fingered quote marks in the air—"'wring her neck' for upsetting his wife."

"Oh, for heaven's sake," I said, "people don't mean things like that literally."

"That's on me," Esme said, leaning away from the sizzling bacon. "I'm the one who prattled on to the detective about that little dust-up. I let my mouth get away from my brain. But it's no more ridiculous than the police suspecting us, Sophreena. And people have killed for less."

"I smell bacon!" came a shout from the front hall. "You can smell it all the way down the sidewalk," Jack said as he came into the kitchen. "That smell's enough to make an orthodox vegetarian backslide."

Coco raised her hand. "Me. I allow myself one meat a month, and it's almost always bacon, then I send PETA a check. Call me a hypocrite, but that balances for me."

"You want to join us?" I asked. "There's plenty. And Coco promises me these tomatoes taste better than they look." I sawed away, mounting up amoeba-shaped slices on the cutting board.

"Love to," he said, "but can't. I'm taking Julie to dinner. Thought maybe I could set her straight on this whole thing about you and Esme being under suspicion and all that."

"Well, you *do* that," I said.

Coco winced. The words had come out the way I'd thought them, not the way I'd meant to say them out loud.

"Good then," Jack said, frowning as he studied my face. "I just came by to see if you wanted me to put in those succulents you got at the nursery. I saw last night they were still in the garage and I know you two are probably up to your eyeballs in Pritchett family scrapbooks now you've gotten the go-ahead."

"And how do *you* know this?" I asked.

"I heard it from Marydale who I guess heard it from Linda Burnette, Dorothy's housekeeper, who heard it from Vivian, maybe? Don't know where she heard it."

"Well, anyhow, you're right," Esme said, "we are up to our eyeballs with this thing and yes, please, we'd appreciate it a bunch if you'd put those plants in for us."

He glanced at his watch. "Got just enough time before I need to get home and clean up to meet Julie."

I had a sneaking hunch I wasn't going to like Julie.

nine

I CALLED JACK THE NEXT MORNING WHILE I WAS WAITING IMPA-
tiently for Mr. Coffee to give up his last gurgle. It doesn't
take much to make me peevish in the morning, but I was
determined to make nice.

"Thanks for putting the plants in," I said to get us right
off on a positive note. I stood on tiptoes and peered out the
kitchen window at the patio. "They look great."

"No problem. Man, you're up at early-thirty. This deadline
must have you desperate."

"No kidding." I steeled myself and asked what was really
on my mind, trying my best to keep the snarkiness out of my
voice. "So how was your dinner last night?"

"Okay, only I think my plan backfired."

"What do you mean, 'backfired'?"

"I explained all about you and Esme. What you do and
the job you were doing for Dorothy—all of it. But now Julie's
thinking maybe you uncovered some deep, dark family secret
and that's what got Dorothy killed."

"Oh, good grief," I muttered. "Other than a couple of

disreputable distant ancestors the Pritchett family was pretty much mom and apple pie, at least the public face of it. I mean, Dorothy's father, William, was a lout, but I think that's probably the worst-kept secret in town. We're not muckrakers, you know. We just look at what's on the public record and in their personal papers if we're lucky enough to find those. People don't usually post their dark secrets in those places. Though in years to come Facebook is going to be a treasure trove of *way too* personal info for future genealogists. I hope I'm out of the business by then."

"Yeah, well, I wanted to give you a heads-up in case Julie comes around trying to score an interview with you or Esme."

"That won't be happening," I said.

"Maybe she won't even try," he said. "I think she's following up more reasonable leads. She says there's a witness who saw someone in the vicinity of High Ground around the time Dorothy died."

"Really?" I asked, perking up despite the delay in my caffeine infusion. "Does she know who it was?"

"The witness or the lurker?" Jack asked.

"Either."

"Not that she was willing to tell me," he said.

Much as I wanted the info, the fact that Julie had been unwilling to share something with Jack just tickled me pink. What was wrong with me?

"Gotta go," Jack said. "I'm at the job site."

"Later," I said. When I put back the receiver I noticed Esme's coffee cup already in the sink. I thought I'd crawled out of bed before she did, for once.

I went to the workroom and found her at the scanning station.

"What time did you get *up*?" I asked. "It's only seven-thirty."

"Couldn't sleep. Figured I might as well do something productive."

I stood in the doorway sipping my coffee. We have an ironclad rule, no food or drink in the workroom. I told her about Jack's failed tactic with Julie and about the lurker.

"Good. Maybe this witness will break the case, but if not we're gonna have to accept that this thing is going to take a while to run its course and there's not much we can do to speed up the process."

"Since when did you get so zen? Yesterday you were ready to put on the boxing gloves and climb in the ring."

"I know," she said, resting her elbow on the desktop and cradling her forehead with her hand.

I set my coffee mug on the occasional table just outside the door and went to sit beside her. "You okay?" I asked, reaching over to clasp her arm.

"Yes, I'm fine—sorta fine," she said. "Another nighttime visit, but at least this time I know who it is. It's Dorothy's grandmother, Sarah. She's reached out again. Seems we're buddies now."

"Yeah?" I asked. "What'd she have? Does she know who killed Dorothy?"

"No, nothing that helpful," Esme said. "As usual the message is open to interpretation." She gave another heavy sigh as she carefully placed an old cabinet card photo of Sarah

Malone Pritchett into a protective sleeve. "She says, and I'm quoting here: *The time is nigh. All the black-winged ravens may come home to roost for no innocent will suffer.*"

"What is that, some kind of failed haiku? What does it mean?"

"How I wish I knew, Sophreena. I swear I don't understand why they ever started calling this thing a gift. Most times it's more like a curse."

I picked up the protective sleeve and studied the photo of Dorothy's grandmother. Sarah Malone Pritchett. It was a cabinet card, popular in the late 1800s and into the early 1900s. The paper photograph was affixed to a commercially produced mounting card with the name and location of the studio in elaborate calligraphy on the back. These images were larger than the older tintypes or ambrotypes. They could be viewed from a distance when they were set on a cabinet in the parlor, hence the name.

Sarah Malone had been a hauntingly beautiful woman. As was the convention of the day, in this headshot she was looking off into the distance, not directly at the camera. She was smiling but it was a wistful, Mona Lisa smile. No say-cheese grins back then. Her hair was piled on top of her head and clasped with a jeweled sunburst. A matching brooch was pinned to the scooped-neck bodice of her fru-fru dress, which had all manner of gathers and ruffles and tulle puffs for sleeves. Neither her ears nor her peaches-and-cream neckline were adorned. The photograph had an ethereal quality to it and as I studied it somehow it didn't seem unnatural that this woman would be contacting Esme from beyond the great divide.

"Sarah Malone Pritchett seems to have something she

needs to get off her chest. Let's see what all we know about her." I turned to the computer and started to open folders.

"Sophreena, you do *realize* we only have a few days to finish all this, right? We've got to stay on task. That'll have to wait."

Esme was right and I dutifully buckled down to work. We scanned for hours and *hours*, stopping only for a scarfed-down salad for lunch. By mid-afternoon I was sick of the hum of the motors and the strobe of the light. My back hurt and my bottom had gone completely numb. So when Winston tapped on the door announcing he'd brought fresh raspberry scones I wanted to kiss his feet.

Esme asked for a few minutes to finish her stack of photos and I tried to admire her work ethic, but really I was just annoyed that she was keeping me from those scones.

Obeying the workroom rules, Winston set the bag on the table outside and strolled in to marvel at the piles of material covering every available surface. He gave a long, slow whistle. "Whatever you two are getting paid, it's not enough."

"You're telling me," I said. "I underbid. I had no idea there'd be this much material."

Winston pointed to a photograph on the top of a pile. "See there, told you she was a pretty girl. I think I remember this picture. Must have been her high school graduation."

"Right you are," I said. "Nineteen fifty-seven."

Winston smiled. "Dorothy was the queen of the school, pretty, popular and from a wealthy family. I was a lowly freshman, the awkward offspring of a cabinetmaker and a grocery store clerk. Her daddy had hired me in the summertime to cut their grass and do little odd jobs around High Ground so she knew me. And she was very nice to me. Would always say hello to me in school and not stick her nose up and walk by like she couldn't be bothered like most of the girls from up on Crescent Hill did."

I've always believed a good family history should put family dates and events into the context of their time, and I've been at this so long I now have a mental almanac that starts to run in my head at the mention of a date. "Nineteen fifty-seven," I repeated slowly. "Eisenhower president, Sputnik launched, mob threatened nine black kids integrating Little Rock schools, Asian flu pandemic, Jack Kerouac's *On the Road* published, new cars cost less than three thousand dollars and sported huge tail fins, gas at twenty-four cents a gallon, hula hoops and Slinkys the hot toys, and black and white TV premiered *Leave It to Beaver* and *Perry Mason*."

Winston chuckled. "It's like you were there. Course, I was probably more concerned with where I was going to scrape up the money to go see Elvis in *Jailhouse Rock* at the movie theater over in Chapel Hill than with any of those things."

He picked up another photo safely tucked inside its protective sleeve and looked at it more closely, "That baby she's holding in this one, that's Ingrid, right?"

"Right again," I said. I raised my arms and stretched, trying not to drool as I thought of those scones out there waiting for me.

"Dorothy was really attached to her baby sister, looked after her night and day. Mrs. Pritchett was a frail little woman and I think something went wrong when Ingrid was born. She never really recovered and died a couple of years later."

I glanced up at the timeline we had tacked up on the wall. "Yes, I think Dorothy would have been about twelve in that photo. Expecting a girl that age to take care of a baby all the time was a lot to ask."

"They had a nanny for a while, I think," Winston said. "Or a governess or whatever you want to call it. Some gal they brought in from out in the country. Anyhow, she didn't last long. Old William Pritchett was a hard man to work for; I can attest to that. Dorothy had to take on a lot of responsibility. Then after Mrs. Pritchett passed, William hired an older widow woman as a live-in housekeeper to cook and clean and look after Ingrid. Mrs. Stoddard was her name, cranky old fussbudget. Really, I think Dorothy still looked after Ingrid most of the time, or looked *out* for her anyway. You know how it seems like the baby usually gets doted on? Well, their daddy not only didn't spoil Ingrid, he singled her out as a target for his meanness. He was awful hard on her."

"Might have blamed her for his wife's death," Esme said. "That happens sometimes in situations like that."

"Could be." Winston shrugged. "Though, truth be told, he didn't seem that attached to his wife either. All I can say is it didn't surprise me when Ingrid ran away."

Esme closed the lid to the scanner and clicked it off with a flourish. "Lead me to those scones, my dear man."

We fixed iced tea and went out onto the patio. It was hot out, but there was a breeze and it felt great to be outdoors.

"I ran into Vivian Evans this morning," Winston said. "She didn't look too good. She's taking Dorothy's death hard."

"They've been close friends for a long time, I take it," Esme said.

"Not really," Winston said, frowning. "I mean, maybe the close part, but not the long. There's a big age gap. I think

Vivian's more Ingrid's age. Vivian didn't grow up here in town, though I think their families might've known each other. But Vivian and Dorothy surely got to know each other real well during Dorothy's beautification campaign."

"Maybe that's why they were close, they were joined in the cause," Esme said.

"Oh, no," Winston said with a chuckle. "That's not how it was at all. Vivian's husband, Frank, owned a little diner right downtown. It's the Sunrise Café now, but it used to be just a plain storefront diner. Didn't even have a name. Everybody just called it the Diner. When the pressure came on the downtown businesses to pretty up their places Frank didn't comply. He was barely holding on as it was and didn't have a nickel to spare. When Dorothy pushed through all the new ordinances he couldn't afford the upgrades and had to sell out."

"Dorothy put Vivian's husband out of business?" I said. "And yet they became friends? How did that work?"

"I'm not sure," Winston said with a shrug. "Frank died not long after that—heart attack. Shame. He was only in his late forties. Maybe Dorothy felt bad. There's some around who'd say she *should* have felt bad. I know she helped Vivian get started in her event planning business after that. It was a peculiar start to a friendship, I'll grant you that, but it seemed like they got real close over the years."

I'd polished off my scone and I was ogling another one, which I didn't need. I distracted myself by asking Winston how his research was going.

"That's one reason I came by," he said. "I just had to tell y'all the latest."

"And?" I prompted.

"Got a call from that woman at the historical society down in South Carolina and she's located a relative who has lots of information about the Lovett family. We had a long phone conversation this morning. Erik is his name. He lives up in Maryland, sounds like he's not much older than my oldest grandson, but he's graduated from college already. Smart fella and nice as he could be—"

"*What* did you find out?" Esme cut in.

"Sorry," Winston said. "He says he's got an old diary I need to read. He's going to send me a digital copy."

"So you haven't really found out anything concrete yet," I said.

"No particulars, but this fella says it's certain my twelve fathered children with a slave woman and that I'm a descendant of theirs. But he tells me there's lots more to the story and I shouldn't judge the man until I know it all."

"Always good advice," I said, thinking of how I'd judged Dorothy without knowing much about her life. I knew about her ancestors and had admiration for some of them, but I'd dismissed Dorothy as nothing more than a society matron with entitlement issues.

Just then I heard the bells tolling at the Presbyterian church six blocks away: Dorothy's church. I glanced at my watch. The funeral was over. Dorothy herself had now passed into the Pritchett family history.

When the day's scanning was done I organized the electronic files while Esme set out the scrapbooking supplies on the long table in the middle of the room.

As I was going through the folders I ran across a photo of the Pritchett ring I'd taken with my cell phone just after we found it. I'd completely forgotten about it with all that had happened afterward. It was a close-up shot and not the best quality, but not bad for a cell phone camera.

Esme wasn't happy but after some discussion we decided we needed to call Detective Carlson. If this had been a robbery the photo could be helpful to the case.

When Carlson arrived an hour later he was dressed in jeans and a T-shirt. He was off duty, though as he said, "Nobody's gonna be *really* off-duty 'til this one closes."

I'd printed off the photo with the best resolution I could get and burned it onto a disc in case the department techies wanted to take a whirl at enhancing it.

"What else do you know about this ring?" he asked, absentmindedly reaching to a breast pocket that wasn't there. He seemed a little off his game without his trusty notebook and ballpoint. I slid a stack of sticky notes and a pen across to him.

"We don't know anything else about it," I said. "But I'm sure it's quite valuable."

"Seems odd, though," Carlson said, almost to himself. "If robbery was the motive why didn't they snatch the other stuff, too? She had on another impressive ring plus one of those tennis bracelets and earrings, all diamonds. And I'm pretty sure they were the real stuff. Why didn't the perp take those?"

"Interrupted?" I offered.

Carlson pursed his lips. "Could be."

"The pearls, too," Esme said, reluctantly joining the conversation. "Those weren't cultured pearls, they were the real thing. A whole lot of oysters put up with a whole lot of aggravation to make those. They were very old. Dorothy told us her grandfather brought them back from the Orient. I expect they were expensive."

"Pearls?" Carlson said, frowning. Then he repeated the word, almost in a whisper, and I could see his mind was somewhere else.

"Pearls," Esme said impatiently. "She was wearing them when we saw her that day. Three strands around her neck?" She demonstrated by gesturing arcs across her chest, then her eyes grew wide. "Oh, dear Lord," she said. "Was she strangled with the pearls?"

Carlson scribbled something on the sticky note but didn't reply.

"You didn't find her pearls," Esme said, more a statement than a question.

Again Carlson didn't answer. He pulled off the sticky note and stuffed it in his jeans pocket. "Thanks for calling me about this," he said, picking up the envelope with the photo.

"You're welcome," Esme said, briskly. "Now did you talk to the gal at the gas station? Are we free to leave town?"

"You planning a trip?" he asked.

"No," Esme answered. "But *could* we if we wanted to?"

"Yeah, sure," Carlson said with a shrug. "I did talk to the clerk and she remembers you being there. You're free to do whatever you please. But I—we—may still have some questions. I hope y'all will make yourselves available if we do."

His eyes never strayed from Esme. I might as well have been a chair. As I watched a smile crinkle up the corners of his eyes, the dime finally dropped.

Somebody was sweet on Esme.

ten

In summer Esme and I try to get in our walk before it gets too hot. This morning we were doing our routine three-mile loop, with a stop at the coffee shop at the halfway point. I get a lot more exercise on these outings than Esme does. For every stride she takes I have to take two. She claims I have the advantage of youth so she cuts me no slack.

As we walked by the main administration building of Morningside High School on Parsons Street, Esme pointed. "I've been thinking about what Winston said about how much the town has changed. Is this what the high school looked like when you graduated?"

"Pretty much," I answered, trying not to huff and puff. "There's a new football field and the music building was built since then. Everything's been spruced up and there's nicer landscaping, but other than that it hasn't changed much."

"What year did you graduate?" she asked, and I noticed with some irritation that she wasn't even breaking a sweat.

"Nineteen ninety-eight," I said. "Bill Clinton was president and embroiled in the Lewinsky scandal; Carl Wilson, my favorite Beach Boy, died that year and so did Linda McCartney, another favorite. The embassies were bombed, Hurricane Mitch hit Central America and killed a bunch of people and an earthquake in Afghanistan killed even more."

"I see," Esme said. "Tell me, Sophreena, did anything good happen in 1998?"

"I'm sure it did, but I was in a bad place so I guess I only noticed the bad. Let's see, there was peace in Northern Ireland, that's good. Europeans adopted the euro, is that good or bad?"

"Jury's still out," Esme said. "How about music, movies, things you enjoyed?"

"Let's see, for movies it was *Saving Private Ryan, Armageddon* . . ."

"Okay, let's forget movies," Esme cut in. "How about music?"

"Green Day, Spice Girls, Alanis Morissette," I rattled off. Esme made a face like she smelled something bad.

"Television?"

"*X-Files*," I said. "I *loved* that show."

"Me, too," Esme said. "It seemed like a documentary to me."

"Oh, and gas was a buck a gallon," I added.

"Now that's enough to make a person nostalgic," Esme said as we turned onto Sandhill Avenue.

Esme and I are creatures of habit. We like taking the same route every day and I knew this stretch on Sandhill was the best time to bring up a delicate subject. At least going downhill I stand a chance of keeping up if she gets steamed and starts truckin'.

"So what do you think of Detective Carlson?" I asked, trying for casual.

Esme wasn't buying it. "Say what you mean, Sophreena. Are you asking if I think he's good at his job?"

"Do you think he's handsome?" I asked.

"Yes, he's a good-lookin' man," Esme allowed.

"He's crushin' on you, Esme," I teased as I turned to dance along backward in front of her.

"Yes, I can see that," Esme said flatly.

This bummed me out. I'd been pretty proud I'd picked up on it and I'd thought I was the only one so astute. "Well?" I asked.

"Well, nothin'," Esme said. "I told you long ago, Sophreena. I am done with men. I walked down that long aisle to one man and I gave him everything I had and he *took* everything I gave and then some more. After him I took back my name and my life. I'm better off on my own."

Esme had married young. She'd fallen for the very kind of man her mother had warned her against, a musician. He'd broken her heart over and over again but she kept struggling to make it work. Six years into the troubled marriage, he'd set out in a van with four other musicians bound for a gig in Chicago. Somewhere in southern Illinois they were t-boned by a semi. No one survived the crash. I'd asked her once if he's ever tried to contact her from beyond the grave and she'd said, "Roland was never good about calling when he was out on a gig. Said long distance was too expensive. Well, this is *way* long distance, so no, not word nor sign."

"But Esme, every man's not like that," I said now. "And

anyway, you wouldn't have to marry Carlson, for heaven's sake. You could just go out with him. Have some fun."

"I have fun already, Sophreena. End of subject."

We'd reached Top o' the Morning, the coffee shop everyone in town frequents to get their caffeine and town news. Esme stopped at one of the outside tables to say hello to a friend from church and I went inside and got in line. I spotted Jack standing near the pick-up counter, clicking away on his BlackBerry as he waited for his coffee. He looked up as if he'd felt my eyes on him and walked over.

"Hey, I was gonna call. You want to catch a movie tonight or something? I've been working too hard, I need a break and I'm bettin' you're in the same boat."

"Wish I could," I said, surprised by how big an understatement that was, "but we're going to have to work overtime to get the Pritchett family scrapbooks done in time."

"Okay, then," Jack said as the young barista called his name and set his order on the counter.

Two cups. Not good.

"Well, step over here after you get your coffee," Jack said. "I want you to meet Julie."

He picked up a coffee in each hand and gestured toward one of the bistro tables in the front window. A woman was sitting with her long legs crossed, talking on her cell phone. She was blond and willowy, nicely dressed, beautifully groomed and a perfectly dreadful human being. I was certain of it. Julie was going to be easy to hate.

But after I got our coffee I trudged over dutifully to be introduced, hyper-aware of my sweaty clothes and droopy hair divided into two messy ponytails.

"It's nice to meet you," Julie said, putting out a hand then realizing I didn't have one free to shake. "Jackie's told me so much about you."

"Really? Has Jackie?" I turned toward Jack.

"I know Julie from college days," he said. "That's what everybody called me then."

"When we weren't calling you Mr. McStudly," Julie said with a laugh. She reached over to touch his arm.

"Nice to meet you, but I gotta get this coffee to Esme before it gets cold."

"But wait," Julie called as I turned to go. "I'd like to talk to you about—"

"No comment," I said over my shoulder. "Absolutely *no* comment."

Esme had grabbed one of the tables outside. She passed over a water bottle from her waist pack as I set the coffee in front of her. "Water first," she instructed. "Now, what's that scowl on your face all about?"

"Nothing," I said.

"It's somethin'," Esme insisted. "But I suppose you'll tell me when it suits you."

I glanced over and saw Vivian Evans writing furiously in a big notebook and when she looked up she held up a wait-a-minute finger as if I'd asked her to come over, which I hadn't. She looked worse than I did. Vivian was normally very polished, but today her eyes were red-rimmed, her clothing rumpled and her hair was in a bun, skinned back so tight it looked like it hurt.

She came over and went into a passive-aggressive scolding. "I'm surprised you two have time for lingering over coffee with the scrapbooks due. Now, remember, Dorothy would've wanted you to cover *absolutely* everything concerning the family. Double- or triple-check if need be."

"So you've said," I replied, trying to give the woman the benefit of the doubt. "Look, Vivian, I know Dorothy was your friend. This must be a very hard time for you. But you have to believe me, we'll deliver what we promised her."

Vivian's eyes filled with tears and she bit her bottom lip. "I'm sorry," she said. "Nobody seems to understand how close Dorothy and I were. No offense to Ingrid, but I was more a sister to Dorothy than she was. Surely you, of all people," she said, looking from Esme to me, "can understand that."

The most I expected of Esme was that she'd hold her tongue after Vivian had questioned our professionalism, but she surprised me by offering Vivian words of comfort. "It's hard to lose a friend. It's good you want her memory to live on."

"I do," Vivian said, wiping at her eyes. "I want that."

Just then three women walked by. The younger one I recognized from my yoga class, Sherry something. But the others I couldn't place. They were blatantly staring at us and I felt the color go to my face. Would this never end?

"Here we are," I said to Esme in a low voice, "the Thelma and Louise of Morningside."

"Don't mind them," Vivian said when the women were out of earshot. "The tall one's Leticia Morgan. She's overly suspicious, probably because she was once married to a cop—that Detective Carlson. She's married to a banker now. She takes a couple of the bank employees out to coffee or lunch occasionally. Makes her feel good about herself."

So the rumor mill was still grinding. Esme was right, we were just going to have to hold our heads high, which is exactly what she was did when the women came back out of the coffee shop. She stared right back.

I had to hand it to Carlson, he had good taste in women. Leticia Morgan was a beauty, though she didn't hold a candle to Esme.

Vivian started to tear up again as she watched them walk away. "Poor Dorothy, she would've hated being the subject of this horrible spectacle. This is not the way a Pritchett should be remembered."

"Vivian," Esme said, her voice gentle, "can I ask you a question?"

"I guess," Vivian said, wiping her red nose with a hanky.

"I'm sorry to be so blunt," Esme said, "but how is it you could become friends with the woman who helped put your husband out of business? I don't understand that."

"Oh, that wasn't Dorothy's doing," Vivian said. "It was just circumstances. And anyway, in the end it was the best thing that could have happened to him—to us. When Frank was running the diner he put in *such* long hours and I was working for the phone company over in Chapel Hill. We never saw each other. After Frank sold out we had time together, for a little while anyway. It was a blessing really. And Dorothy helped me get started in my own business after Frank died. Something I could throw all my energies into. She made sure all the right people hired me for their events and coached me on what discriminating clients expect. She said I was a natural, that I had exquisite taste." Her face contorted and the tears came again.

Esme patted her hand. "I'm sure Dorothy will be smiling down on you on her memorial day. And you needn't worry, we won't let you down."

Vivian nodded, fighting to keep her emotions in check, and went back to her table to scribble some more in her notebook.

"That was very kind of you," I said.

"I'm a very kind person, Sophreena," Esme said. "Just because I don't enjoy putting up with people's nonsense doesn't mean I can't see when they're in pain. And she is *racked* with it."

I called Ingrid when we got home to let her know we were about to begin work on the scrapbooks. Less than an hour later she arrived looking like she'd had another hard night, but smiling gamely. "Sophreena, thanks for letting us do this. Cassidy'll be here soon. Her daddy's spending some time with her this morning then taking her out to an early lunch."

"How're you doing?" I asked, as I guided her toward the workroom.

"I think I'm still in shock. Dorothy was always healthy as a horse, so I guess I got the idea that we'd have plenty of time to fix what was broken between us. I didn't count on anything like this."

When we stepped through the doorway Ingrid looked around. "Wow, how much of this is from the Pritchett family?"

"All of it," I said.

She gave me a jaw drop, then walked over to the scrap-booking table where we had the first few pages in progress. "Is it okay to touch?" she asked, eyeing the cotton gloves Esme was wearing.

"Oh, yeah," I said. "She's been filing originals, but the scrapbooks are meant to get handled."

I attempted an abridged version of what we'd done as Ingrid looked at the pages. "Dorothy was our *proband*, to use a word borrowed from the medical field. That's the family member first studied in a genetic investigation that traces back from him or her. Since Dorothy was our client she was our proband—our generation one. We worked our way back through six generations in the Pritchett line before we hit a wall with Edmund Thomas Pritchett, your ancestor who emigrated from England to the United States in the mid-1700s. To go further would have required more time, travel and some heavy expenses so Dorothy had us stop there."

I'd been working on the family tree in the hour before Ingrid arrived, filling in a decorative chart in my best calligraphy. It looked great if I did say so myself.

"Interesting," Ingrid said as she studied it. "It's beautifully done, but I don't think I ever heard any of these names. Course, I was young so maybe I did and I just don't remember. In case you haven't figured it out already, I'm the official black sheep of the Pritchett family. And now the Pritchett name has ended." Her voice caught, then came out as a growl. "Pity it didn't end sooner."

Shock must have showed on my face, because when Ingrid looked up she blanched.

"Oh God, I didn't mean Dorothy. My father was the only window I had into the character of the Pritchetts and let's just say it was a dark and frightful view."

"We know you left home when you were young," Esme said, "but in some of these old pictures it looks like you and Dorothy were very close at one time."

Ingrid smiled, a real smile this time. "We were," she said as she turned to a new page. I wasn't sure she was taking in anything in front of her; she seemed lost in her own memories. "Dorothy was like a mother to me when I was little, or at least what I imagine a mother to be. At the very least she was a protective big sister." She laughed, but tears welled in her eyes. "As long as she could be, anyway."

"You can see it in the pictures, how much you loved each other," Esme said softly.

Ingrid shook her head "Yes, we did then and we still did, despite everything. Things just got all scrambled up somewhere along the way. Our father was a tyrant, there's no other way to put it. He wanted to control every aspect of our lives. Dorothy was the good, obedient daughter, but I couldn't take it."

"Ingrid, forgive me for prying, but was there abuse?" I asked.

"He didn't hit and he wasn't a pervert, if that's what you're asking. But he was controlling and cruel—psychologically abusive. I ran away when I was not quite fifteen and he disowned me on the spot. Never looked for me and never spoke to me again. Dorothy tried to be the peacemaker a few times over the years, but I got angry because I thought she was taking his side. It drove a wedge between us. And, of course, since I was already dead to him he didn't leave me a penny in his will. The entire estate passed to Dorothy. That fact has the cops all a-twitter and tongues wagging all over town. They assume I'll inherit everything now, which I seriously doubt. And it doesn't help that Dorothy and I quarreled so much."

"The police questioned you?" I asked.

"Yes, but I'm fine with that. They're doing their job and if I were in their position I'd be looking hard at me, too. Thankfully, I have an airtight alibi. One of the doctor's patients, the youngest Cahill boy, fell off his bike doing one of those fancy tricks and cut his arm on a metal railing. He needed sixteen stitches. I stayed with his mother while the doc fixed him up. She gets queasy at the sight of blood, and there was plenty of it. She was holding on to my hand the whole time, I mean *really* holding on to my hand." Ingrid flexed her fingers as if she could still feel the woman's grip.

"Still, I'm sorry you had to endure the questioning," I said. "We got a little taste of it ourselves and it wasn't pleasant."

"It's the gossip that bothers me. People think they've got the story, but they don't know what Dorothy and I were going through. We were trying to work things out. I know you two had the unfortunate opportunity of seeing what that looked like. I'm embarrassed at how I acted with her sometimes, but we are—were—both so stubborn." She sighed. "If we hadn't run out of time we'd have sorted out everything. We both agreed we owed it to one another and to Cassidy."

"Cassidy really loved Dorothy, didn't she?" Esme asked.

"And Dorothy loved her right back," Ingrid said. "I admit I didn't like that at first. *I'm* Cassidy's grandmother. I thought

Dorothy was trying to horn in on that and I was jealous. But gradually I realized it was good for Cassidy to have Dorothy in her life, too."

I wanted very badly to ask about Dorothy's estate. But first off, it was totally insensitive and second, it was none of our business anymore, we'd been paid. I just wanted to satisfy my curiosity. If Dorothy had rewritten her will recently my bet was on Cassidy as heir. But she was a minor, so who would really have control of Dorothy's fortune?

Just then the doorbell rang and Esme went to get it, returning a few seconds later with Cassidy and her father. I noticed Jeremy sneaking a peek at his watch. He nodded a greeting at Esme and me. "Thanks a lot for letting her come do this," he said, looking around the room with a decided lack of interest. He didn't wait for a reply but slapped his hands together. "Hey, Tadpole, I gotta get to work. See you tonight."

"Okay, Daddy," Cassidy said, giving him a big grin. "I liked going to lunch and thank you for the—" She glanced over at Ingrid then put her finger to her lips.

"Let me guess, the chocolate sundae?" Ingrid said in a mock scold.

"Just a little one," Jeremy said, holding out a cupped hand and grinning as he backed out of the room. "A little baby sundae."

Cassidy giggled and ran to him. He scooped her up and they gave each other a fierce hug. I'd never had the warm fuzzies for Jeremy Garrison, but he was obviously a devoted father and that earned him points.

Cassidy was still carrying around the little cloth bag with

her assortment of busy work inside and she began to unload it on the table. She set out a small stuffed dog, a sketchbook and crayons and the puzzle box. She looked them over carefully then picked up the puzzle box.

"Have you solved it yet?" Esme asked.

"No," she said, rubbing her fingers across the wooden surface studded with opalescent inlays. "It's hard."

"I'm betting you'll get it," I said. "But it's okay if you don't. It's just a game."

"Auntie Dot said I'm stubborn as the day is long," Cassidy said, "but she said sometimes that's a good thing."

"My mom used to say the same thing about me," I told her. "But I say we're determined, not stubborn."

Cassidy smiled. It was a weak one, but it was a smile.

"I see you brought your art supplies," I said, nodding to the crayons and sketchbook. Would you like to draw a picture for the scrapbooks? Maybe you could draw your Aunt Dot's house."

This got a grin and she set the box aside and began to draw, her tongue curled around her lip as she concentrated.

I told Ingrid I was just about to start working on the pages for her grandparents, Harrison James Pritchett and Sarah Malone Pritchett. I did *not* mention that Esme had been having a very long-distance tête-à-tête with Sarah.

"I don't remember them all that well," Ingrid said. "They're more of a feeling for me than a true memory. Do you know what I mean?"

"Oh, do I ever," Esme said, low enough so that only I heard her.

"But it's a good feeling," Ingrid went on. "Dorothy adored

Grandpa Harry and Grandma Sarah and she told me lots of stories about them."

"Great," I said. "If you know any information about any of these photos speak up and I'll make sure it gets noted in the scrapbooks."

"Me, too?" Cassidy asked.

"Definitely," Esme said. "I'm sure your Aunt Dot told you lots of family stories."

"Uh-huh. She said knowing where you came from is what keeps people rooted." Cassidy frowned. "I thought that was silly. People don't have roots, trees have roots, oh, and plants and stuff. Can I look at the pictures?"

"You can do more than that," Esme said. "You can help put them in the scrapbooks. How about you come around here and work with me."

Ingrid watched as I worked on the two-page spread for Harrison James Pritchett and Sarah Malone from 1893 to 1894, the year before they were married. There were three photographs of Harrison Pritchett, taken at different times, by different photographers during that time period.

"He was quite a dandy, wasn't he?" I said.

Ingrid laughed. "Dorothy preferred the term *bon vivant*. I remember he was a sharp dresser even when he was old. He was quite handsome back then," she said, studying one of the photos, "and rich to boot. No wonder everybody thought he was such a great catch for my grandmother."

"Actually, he wasn't rich back then," I said. "In fact, he grew up in somewhat diminished circumstances."

"You're kidding," Ingrid said. "I thought the Pritchetts

came from old line money. Like really old line, back to England or wherever."

"As near as we can tell, your immigrant ancestor, Edmund, arrived in this country with the proverbial shirt on his back just before the American Revolution," I said. "He settled in the tidewater area of Virginia and through the next couple of generations the Pritchetts became small plantation owners and acquired some degree of comfort. But Harrison's father, Lawton, was killed in the Civil War, leaving his wife with a baby to raise and a plantation to run on her own. In those reconstruction times it would have been a challenge even for the most experienced overseer and she couldn't keep it afloat. She managed to keep the house, but had to take in boarders to make ends meet."

"I never knew," Ingrid said. "So how did Grandpa Harry get his money?"

"By his own ingenuity and hard work," I said, making sure Cassidy was listening. "He had a dream and he worked hard. He came to this area and saw all it had to offer and brought his bride here to start a new life, though it surely wasn't a life of luxury back then. He bought land on the highest point for the house he wanted to build for his wife one day. He also purchased a plot down by the river and built a sawmill and a modest little house for them to live in while he got his business going. That was the beginning of what grew into Pritchett International."

"Where did he get the money for the land?" Ingrid asked.

"Good question," Esme said. "Things were a whole lot different back then as far as reporting income so there doesn't seem to be a paper trail. He bought the land for cash on the barrelhead."

"Wow, there's a blank I'd like to have filled in," Ingrid said, then whispered, "Maybe the Pritchett men weren't stuffy old bores after all. Maybe he robbed a bank or something and there's an outlaw in the clan."

"Well, however he got his start," I said, "he really did build his fortune on his own and I can tell you in all our research we never found anything that assailed his character. He seems to have been a very principled and generous man."

"Guess things really do skip a generation," Ingrid said, giving me a rueful smile. "My father looked nothing like him. I guess he got all Grandmother Sarah's genes from the Malone side, though he surely didn't get her temperament if what I remember about her is really how she was. I think of her as a gentle, kind person. My father was neither of those things."

I let that comment lie, since from everything we'd discovered it was true in spades. Ingrid and Dorothy's father, William, did not leave shiny testimonials in his wake. By all accounts he'd been a disagreeable man and not one to be trusted in business dealings. We'd interviewed an older gentleman who'd known him who'd said, "Will Pritchett was so crooked when he died they didn't need a coffin, they just corkscrewed him into the grave."

I showed Ingrid the pages we'd made for Sarah Malone from that time period. "Your grandmother was a beautiful woman. I think you look like her."

"Do you? Well, that's a compliment. And I did know that she grew up in—how did you put it?—diminished circumstances. Actually, I think her family had always been poor so I guess there was nothing diminished about it. That's sort of the family fairy tale, that Grandpa Harry took the poor little matchstick girl and made her queen of his castle."

"Well, now, hold on," Esme said, holding a photo down while Cassidy concentrated on painting the back with a glue stick, "the Malones weren't well-to-do, but I think that might be a bit of an exaggeration. Her parents owned a small mercantile store that did tolerably well, so your grandmother had all her needs met, though there probably wasn't much left over for luxuries."

"And her family wanted her to have some advantages. Her parents sent her to live with relatives in Richmond for a while so she could experience the cultural activities the city offered."

Ingrid chuffed. "Did Dorothy tell you that?"

"Yes," I said, puzzled by her reaction. "But we verified it through other records. She lived with the Spencer family for almost two years."

"But not as a guest," Ingrid said. "She was a live-in babysitter. Practically an indentured servant."

"Are you sure?" I asked. "Everything we've found describes her as a guest in the Spencer household."

Ingrid shook her head. "I remember distinctly hearing that Grandmother looked after the two Spencer boys. I even remember their names, Lyle and Lawrence. She used to tell Dorothy stories about what horrid little boys they were and how mean Mrs. Spencer was to her. All very Jane Eyre, but without the Mr. Rochester romance."

Esme and I exchanged glances. If that was true, what else

had Dorothy intentionally misled us about to buff luster onto the Pritchett family story?

Ingrid's account made more sense as I studied a photo of Sarah with the Spencer family. Families were usually posed in some kind of pecking order and in this photo Raeford Spencer stood beside his wife, Agnes, who was seated in an ornately carved chair. Sarah was perched on an upholstered bench off to the side with a young boy on either side of her. As was also common the subjects were not looking directly at the camera, but staring off as if viewing some oddity in the far distance—with the exception of Sarah Malone. She was looking straight into the lens and her expression could only be described as defiant.

Agnes' face indicated either deep unhappiness or severe indigestion and I could only take from Raeford's expression that he really wished he were somewhere—*anywhere*—else at that moment.

"Look, Cassidy, this is my grandmother, like I'm your grandmother," Ingrid said.

"You're my Gigi," Cassidy corrected, using her pet name for Ingrid.

"You bet I am," Ingrid said. "Come see if you think I look like my grandmother."

Cassidy puckered her lips and put on a thinking frown. "Um, maybe. Your eyes are like hers." She studied the picture some more. "Why is that lady wearing Auntie Dot's pretty new ring?"

I looked again at where Cassidy was pointing and nearly yelped. There on Agnes Spencer's chubby hand was a ring that looked remarkably like the Pritchett family heirloom.

"Auntie Dot had a new ring?" Ingrid asked. "I doubt that. Or if she did it must have been costume jewelry. Dorothy quit buying real jewelry a long time ago when she realized the people she was trying so hard to impress couldn't tell the difference between the real thing and cubic zirconium."

I was surprised the cops hadn't questioned Ingrid about the ring already and I could tell Esme was thinking the same thing.

"Auntie Dot did have a new ring, Gigi," Cassidy insisted. "That one." She pointed again to the ring on Agnes Spencer's finger. "Miss Esme and Miss Sophreena gave it to her."

Ingrid frowned, looking from me to Esme.

"Well, it did look a lot like that one," I said.

"A *lot* like that one," Esme echoed.

"The Pritchett family ring," I said, by way of explanation. "We returned it to Dorothy on the day—that day. We found it in your grandmother's belongings."

"You mean that thing is real?" Ingrid asked. "There really is a Pritchett family ring? I always thought that was just another of Dorothy's tales to try to glam up the family. Where is it now?"

"We're not sure," I said, letting my eyes come to rest on Cassidy.

Ingrid got the message, her fingertips flying to her mouth to suppress a gasp.

"I think we could use some coffee right about now," Esme said. "And Cassidy, I'll bet you could use a cup of hot chocolate. How about we go out to the kitchen and fix it?"

"Okay," Cassidy said. "But how do you *use* hot chocolate?"

Esme laughed as she took her by the hand.

"I'm sorry we didn't tell you about the ring," I said once they were out of earshot. "I assumed the police filled you in."

"Not a word," Ingrid said. "So I take it this ring is missing? Wait, does that mean Dorothy was killed for that? Oh God, yet another curse from the Pritchett family."

"I don't know any more about that than you do, Ingrid," I said. "All I know is we found it and gave it to Dorothy that afternoon." I told her about the photo I'd taken and about giving a copy to the cops.

"Do you still have a copy? Could I see it?"

The way I figured it, the ring was from Ingrid's family and she had more right than anyone else to know about the family heirlooms. I fetched the photo.

"Wow, that's big and ostentatious—a perfect symbol for the Pritchetts," Ingrid said. "You know, I think I do have some vague memory of my grandmother wearing a ring like that on special occasions. Are the stones real?"

"I didn't have it appraised." I shrugged. "When we found it we gave it to Dorothy straight away, but they sure looked real to me."

Ingrid bent to study the Spencer family portrait again, looking at the portrait then back to the photo of the ring. "They do look the same. Maybe it was a popular design of the day or something? Some sort of fad?"

"I'm not a jewelry specialist," I said, "but I know a little. Certain types of pieces were in vogue in the Georgian period when the ring was probably made. Memorial brooches made from a lock of a deceased loved one's hair, cameos, miniature portraits and lover's eye lockets that featured a small painting of the eye of a beloved were all big, as were chokers and necklaces called rivieres made of multiple strands of gems. But most wealthy families wanted their signature pieces to be distinctive and I suspect this ring was."

I pulled a magnifying loupe out of the desk drawer. I studied the ring in the photo then handed the loupe over to Ingrid. "Like I say, I'm no expert, but that sure looks like the same ring to me."

"Me, too," Ingrid said. "But why in the world would this Spencer woman have been wearing it and how did it make its way into my grandmother's possession? From what I heard about their relationship Agnes Spencer surely didn't give it to her. Maybe Grandma Sarah wasn't as upstanding as everybody thought."

eleven

HEAT AND FATIGUE MADE THE THOUGHT OF COOKING SUPPER repugnant so after Ingrid and Cassidy had left, Esme fixed us a salad with iced tea. We were in the process of some listless eating when Jack let himself in the front door.

"You're gonna need more fuel than that," he said. "Have some toast or something. I'll go get your bike out of the garage."

"And why do I need my bike?" I asked. "Did I miss a memo?"

"You've been sitting all day, right? You need fresh air and exercise. It's cooled down outside and we've got two hours of daylight. Let's go ride around the lake. Come on, chop, chop!"

I looked over at Esme, my eyes pleading with her to help me think of an excuse. She threw me under the bus.

"You heard the man, chop, chop," she said, getting up to put her dishes in the sink. "I, on the other hand, will be doing a little yoga, taking a nice long bath, watching a smidge of telly then turning in. You kids have fun."

"Okay, but before you go, let me tell you what I found out from Julie," Jack said, turning a kitchen chair around to straddle it.

I was immediately suspect of whatever information he had, considering the source, but Esme had no such reservations.

"Whatcha got?" she asked.

"According to Julie, the police are now leaning toward the theory that this was a robbery gone bad. Apparently Linda, Dorothy's housekeeper, told the police she saw a man on the front porch when she pulled out of the driveway headed for the grocery store that afternoon."

"What did the guy look like? Did she recognize him?" I asked.

"Nuh-uh. Too far away. But she thinks he had blond hair or maybe was wearing a yellow cap, she can't be sure which. But anyhow, Julie says she's heard there was valuable stuff missing and that adds up to a crime of opportunity."

"Stuff?" I said. "So the press hasn't found out about the ring yet?"

"Nope," Jack said, "but it's sure not from lack of trying. I've had doctor's exams where I got less prodding and probing than I got from Julie."

Because I was miffed at Jack I hated to admit the bike ride had been a good idea, but it was great to be in the fresh air and moving after being hunched over a layout table all day.

Misty Lake is a manmade body of water formed when civil engineers dammed Potters Creek back during the

1930s. The eastern shore is lined with nice middle-class homes of differing sizes and architectural styles. A bike and hiking path snakes through the neighborhood along the waterfront.

Across the way the west side lakefront is dotted with private piers and gazebos. No public access on the western shore. The land slopes up to the most expensive homes in Morningside perched along the ridge known as Crescent Hill. The Pritchett house, known as High Ground, is located on the highest point.

Motorboats are forbidden on the lake, but rowboats, kayaks and canoes are encouraged. There's even a reasonably priced pedal-boat rental on the southern end where the lake borders the golf course. I spotted a family of four in a rowboat. The dad and the daughter were fishing over the side while the mom lounged in the aft section with an e-reader and the son punched away on what looked like a handheld video game. Maybe not Norman Rockwell, but they looked happy.

We pedaled along at a leisurely pace and chatted about our day as we rode side by side. I wanted to ask him more about Julie, but I couldn't bring myself to do it. Instead he told me about the landscaping jobs he had yet to finish before the Honeysuckle Festival and I filled him in on what Cassidy had noticed about the ring in the Spencer family photo.

"So, are you thinking Dorothy's grandmother stole it from her employer?" he asked. "Is that it?"

"I don't even know for sure it's the same ring. But I'll be trying to find out more about that bit of bling and about the Spencer family, too."

"You think it's strange the police never asked Ingrid about the ring?"

"Yeah, I do. And maybe we weren't supposed to say anything, but the detectives never told us to keep quiet about it."

"And you're sure she really *didn't* know about it 'til today?"

"If she was acting she missed her calling. But the thing I don't understand, if this was robbery why didn't they take it all? Dorothy was wearing a diamond ring and a tennis bracelet worth thousands. Why not grab it all while they were at it?"

"Wait, you were talking about her pearls before, didn't you say those were heirlooms, too? So they only took the family jewelry?"

"Appears that way," I said.

We'd gotten about halfway around the loop when Jack frowned, looking toward the lake. "Hey, isn't that Joe Porter over there?" he asked, dipping his head toward a bench near the water's edge.

"Do you know him?" I asked, squinting to get better focus.

"Yeah, I did some landscaping work up at High Ground a while back. Dealt mostly with him, except for times when Mrs. Porter would come out and make me plant or uproot things on some whim or another. He looks lonesome. Let's go over and say hello."

"Maybe he'd rather be alone," I said, thinking of the unease I'd felt as Porter and his mechanic had watched me as I was leaving his service station.

Jack frowned. "What's up with you? You don't seem like yourself."

"You mean other than one of my clients being murdered and my name being bandied about as a suspect all over town?"

"Yeah, other than that," Jack said with a smile. He pulled out ahead of me and cut across the grass heading for Joe Porter. I had little choice but to follow.

"Mr. Porter," Jack said as he came to a stop and dismounted. "Hope we're not intruding, I just wanted to say I'm really sorry about Mrs. Porter."

"Jack? It is Jack, am I remembering that right?"

"Yes sir, Jack Ford. And I think you know Sophreena McClure."

I was out of breath so I gave a little wave.

"Sure do," Porter said, nodding. "Thank you for your condolences, Jack. This is hard on everybody."

"I see you've got some friends there," Jack said, pointing to the raft of ducks bumping into one another as they crowded close to the water's edge. There were so many it looked like a carnival game.

"They're waiting for me to throw out some more cracked corn," he said, holding up a paper bag. "I come down here about once a week to bring them a treat. They know me on sight now."

"My dad and I used to bring stale bread to feed them," I said. "It was my reward for getting my homework done."

"Here, come give it a whirl," Porter said, patting the bench beside him. "I used to bring bread, too, until I read somewhere that's bad for 'em, kind of like fast food. Fact, I guess it's bad to feed them at all. Makes them lazy about finding their own food and they get aggressive toward one another. Sort of like people who never have to work for a living, I suppose. But surely a little cracked corn once in a while can't hurt."

I took a handful of the proffered corn and threw the pieces into the water one by one. The ducks paddled and bobbed turning their tails skyward as their heads went below the surface.

"How're you coming on Dorothy's scrapbooks?" he asked as we watched the ducks' antics.

"We'll have them all done as promised by the day of Dorothy's memorial. I don't think I ever said thank you for giving us the go-ahead with them."

"And you're wondering why I'd bother with it, aren't you?" Porter asked. "Given that Dorothy and I were having our troubles."

"It was a nice gesture," I demurred, giving Jack the evil eye as he settled onto the grass a few feet away. He'd gotten me into this sticky wicket and he was making no effort to get me out of it.

Porter kept his eyes fixed on the ducks. We sat in silence for a few beats and then he said, "I knew your daddy; he was a good man. Knew your mama, too. You look like her. Your daddy was a straight shooter. Always said exactly what he meant and meant what he said."

"Yes, he did."

"I appreciate that in a person," Joe Porter went on. "So instead of dancing around it, why don't you just come out and ask me what it is you'd like to know about me and Dorothy. I know how it is in a small town. I'm sure there's people saying

harsh things about me. Some maybe even saying I killed her."
He swallowed hard and looked out across the lake, wincing.

"No one's saying that," I said.

"Yeah, they are," Jack countered from his seat on the grass.

I gave him my most withering look.

"What?" Jack protested. "They are. I'm just saying Mr. Porter's right, it's a small town and people who don't know what they're talking about still talk."

"Call me Joe, I'm not much on ceremony," Porter said. "People talk, it's just the nature of things. As long as people who know me don't doubt me the others can blather on much as they please. Me and Dorothy, we'd been through a lot."

"I've seen the photos," I said. "You two looked very happy in the earlier days."

"We were," Joe said. "As happy as Dorothy ever allowed herself to be, anyway—*despite* her daddy's interference. You know we weren't exactly kids when we married. She was forty-three years old and me a few years younger. She defied her father to marry me, the one and only time she ever did that. He made it hard on us, but I think in some ways that brought us closer, for a while anyhow."

I found myself liking Joe Porter, but I decided to test out his claim that he liked straight talkers.

"I think one thing that's feeding the rumor mill is the speculation about who'll inherit the Pritchett estate," I said. "Do you know what's in Dorothy's will?"

Joe pulled back as if I had bad breath and I saw Jack's eyes go wide.

"Sorry, you said you like things straight out," I said.

"Eh, so I did," Joe said, tossing out more corn to the squawking ducks. "I have no idea who'll inherit the Pritchett estate. If there's any justice in the world it'll be Ingrid. But I know for sure it won't be me. We had a pre-nup."

"Her father's insistence?" I asked.

Joe smiled and shook his head. "No, mine."

"To prove to her father you loved her and weren't marrying her for her money," Jack said. "That's radical."

"Nothing quite so chivalrous, I'm afraid," Joe said. "The truth is I was protecting my own interests. I'd built up a good business over the years and my net worth far exceeded hers, even after she inherited. I wanted to make sure my money went to support the employees who helped me. They're loyal to me and I try to return that. I didn't want my money to get poured into that big old house and go to keeping servants and throwing parties and what-not."

I stole a glance at Jack and I could see he was as shocked as I was. In the in-for-a-penny tradition I asked, "Who do you *think* will inherit the estate?"

"Given her druthers I think Dorothy would've named Ingrid as her beneficiary. I know she felt guilty about getting the whole she-bang. But old William was determined that Ingrid was never to get a dime and I don't know if Dorothy could have brought herself to defy her father's wishes, even though he's been in the ground for more than two decades. That's how strong his hold on her was. She spent her whole life trying to be worthy of the Pritchett name. I purely hated that. I wish she could have realized . . ." His voice trailed off.

"Joe, what do you know about the Pritchett family ring?" I asked.

"Not a blessed thing. Don't even know if the dang thing exists. Why are you asking about that?"

I hesitated. So the police hadn't asked Joe Porter about the ring either.

After a moment of indecision I spilled, telling Joe about finding the ring, returning it to Dorothy and the fact that it had not been found at the crime scene.

"You mean somebody killed her for a finger bauble?" Joe made a groaning sound and leaned forward, both hands cradling his head. "Dorothy hunted for that stupid ring for years and for the last little while she'd been obsessed about it. I know it was supposed to be valuable, but that wasn't what it was about for her. It was about being a blasted Pritchett. Everybody thinks she was a spoiled uppity woman, and she could be that," Joe said with a sad smile. "But she *paid* for everything she had in one way or another. Her father put a really bad head trip on her. She could never do enough to please him. He used to bark things at her like "Pritchetts don't cry" or "Pritchetts don't apologize" or "Pritchetts are made of better stuff." He expected too much out of her."

"Like taking care of Ingrid?" I asked.

Joe nodded. "Just about raised her," he said. "It hit her hard when her and Ingrid parted ways. But with just a little more time they could've been sisters again. Dorothy was making her peace with lots of things in the last year. She was just getting to where maybe she could be happy again and now she's gone."

"What about her relationship with Jeremy?" I asked, half expecting Joe to tell me I'd abused the straight talk privilege.

"Jeremy's a good man," he said, his tone indicating there were some conditions on that testament. "He's angry, but I reckon he's got some things to be angry about. Since him and Ingrid moved back here it's been constantly in his face, the difference in how Dorothy lived and how his mother struggles. Plus Dorothy gave him an awful hard time about some investments he recommended. I mean, she asked his advice and he didn't stand to make a dime from it. I think he was trying to show her he was smart about money. Nobody could have seen how things would go south in the market so quick. But she blamed him." Joe stopped suddenly and gave me a scowl. "Wait a minute, you've not got it in your head that Jeremy had any part in Dorothy getting killed, have you?"

I opened my mouth to deny it, but Joe plunged on, picking up volume and outrage.

"First off, he just wouldn't do that. He had problems with Dorothy, but he's not that kind of man. And secondly, Cassidy loved Dorothy. Jeremy would never do anything that would hurt his daughter, *come what may*."

"I don't think Sophreena was insinuating that," Jack said.

"No, I wasn't," I said quickly. "I wasn't insinuating anything at all. I was just trying to understand the whole situation better, that's all."

Joe relaxed his shoulders and I said the only thing I could think of to end our visit on an up note. "You're sure right about Cassidy. She loved Mrs. Porter and it was clear it was mutual."

Joe smiled, rocking back on the bench. "Oh yeah, she

was crazy about that child. I am, too," he added, seemingly embarrassed by the confession. She's cute and she is *smart*. Funny, too. Has she told you her knock-knock jokes?"

"No, she hasn't," I said.

His face went solemn. "No, I don't suppose she's joking much these days."

I caught Jack's eye and he got up from his resting place and swiped at his clothes. "We'd better ride on before we lose the light. It was good to see you, Joe."

"Good to see you both," he said. "I'd better be getting on home myself." He scattered the remnants of the cracked corn at the water's edge before crumpling the bag and putting it into the pocket of his windbreaker.

As we mounted our bikes and rode away I looked back to see Joe staring out across the water. He reached into his pocket for a hat that he hooked onto his head before walking off toward the footpath. I nearly fell off my bike.

It was a golf hat. A *yellow* golf hat.

twelve

On Saturdays Esme and I usually treat ourselves to a sleep-in as a pre-reward for the work we *intend* to do later in the day—yard work, DIY projects, car washing and other Saturdayesque activities. But today we'd crawled out at an uncivilized six a.m. and were in the workroom and scrapbooking by seven. We'd been at it for an hour when Detective Carlson showed up at our door.

Seeing as how we were no longer suspects, I greeted him cordially and invited him back to the workroom. His eyes ended their sweep of the room and came to rest on Esme. He doffed an imaginary cap by way of greeting. "Ms. Sabatier."

"Esme's fine," she conceded, "now that you don't think we're murderers. Why are you here?"

"Esme, that's not very hospitable," I said, which earned me an eye roll. "Would you like a cup of coffee?" I asked Carlson.

"For that we'll all have to traipse out to the kitchen," Esme said ungraciously. "We don't allow food or drink in here around these things."

"I'm fine," Carlson said, giving me a thanks-anyway smile. "And I'll get right to why I'm here. First off, I want to ask you both to keep an open mind, please. I'm going way out on a limb here. This is—and I can't emphasize this enough—a strictly unofficial visit. This case has got the whole town in turmoil and the longer it goes unsolved the more people start looking cross-eyed at their neighbors and the more outland- ish the rumors get. I hate seeing this happen to our town."

"It's terrible," Esme agreed. "And we don't like it either considering we're two of the people getting the evil eye everywhere we go."

Carlson pointed to a chair for permission to sit.

Esme nodded and he sat down but seemed to need some time to gather his thoughts. "Look, I'm a good cop," he said finally. "But Morningside's usually a peaceful town, thank God, and I've only done a handful of murder investigations. Most were drug related and not all that complicated. I've got a lot on the line professionally, me and Jeffers both, but that's not the topmost thing on my mind. I hate what this is doing to my town, to my friends and neighbors. Normally we'd look for a motive and follow where it leads but in this case there seem to be motives aplenty, which frankly has us chasing our tails. Jeffers would pull a muscle yelling at me if she knew I was here," he said, rubbing his temples, "but I've just got this feeling that won't go away telling me I needed to come talk to you two. I don't know how else to explain it and I know that sounds peculiar."

"Not too peculiar, really," Esme said, giving me a sidelong glance. "What is it you believe we can do?"

Carlson threw up his hands. "I don't know. I just have this

gut feeling I need to work with you two. Look it, you might know this family better than anybody around since you've spent months studying the Pritchetts."

"The Pritchett family *history*," I said. "We weren't really learning much about the live ones."

"Still," Carlson said, "you probably know a lot about Dorothy Porter and how she lived and what was important to her. We surely learned a lot from you in that first interview on the day of the murder, Esme. You were able to point out several avenues we should investigate."

"Detective Carlson," Esme said, "please, do not remind me of that. I was in shock and mad. Those are not conditions I handle well when they come one-by-one. Getting them in combination turned me into a reckless tongue wagger."

"Still," Carlson said, "just shows you may know more than you think."

"Actually," I said, "we were planning to touch base with you later today about something." I told him about how we'd found a ring with a similar appearance in the photograph of the Spencer family and how that family was connected with Dorothy.

"And you're convinced this is the same ring you returned to Mrs. Porter on the day she died?" he asked.

"No, we're not," I said. "We genealogists have rules of evidence just like you cops. So, no, we're not convinced. I'll use one of our favorite wiggle phrases and say the ring could possibly be the same but there's no proof as best as can be determined to date."

"What Sophreena's tryin' to say," Esme said, "is the ring we gave Dorothy looked just like the one in that picture but we got nothing but our four eyes to tell us that. You'll have to judge for yourself." She motioned him to the end of the table where the scrapbook pages were stacked in their protective sleeves. She handed him the magnifying loupe and pointed out the photo.

Carlson took his time, studying the image carefully. Finally he handed the loupe back to Esme. "Make that six eyes. Sure looks like the same ring to me."

"Even if it is, we have no idea what it means," I said.

"What do you know about this Spencer family?" Carlson asked. "Could this turn out to be some kind of Hatfield/McCoy deal?"

"We know very little about them," I said. "But I plan to do some investigating when I get a free minute. As Vivian Evans keeps reminding us, we were hired to do a thorough job of documenting the Pritchett family and it seems the Spencers have become a part of that."

"Vivian's on your case, too? She calls the station four or five times a day wanting to know why we haven't arrested somebody. She's offering up lots of leads, most of 'em far-fetched. Jeffers is out chasing down some of those." Carlson puffed out a breath. "Okay, well, I'll get out of here and let you get back to work. Just think over what I've said and maybe when you've got some time we can talk." He started for the doorway then turned back. "Listen, I hope you don't think I'm some kind of nut job with all this folderol about feelings and hunches."

"I wouldn't worry about that," I said, giving Esme an arched eyebrow.

"Sophreena and I don't judge," Esme said. "Now, as you

can see we're swamped right now, but I suppose later we could have coffee and talk more."

Carlson nodded. "Great, that'd be great. You've got my number."

I walked him to the door and when I returned to the workroom Esme was holding up her stop-sign hand. "It's only coffee, and it's only for the case, Sophreena. Don't go getting romantic notions in your head."

We worked for two more hours then broke for a lunch of flatbread veggie sandwiches with yogurt sauce. We congratulated ourselves on eating healthy, neither of us mentioning this would nowhere near offset the calories we planned to consume later. We'd agreed to reward our hard work by going out to The Morningside Café for a fried fish supper complete with home fries, hush puppies and creamy coleslaw—and maybe topped off with apple dumplings.

"If we make as much progress this afternoon as we did this morning I'll take an hour tonight and see what I can find out about the Spencer family," I said.

"You go for it," Esme said. "After we get back from supper I'm going to work a while longer and then I'm planning a rerun of last night's hot bath and early to bed with a good book."

As I was loading the dishwasher my friend Gina Bradford returned my call. I'd known Gina since we were college roommates. She works at the State Archives in Raleigh so I get to see her often since that's one of my regular research haunts. She and her husband, Sam, have an eight-month-old daughter named Ella who's the light of their lives, but from time to time even a devoted mama needs a break. We were scheduled for a girls' night dinner and movie on Monday and I'd left her a message that I needed a raincheck.

"Why are you bailing on me?" Gina asked without preamble. "This better be good. Tell me you've got a date with a great guy and I'll totally forgive you."

"No, but thanks ever so much for rubbing that in. It's work." I told her about our deadline.

"They haven't found out who did it, have they?"

"No, not that I've heard, and believe me, I would've heard. Nobody's talking about anything else."

"Hey, I've been meaning to call to tell you this," she said, "but it's been crazy around here. Ella's teething like crazy and Sam's been out of town and the nanny called in sick twice this week. Anyhow, somebody's doggin' your steps on the Pritchett family research."

"What do you mean?"

"There's a guy who's come into the Archives a couple of times recently. I've never assisted him but I overheard a couple of the staff talking about it after the Pritchett woman was killed, you know, like how weird it was that there were two people researching the Pritchett family and then she gets murdered."

"Do you know what his name was?" I asked.

"I forgot, but I wrote it down. Hold on a minute, let me get my bag."

I could hear Ella wailing in the background and had the thought maybe she'd grow up to have a career in opera. After some scrambling noises Gina came back on the line, talking between vain attempts to shush the baby. "His name was Spencer, Henry Spencer. He lives here in Raleigh someplace. I don't have contact information, but I'm sure you can ferret that out in a heartbeat. Sorry, Sophreena, I've really gotta go."

I hung up, marveling that there was a mother left the wide world over with her hearing—and her sanity—intact. I filled Esme in on what Gina had told me.

"Spencer? Well, that surely can't be a coincidence. Maybe Mr. Henry Spencer would be interested in pooling our resources," Esme said. "Should we try to find him and ask him?"

"My thoughts exactly," I said.

Some people have mixed feelings about the way the Internet is remolding society, but for genealogists it's been a gift from the technology gods, for the most part. I had contact info for Henry Spencer in less than sixty seconds; phone number, address and a map to his house. Plus I'd learned he owned a travel agency specializing in historical destinations.

I called his home number and a female answered—either that or Henry had a voice in the Michael Jackson register. I asked for Henry and the woman got cagey.

"Can I ask who's calling?"

I summoned my friendliest down-home manner and told her I'd been doing some family history research and I'd heard that Henry was interested in the family, too. I allowed as how we might could share information.

"Oh, that," the woman said and I sensed she wasn't a fellow traveler when it came to the family history hobby.

She covered the mouthpiece, but not very well, and yelled, "Hank, phone, pick up." She sounded like a quarterback getting ready to take the snap. I was half expecting her to add *hut hut*.

After some confusion and rustling in the background a male voice announced, "Hank Spencer." He sounded younger than I'd expected.

Again I explained why I was calling. I may have misrepresented a tad, but only by omission. He apparently got the idea I was researching the Spencer family and I didn't disabuse him of the notion.

"Maybe we're distant cousins or something," he said, seemingly pleased at the prospect. "Yeah, I'd love to exchange info. When could we do that?"

"No time like the present," I said. "How does your afternoon look?"

"Uh," he said hesitantly, "let me think. Well, I can't invite you here. My wife's giving a baby shower and I'm going to have to vacate the premises in a few minutes. I could come to you if you live nearby."

While we'd been talking I'd been searching one of those meet-halfway websites and found a coffee shop just off I-40 that fit the bill. I threw out the suggestion and Spencer said he could be there in less than an hour.

Esme wasn't about to miss out on the sleuthing and we agreed, grudgingly, that we'd have to give up our planned supper out and work into the night to make up for lost time. I resisted the urge to say we had bigger fish to fry. I love a good pun, but Esme's not a fan and I fear one of these days she's going to take the eye roll too far and never be able to see straight again.

I printed extra copies of the three photos we had of the

Spencer family and put them into a folder along with the timeline I'd drawn up for Sarah Malone and we set out for our meeting with my long-lost cousin.

Esme and I both spotted Spencer straight away then looked at each other, gaping. We really need to work on our poker faces.

The guy had blond hair of a hue usually seen only on fifties-era starlets and Scandinavian children. He was handsome and well dressed but his motions were hyperkinetic, his leg bouncing and his eyes flitting around the room. Too much caffeine maybe.

We introduced ourselves and I could see confusion register on his face as he glanced from Esme to me then back again. No doubt he was wondering which of us he could possibly be related to since neither of us is anywhere near Anglo enough to be a Spencer.

Esme went off to get us coffee and I sat down in the chair Spencer pulled out for me. "Okay, then," he said, "tell me, how exactly are we related? I know I have lots of distant Spencer cousins but I haven't been at this long enough to get them all straight."

"Is this a hobby?" I asked, avoiding the question. "Or is there some particular reason you're researching the family tree?"

"Hobby," he said. "Well, sorta hobby, sorta work. I own a travel agency and we specialize in trips to different historical sites—Revolutionary and Civil War battlefields, birthplaces of presidents, monuments, stuff like that. So our clients are all history buffs. Most of them know their family trees back to Methuselah. I got tired of answering 'I have no idea,' when they asked me about mine. So I started it because I thought it would help my business, but then I got hooked. You know what I mean?" He pointed to my folder and laughed. "Well, course you do."

He opened a notebook and flipped through pages of scribbled notes until he came to a clean page. "Okay, tell me your name again and how we're related."

Esme joined us with the coffee and raised an eyebrow at me. I'd been stalling until she got back so we could both see his reaction.

"I'm not certain we are," I said. "Actually the family line I've been tracing is the Pritchett family."

"Okay, yeah. That's way distant. Wait, no, that's not even a blood relation to me," he said. "The Spencers and Pritchetts had some connection way back, but they aren't related."

I glanced over at Esme. The mention of the name hadn't unsettled him so I took a more direct approach. "Did you know Dorothy Pritchett Porter?"

"Know her? Well, no, I can't say I know her. I met her once, man, what a clusterf—" He caught himself before he uttered the expletive. "What a disaster that was. How is the grand dame?"

"Dead," Esme said flatly.

Hank Spencer looked like a pole-axed steer, as my grand-dad used to say. His eyelids fluttered and he seemed uncomprehending. He worked his mouth for a couple of seconds then sputtered. "Geez, I'm sorry. It must have been sudden."

"Real sudden," Esme said. "She was murdered. You haven't heard this? It's been all over the news."

Spencer shook his head. "No, I've been out of town—a tour to Antietam. Didn't get back until about four this morning. I slept in then did a couple of chores for my wife and then you called. Martians could have landed on the White House lawn and I wouldn't have heard about it. Who killed her?"

"That's the big question right now," I said. "When did you meet Dorothy?"

"Earlier in the week," Spencer said, still frowning. "I don't remember which day it was. Let's see, it wasn't Monday, I had a meeting that night. Must have been Tuesday. Tuesday afternoon."

"And where was this?" I asked, trying to keep my voice casual.

"At her house. I'd come across some info written in my, let's see"—he shot his eyes upward and tapped the table with his finger to keep count—"my great-great-aunt's diary while I was doing my family research and there was a wicked funny story I thought she'd find amusing. Boy, was I wrong about that."

His posture stiffened and he looked at each of us through narrowed eyes. "Wait a minute, when did you say was she killed? Are you cops or something?"

"No," I said, drawing out the word, "we really are genealogists researching the Pritchett family. But the police *are* going to want to talk to you. You may have been the last person to see Dorothy alive, other than the killer."

Esme started in on one of her low decibel mumbles and I knew she was already building a case against Spencer in her head. And on the face of it things did look pretty bad. But if he was acting, he was ready for the next Scorsese film.

His hand shook as he took a sip of his coffee. "Man, oh man," he said. "I can't believe it."

"Could I ask about the story you told Dorothy?" I asked. "You say she wasn't amused?"

"That's putting it mildly," he said, looking around as if he'd lost something. "Do you think I should get a lawyer or something? That's going to cost a bundle, isn't it? My wife's gonna kill me. She told me I shouldn't go to see the woman, but I thought it would be good to connect. Most people like to talk about their ancestors, you know?"

"Yes, I know. I'm a genealogist, remember?" I said with a smile. "I'm sure you'll be able to get this all cleared up. I wouldn't worry."

Esme grunted and I gave her a nudge under the table.

"The truth will set you free," she said with a tight smile. "So what was this story?"

"Okay," Spencer said, talking rapidly now. "So my folks were thrilled about me getting interested in this family history thing. For one thing it was their chance to get rid of the boxes of family crap that had accumulated in their attic. Some branches of the Spencer family are not what you'd call sentimental. As each generation died out they dumped the stuff on anybody who'd take it and my folks ended up with a ton of it. I drove to Virginia and loaded up as much as I could fit in my car. That's another reason my wife's not thrilled. I took over the spare bedroom to sort through it all."

"And there was something that would have interested Dorothy in this diary you're talking about?" Esme asked, trying to steer Spencer back on track.

"Yeah, sorry," he said, tapping his pen nervously on his notebook. "I found a diary from my great-great-aunt Agnes, except she wasn't related to me except by marriage, so whatever that makes her."

I opened my mouth to educate Spencer on the affinity of in-laws but it was Esme's turn to silence me. "Yes, go on," I said, rubbing the shin she'd kicked.

"Okay," Spencer said, squeezing his eyes shut. "Let me get this right. My great-great-uncle Raeford Spencer and his wife, Agnes, lived in Richmond sometime late in the 1800s. And Agnes, who just between you and me and the fencepost sounds like a primo shrew if ever there was one, wanted someone to help take care of her hellion kids. Two boys, some kind of old-fashioned names I can't remember, but I've got them written down in here somewhere," he said, placing his hand on the notebook as if he were swearing on a Bible. "Anyhow, Agnes remembered some distant cousins of hers out in the tidewater who had daughters. She got to thinking one of them might like to come live in the city a while so she reached out. She writes all about how happy she is when Sarah Malone accepts the invitation, yadda yadda, all is well."

"We found a picture," I said, pulling the copy of the cabinet card photo out and handing it to him. "I think this is Raeford and Agnes Spencer."

"Yeah, yeah," he said. "I've got that same one. Mine has names on the back. They're in pencil and whoever wrote it had terrible handwriting, but you can make it out. That picture tells a lot, doesn't it? Look at those boys. You can tell they were the spawn of the devil, can't you? And Agnes, whew boy, a face that could stop a train, and not in a good way. And I think there was a little bait and switch going on with Sarah Malone. I'm not sure it was made clear she was coming to be a servant. From some of the entries in Agnes' diary it sounds like they had some disputes about that. A couple of times Sarah threatened to pack up to go home, but something convinced her to stay."

"One thing that we're interested in," Esme says, "is this ring right here on Agnes Spencer's finger."

"So she told you?" Spencer asked. "From the way she was acting I didn't think she'd tell anybody."

"Who told us what?" I asked.

"Mrs. Porter," Spencer said. "She told you the story about the ring?"

"No, she didn't," Esme said, using her running-out-of-patience voice. "As we told you, Mr. Spencer, you were prob-ably the last person to see Mrs. Porter alive."

"Oh, yeah," he said, running his hand through his thatch of blond hair.

The late afternoon sun was bathing the western window in a golden light that gave the entire coffee shop a sepia hue as if nature was adjusting the lighting so we could picture the tale Spencer began to unfold.

"According to Agnes Spencer's diary this ring was made by some famous jeweler in England back in the mid-seven-teen hundreds. It was like a big deal thing in the Spencer family. Anyhow it came down through the gencrations, always through the oldest son in the family, natch. It missed my line."

"So your great-great-granddaddy wasn't in line for it," Esme said, following the thread.

"No, his older brother. Raeford was the last Spencer to have the ring, or rather his wife, the not-so-lovely Agnes, was," he said, pointing to the photo. "They got married sometime in the 1870s. But apparently Raeford's mother didn't much take to her son's intended. Instead of giving over the ring for the engagement like was the family custom she held on to it long after they got hitched. It made Agnes furious. She wrote pages and pages about that in her diary. She wanted that ring in the worst way."

"Apparently she got it eventually," I said.

"Yeah, Raeford's mother took ill and on her deathbed she finally gave the ring to Agnes. But the universe had a little joke in store—the old broad surprised everybody, including herself, and made a full recovery."

"I don't suppose Agnes offered to return the ring," I said.

"Nuh-uh," Spencer said. "Wore it twenty-four-seven. Gloated about it constantly in her diary."

"But that still doesn't tell us how it went from being the Spencer family ring to the Pritchett family ring," Esme said.

"I'm getting there," Spencer said, holding up a hand. "So it seems old Raeford Spencer had what these days we'd call an addictive personality. He overate, you can see he's a tubby guy. And he drank a lot, but I think one look at Agnes explains that. Anyhow, he also had himself a bit of a gambling problem—and a poker buddy by the name of Harrison Pritchett."

"Dorothy's grandfather," I said, starting to see where this was headed.

"Yep," Spencer said. "And here's where the two families connect, and clash. Agnes wrote quite a bit in her journal about Sarah Malone. She'd come to loathe having her in her house. She didn't like that Sarah got so much attention from the men. Well, duh. Look at her; she's gorgeous."

"She caught Harrison Pritchett's eye," Esme said, picking up the photo and staring at it. "She was radiant and he was totally smitten," she said, stating a fact rather than asking a question.

"Oh yeah," Spencer said. "Agnes thought it was 'vulgar the way Harrison looks at her,'" he said, adopting a snooty voice as he recited lines from the diary. "'She plays the shy kitten but that is all artifice.'"

"Am I to take it gambling was involved with the ring passing hands?" I asked.

"Yep," Spencer said. "Raeford went all in on a game of five-card stud. He couldn't cover his bet so he crept into the bedroom and took the ring right off the sleeping Agnes' hand. Harrison Pritchett cleaned him out that night, taking not only the ring but the backstory about a family heirloom that went with it."

"I can see why Dorothy didn't care for that version," Esme said.

"Yes," I said, remembering how grateful Dorothy had been that we'd found the ring that was the emblem of her *illustrious* family. "She would have been appalled to learn it was poker winnings."

"You got that right," Spencer said. "She took the ring off and put it in her pocket after I told her the story. Then she just went berserk and threw me out. All I wanted was to share a good story. I tried to tell her that but she wasn't in a listening mood."

"Did you see anyone else at Dorothy's house?"

"No, only her."

"Did she answer the door herself?"

"Yes," Spencer said. "This is starting to sound like a grilling."

"I'm sorry," I said. "But imagine how you'd feel if one of your clients got murdered on a trip. Dorothy was our client and we'd like to do everything we can to help find out who did this to her. Can we ask just a couple more questions?"

I've got a pretty good pitiful look that I can deploy when I need it and I gave it to him now, looking at him over my glasses and letting my face go slack.

He hesitated then threw up his hands. "Sure," he said. "Go ahead."

I tried to pin him down about the timing of his visit, but he was vague about it. "I'm on an unbending schedule every day with my job," he said, "so when I'm on my own time I refuse to wear a watch. I know I was supposed to be there at four and I think I was pretty much on time."

"And how long did you stay?" I asked.

Spencer shrugged. "I'm not sure. Thirty minutes? Forty-five? It could have been longer, I suppose."

"Did you see a little girl, or the housekeeper or anyone else when you were there?"

"Nobody," Spencer said. "Not to speak to. When I was leaving I did catch a glimpse of a woman taking some bags out of the back of a dark-colored SUV. She was medium tall and medium build, I guess you'd say. Dark hair. That's about all I could tell from a distance. I'd parked on the street and she was at the end of the driveway near the garage. I only saw her for a second or two."

"Must have been Linda coming back from the store," Esme said and I nodded.

"Well, there you go," Spencer said. "She can tell you Dorothy Porter was alive and righteously POed when I left her house."

"Linda's the one who found the body," Esme said.

Spencer slumped back in his chair. "Man, oh man, this is *not* good."

"Were you getting something in there?" I asked Esme as she bulleted up the entrance ramp back onto I-40. "When we were talking about Harrison Pritchett falling for Sarah, you seemed to go somewhere else for a bit."

"There was something incredibly intense about the relationship between those two," Esme said. "And I do mean *intense*."

"They were madly in love, or they despised each other or what?"

"Not sure," Esme said. "Thin line between love and hate sometimes. I don't know what, but it was something extraordinary. Complicated. All tangled up."

"There was quite a difference in their ages. Maybe she didn't marry for love. But then again she didn't marry for money, either. Harrison Pritchett hadn't made his fortune by then. He was working as a blacksmith's assistant back in those days—when he wasn't gambling."

"Well, sounds like he was also a real card shark. Maybe he cleaned out other rich guys besides Raeford Spencer," Esme said.

My phone rang and an irate Marydale barely waited for a hello. "You will not believe this," she said, spitting each word. "Vivian Evans is telling everyone in earshot it might have been Linda Burnette who robbed Dorothy, and maybe worse. I've known Linda my whole life. You have too, Sophreena. She was a friend of your mom's. Linda would never do anything like that, and anyway she actually *liked* Dorothy Porter, despite the demands that woman made on her."

"Why would Vivian say that?" I asked, feeling guilty about my own fleeting suspicion when Spencer told us he'd seen Linda. But that only lingered a nano-second before my left brain gave my right brain a dope slap.

"I have no earthly idea," Marydale said. "She's been spouting off about what dire straits Linda and her family are in with two kids in college at the same time. Of course that's a struggle. Been there, done that. But Linda and Ben are managing fine, thank you very much." Marydale's ire passed and now she sounded simply sad. "I know Vivian is hurting. I know she and Dorothy were close, but, really, this kind of nonsense doesn't help anything."

"No, it doesn't," I said. "Listen, what has Linda told you about that day?"

"Not too much," Marydale said. "She's having nightmares about it."

"Wasn't that late for Linda to be there? Didn't she usually leave around mid-afternoon?"

"She did. In fact Dorothy had cut her back to three days a week. I guess even the rich have to take economy measures nowadays. Linda said she was all ready to leave right after you two did that day but then Dorothy asked her to fix her something for supper and she had to go to the store. You see what I mean? As usual she went way beyond the call of duty."

"Any idea about what time that was?" I asked.

"I don't have any idea, but Linda might remember," Marydale said. "Sophreena, why are you asking about all this?"

"I'll tell you when I see you, Marydale. I'm on my cell and you know it's not a good idea to discuss private stuff on a cell."

"Right," Marydale said. "Where are you anyway? I tried the house. I figured you and Esme would be holed up working."

"We were, but then something important came up. We're on our way back to Morningside."

"Meet you at your house," Marydale said. "I'll put on the coffee."

thirteen

TRUE TO HER WORD, MARYDALE WAS SITTING IN OUR KITCHEN when we got home, the welcome aroma of freshly brewed coffee perfuming the air and a quiche in the oven. And she wasn't alone. Linda Burnette, pale and puffy-eyed, had her hands wrapped around a steaming mug as if the contents were the elixir of life.

I hadn't seen Linda since Dorothy died and I felt ashamed I hadn't reached out. She'd been a good friend of my mother's but unlike with Marydale we hadn't stayed in close touch. Linda had still been parenting teenagers and sometimes working two jobs during the past few years, so there simply hadn't been many opportunities to get together.

"How are you?" I asked.

She turned her face up to me.

"Stupid question," I said, rubbing her shoulder.

"It's bad," Linda said, setting her lips hard to hold in tears.

"Can't help much to have the police questioning you," Esme said. "But if it's any consolation they questioned us, too."

Linda waved a hand. "I don't care. I just want them to find Dorothy's killer. I still can't believe this has happened."

"Remind me again," I said as I helped myself to a cup of coffee, "how long did you work for Dorothy?"

"Nearly seven years," Linda said. "I know lots of people think she was just this stuck-up woman, but she wasn't like that—well, at least not all the time. She could be a really caring person. I like to think we became friends."

Marydale couldn't hold out any longer. "Where have you two been? Was the thing that came up something about Dorothy?"

I looked at Esme.

"Split jury on that right now," she said. "Let's take our coffee to the patio to talk."

Linda drew in a shuddering breath as she rose and I realized Esme had suggested the change of venue to give her a chance to regroup.

Once we'd arranged ourselves around the patio table I told them about Hank Spencer and that he'd freely volunteered that he was at the house that afternoon.

"Did Dorothy mention anything about meeting with him?" Esme asked Linda.

"No. She said she was having a guest, but she didn't say who it was or what it was about. She asked me to make up a pastry tray and set up the coffee service but that was a pretty regular routine, especially lately. She had lots of meetings in the late afternoon and at night. I think she got lonely in that big house since Joe moved out. She looked for any excuse to lure visitors over."

"But this would still have been during the day, right?" I

asked. "In broad daylight. And you can't remember what time it was?"

Marydale glared at me and only then did I realize how accusatory the question sounded.

"I'm sorry, Linda," I said. "I'm going crazy trying to figure out how this could have happened. *When* it could have happened. You okay to go over it all with us? I know you've probably had to tell it a million times."

"It's okay," she said, still clutching the mug so hard her knuckles were white. "I told Marydale I wanted to come talk to you. The police are doing their best, but they don't seem to have much to go on and I'll just come out and say it, I don't like Jennifer Jeffers much. We went to school together and there's something about her that rubs me the wrong way. Anyhow, they seem convinced this was a robbery and I can't see how that makes sense. I couldn't even tell anything was missing. Course, I didn't know about the ring when I found Dorothy."

Esme and I both turned to shoot a look at Marydale and she threw up both hands. "Don't look at me, I didn't blab."

"The police told me about it, or rather questioned me about it," Linda said. "I cannot believe you found that thing. Dorothy and I spent hours up in that hot, stuffy attic going through her grandmother's things and we never found it. I was beginning to think she dreamt it up."

"Oh, it's real," Esme said.

"I can't believe she didn't tell me you found it. But I was cleaning upstairs when you two left, then Jeremy came by to pick up Cassidy and I guess she didn't want to say anything in front of him. She did say she had something to tell me when I got back from the store and she seemed happy about it, whatever it was. But, of course, she never got the chance."

"The ring's gone and we think her pearls as well," I said.

"Pearls?" Linda said, and I remembered Denny had said it the same way, rolling the word around as if trying to divine its meaning.

"The family ones," I said. "She definitely had them on that afternoon when we saw her."

"I didn't remember," Linda said, frowning. "But she had lunch at the club that day and she wore this maroon-colored sweater set that was one of her favorites. She liked to wear the pearls with it so she probably did have them on. But I didn't see them when—" She stopped and swallowed hard. "I didn't see them afterward. The police had me go through the house with them trying to see if anything was missing, but I didn't know that much about Dorothy's jewelry. I just took care of the house. And I think Joe was probably useless, too. He never paid much attention to stuff like that. Vivian would probably have been the one to ask."

"Was Cassidy still there when you left for the grocery store?" Esme asked.

"No, Jeremy came by to get her not long after you and Sophreena were there."

"And you saw Dorothy after they left? Talked to her?"

"Well, no, actually I didn't *see* her," Linda said, frowning. "I was making my list for the store. But after he and Cassidy went out to the car Jeremy came back in after something he'd forgotten. I don't know what. Anyway, he went out to the living room where Dorothy was and I could hear them talking. I took the garbage out and talked to

Cassidy a few minutes. She was restless waiting in the car. I was coming back into the kitchen as Jeremy was coming out the back door. He seemed flustered. He told me Dorothy wanted me to pick up her prescriptions, too, if I had time. I figured she must have asked him to do it and he'd said no. He hated it when she treated him like an errand boy. I tidied up a few things in the kitchen and left a few minutes after that."

"Hank Spencer claims he's not sure when he actually got to Dorothy's. He says he was supposed to be there at four," I said.

"That sounds about right if that was him I saw on the front porch. I went out the side of the circular drive that has the hedgerow, so I only caught a quick glimpse as I was driving by the front of the house."

"And you just went to the grocery store and came right back?" I asked.

"No, no. I was gone a while. Ben was working his side job out at the golf course that night so I decided to take care of a few things while I was out. I drove out to Joe's garage to give him his birthday present from Dorothy, then I picked up her prescription from the drugstore. I dropped some library books off in the drop box then went to the post office to mail a package to our son at school. Then finally I picked up a few things at the grocery store for us and also Dorothy's items and drove back up to High Ground."

"So you were gone for what? Maybe an hour?" Esme asked.

"That sounds about right. Could have been a little longer, I can't be sure. Like I said, Ben wasn't home and Dorothy often ate late so I knew she didn't care. I wasn't watching the time."

"Hank Spencer says he saw you taking bags out of the car as he was leaving. Is that possible?"

"I suppose," Linda said. "I wouldn't have any reason to dispute that. You know how that curve in front of the house is. I wouldn't have been able to see a car parked in front. All I can say is I didn't see him, and honestly what he's saying makes things look bad for *him*, so why would he volunteer it if it wasn't so? I mean, I can't see how anyone else could have come into the house and done something to Dorothy after I got back. Surely I would have heard something. So do you think this Spencer guy did it?"

"I don't know what to think," I said. "I guess you could say he has a motive but it's weak, if you ask me. That ring was originally in his family, but honestly he didn't seem that invested in that. It left the family generations ago and he never stood a chance of inheriting it anyway. He didn't strike me as someone who felt cheated or vengeful about it. But I think maybe Esme has another take on it."

"I'll just play devil's advocate," Esme said. "He seems like a perfectly nice guy. But remember, when you hear people being interviewed on television after some heinous crime they're always saying how shocked they are that their nice, quiet neighbor has been arrested. Co-workers saying the accused was the *last* person they would've thought capable of such a thing. And remember, as a tour director, he's a showman."

"True," I said. "And the timing does look bad for him. Or at least I think it does. Something's just not right. Linda, could we go over a few things again?"

She nodded and I doodled a rough timeline on my napkin as we talked.

"How long would you say it was from when you actually saw Dorothy last and the time you left for the store?"

"Saw her?"

"Or heard her," I said.

"Let's see," she said, frowning. "From the time I heard her arguing with Jeremy until I left for the store was probably about ten, fifteen minutes maybe."

"They were arguing?" Esme asked. "You didn't say they were arguing before."

Linda shrugged. "Not really arguing, it's just the way they were. You know, you've seen them together. Every little thing was a bone of contention."

"And you say he was upset when he left?" I asked.

"Not upset exactly, just, you know, huffy."

I glanced over at Esme and saw an almost imperceptible smile. Dorothy had pushed Esme and me both into the huffy zone on numerous occasions.

"So you didn't see or hear Dorothy again after Jeremy and Cassidy left?"

"No. I called out to her that I was leaving for the store, but she didn't answer. I figured she'd gone into her study or upstairs."

"And when you were out doing the errands, did you have the radio on or notice a clock anywhere, anything that might help nail down the time?"

"No," Linda said, twirling a strand of her dark hair between her fingers. "I've been over this a hundred times in my head and I can't pin it down. I'm trying to learn Spanish with one of those do-it-yourself CDs and I always have that on in the car, so no help there. There was still plenty of daylight left when I got back, that much I know."

"Okay," I said, making myself a note to find out when the sun set that day. "Now, I know this is the hard part," I said, "but can you start with when you got back to High Ground and tell me as much as you can remember?"

Tears pooled in Linda's eyes, glinting like rhinestones as darkness fell and the outdoor light kicked on. She shifted in the chair and started talking, her voice almost robotic. "Okay, I pulled in next to the garage and took the groceries in. I called out, but Dorothy didn't answer so I figured she was upstairs, maybe grabbing a quick nap. I fixed the fruit plate and made some cinnamon toast and hot tea to go with it. I had the thought I might stay and eat with her; I did that sometimes when Ben was working late. But I was tired. Vivian had me polishing silver and washing curtains to get ready for the open house. I went looking for Dorothy to let her know her supper was waiting and that's when I saw—" She choked.

"It's okay," Esme said. "You don't have to go through that again."

"No, you don't," I said. "But on a lighter note, I'm curious. You say you went to take Joe Porter a birthday present from Dorothy? Wasn't their divorce about to be final? I thought Dorothy wanted him out of her life."

Linda smiled and used a napkin to mop off her cheeks. "Yeah." She laughed softly. "Well, Dorothy talked a good game, but she was still in love with Joe, I don't care what she said. Her father really did a number on her and Ingrid both. I don't know which of them got the worst of it. Ingrid got disinherited, but at least she has her own life. Dorothy got the money, but it didn't get her much happiness. Joe really loved Dorothy but it seemed like she did everything she could to test him. He took it a lot longer than most men would have, but about a year ago it got really bad and finally he had to leave. Neither of them was happy about the breakup, I know that for sure. I saw it. Lately they'd been talking more on the phone and Joe would come by on one excuse or another. I wouldn't have been at all surprised if they'd gotten back together. In fact I wondered if that was what she'd planned to tell me that day—that Joe was moving back in."

"And you saw Joe when you went to the service station?"

"No, he wasn't there. I just left the package on his desk."

"Any chance it was Joe you saw at the front door when you were leaving?"

Linda frowned. "He wouldn't use the front door. Wait, surely you don't suspect Joe."

"No, course not," I said, which wasn't entirely true. I didn't *want* to suspect Joe Porter. I liked the man. But I hadn't been able to shake the image of him talking with the mechanic who'd spooked me. Nor the memory of him pulling on that yellow golf hat. It didn't add up to much, but it made my ears prick up.

"Joe is a sweetheart," Linda said. "He would never hurt Dorothy. And neither would I, despite what Vivian might be saying about me. She never liked it that Dorothy was friendly with me. She thought it was *inappropriate*."

"Why?" I asked.

Esme snorted. "Because Linda worked as a housekeeper and that's how service people get treated sometimes."

Esme wasn't exactly clear-eyed when it came to this issue. Her own mother had worked in service for nearly forty years and had gotten very little thanks for her toils.

Linda smiled. "If it had been up to Vivian I'd have had to wear one of those little black and white uniforms with an apron and hat. But Dorothy didn't treat me like a servant. She paid me well and when Ben was sick last winter she sent over meals—okay, they were catered from the country club but that was all the better. Dorothy was a terrible cook." She half-laughed, half-sobbed. "And nobody else knows this, she swore me to secrecy about it, but I guess it doesn't matter now. She gave each of the boys a thousand dollars when they graduated from high school to help out with college expenses. A thousand dollars. You just can't know what a big help that was."

"Very generous," Marydale said. "Maybe I misjudged the woman."

I'd been thinking the same thing, and even Esme had a wistful look.

"I've told you, Marydale," Linda said. "She was a good person. She just had a prickly personality. You had to get used to her ways and lots of people gave up before they got to that point."

"Vivian sure got used to how she was," Marydale said. "She thought Dorothy could do no wrong."

"That's the reason I can't be too mad at her right now, even if she does deserve it," Linda said. "She's grieving and that makes people act crazy sometimes. They wcre really close, but they occasionally fell out over little things. I think maybe that's what's making Vivian behave so badly. She and Dorothy had a set-to—a pretty rowdy one—just the day before Dorothy died. I don't think they got a chance to patch things up."

"Do you know what they fought about?" I asked.

"It was the open house," Linda said. "At least that was part of it. I didn't hang around listening but it was so loud I couldn't help but hear some of it."

"What did you hear?" Esme asked.

Linda sat for a moment, her face contorting, and finally a giggle escaped, then another until she was consumed.

We all looked at one another, eyebrows raised. I wondered if she was hysterical and if I should slap her sharply the way they always do in the movies.

Finally she got control of herself. "I'm sorry, but this is *so* ridiculous in light of everything that's happened. It was the lawn decorations. Vivian had decided a great way to honor Harrison Pritchett was to use the products his company manufactured as part of the décor. I saw her sketchbook. Most of it was quite nice. She had planters set inside coiled garden hoses and garden tools like hoes and rakes teepeed around tiki lights. But she went too far. She'd wanted port-a-potties lining the back edge of the lawn, doors open and bouquets of flowers in the seats and spilling out the doors. I'm sorry," she choked, overcome with laughter again. "I know this is inappropriate but I can't stop."

"I can picture Dorothy's face," Esme said, as she too sputtered a laugh. "She did not like to be reminded the fortune was built on portable necessary rooms."

"And to think we agonized over how to finesse this for the scrapbooks," I said. "We should've put a photo of a port-a-john on each cover."

"But a tasteful one," Linda said, wiping at her cheeks again. "Honestly, it wasn't unusual for Vivian and Dorothy to quibble. They had, let's say, spirited discussions about a lot of things—mostly silly things in my opinion. Clothes, food, even hairstyles. From what I overheard Dorothy must have upset Vivian by saying something critical about her hair that day, too. But I guess all that just proves how close they really were. They squabbled but they stayed friends."

"Vivian told us herself that Dorothy schooled her in the refinements well-to-do clients expect in their events when she was just starting up her business," Esme said. "Guess she missed the lesson about no loos on the lawn."

"No privy on the patio," Marydale chimed in.

"No latrines on the lanai," I contributed.

This instigated another round of giggles and just then Coco appeared in the doorway from the kitchen. She took in the scene with a perplexed expression.

"I don't know this game," she said. "But how about no toilets on the terrace?"

fourteen

I DON'T CLAIM TO BE DEVOUT, BUT ON THIS SUNDAY MORNING I had the urge to attend mass. I craved the solace of ritual and assurances the angels were on our side. Or maybe it was plain old guilt. I'd judged Dorothy Porter without taking the trouble to get to know her. And I should know better.

I've spent my adult life poring over diaries and letters, people's most pressing concerns and private thoughts committed to paper. I've learned things are seldom as simple as they seem and nothing ever really begins when you think it did.

I got to St. Raphael's early and headed for the side chapel to light a candle. I'd done this every Sunday with my mother as I was growing up. During the week we kept a list of people who needed prayers for one reason or another and before mass we'd slip the little piece of paper under a votive holder and Mom would let me light the candle and put the quarter in the slot.

I'd heard the parish council had recently decided the votive candles posed a fire hazard and were soon to be replaced by artificial candles. Say your prayer, deposit your money and

flip a switch. An LED blinks on and even gutters like an actual candle in the breeze.

No, thank you.

I struck the match and set flame to wick, then deposited
a folded dollar bill, the price of sending prayers heavenward
having risen along with everything else. I prayed for Dorothy
and for all those who'd care about her, even the ones who
were presently acting like horse's patoots. I didn't mention
any names; I figured God would know.

My devout grandparents would have been scandalized
by my irreverence. They'd been so devout my mother was
convinced the main reason they'd adopted her was because
they felt like failures as good Catholics because they were
childless. Whatever their motivation, they were loving parents and Mom felt fortunate to be their daughter. But that
hadn't kept her from longing to know more about where
she came from and why her biological parents gave her up.
She'd searched all her life and never found the answers she
was looking for. And now I continue the search for her—
and for me.

I'd been baptized in this church and made my first confession to the priest here. I'd been such a goody two-shoes
I'd had to make up something to confess, and Father Dono-
van had told me gently that was called lying and that I then
had something real to confess. I'd been delighted at how
that'd worked out.

I slid into a pew toward the back of the church and as the
processional started I sensed someone moving in beside me.
Instinctively I shuffled down a spot without looking over.

"Are you out of your mind?" the person hissed in a

whisper and I looked up to see Jack's face looking like a thundercloud.

"What?" I whispered back.

He picked up a hymnal and flipped at the pages, but out of the side of his mouth he hissed again. "You went to see a suspect without even telling the police. What were you *thinking*, Sophreena?"

The music stopped and the woman in the pew ahead of us glanced over her shoulder. She packed a lot of disapproval into that one quick glance and we put our wrangle on hold until mass was over. But the moment the priest urged us to go in peace Jack started in again. "I can't believe you did that, Sophreena. I thought you had more sense than that."

"For pity's sake, Jack, I didn't know he was the guy who'd been at Dorothy's house until after we talked to him. And anyway, it wasn't like he was going to kill me right there in the middle of a coffee shop. And I wasn't alone, Esme was with me."

"Still," he said, grabbing my elbow and steering me out the side door, "Julie says this guy is now the number one suspect in Dorothy's murder. She thinks he looks good for it."

"He didn't kill Dorothy," I said, loud enough to make a couple of people on the sidewalk turn in our direction. "He's not like that," I said, lowering my voice. I wasn't sure if I truly believed Hank Spencer was innocent or if I just wanted Julie to be wrong.

Jack threw his hands in the air and gave an exasperated grunt.

"It looks bad," I allowed, "but I'm telling you, it wasn't him."

"Just don't do anything like that again," he said, as he stomped alongside me to the parking lot. "Where's your car?" he demanded.

"I walked," I said, scanning the lot for Jack's Jeep.

"Great!" he said. "I left mine at the coffee shop. I was gonna ride back with you."

"Well, that gives you six blocks to yell at me some more," I snapped. "Because I'm really enjoying that!"

In the parking lot people were standing around in clusters talking, but it clearly wasn't the usual cheerful chatter about the weather, golf scores and where to go for post-mass brunch. These conversations were punctuated with furrowed brows, pinched lips and long faces. Jack wasn't the only one on edge.

St. Raphael is the patron saint of protection from nightmares. The whole town was living a nightmare right now. I hoped they'd hold out on the LEDs. We needed that whole bank of vigil candles, and we needed the real thing.

Though it was still only mid-morning the temperature had edged up into the high eighties already and was showing ambition. I unwound the scarf I'd looped around my neck to dress up my plain pants and T-shirt and wiped my forehead with it before stuffing it into my bag.

The heat seemed to have knocked the stuffing out of Jack as well and he was quiet as we started our trek toward Top o' the Morning.

I wanted to ask him what was Julie to him anyway, but instead I asked how he was coming on his family history search.

"Still stuck," he said.

"You've been stuck for a long time. Have you lost interest?"

"No, I'm still interested," Jack said. "I want to *know* if I'm related to Robert Ford, but I guess part of me doesn't want to *be* related to him. I've been thinking, do I really want that to be part of who I am? Somebody who'd kill a friend? Yeah, Jesse James was an outlaw, but Robert Ford was supposed to be his pal. Where was all that honor among thieves thing? And the way the story goes, he shot James in the back—the most cowardly thing a man could do back in those days."

"Not too well thought of these days either," I said.

"Right," he said, giving me the lopsided grin. "Anyhow, I'll get back to it soon. You want some help with the Pritchett books this afternoon? I'm not so good at pretty pages, but I'm an ace with a paper cutter."

I was thrilled his afternoon was free—of Julie. Then ashamed. If Jack had reconnected with someone he enjoyed being with I should've been happy for him. What kind of a friend was I, anyway? A grossly inferior one, apparently.

Just as we reached Top o' the Morning I saw Esme getting out of her SUV across the street. She called out to us and though her bearing indicated she thought she owned the street, she let a car pass before she strode over. She always dresses nice, but for church she goes all out. Esme's a big woman, but her proportions are spot on and she was wearing a georgette dress that highlighted that. It had a full skirt that allowed plenty of motion when she walked.

We snagged a table outside while Jack went in to put in our order. Esme filled me in on what she'd gotten accomplished this morning as I brushed crumbs off the table and wiped it with a tissue she'd fished from her purse. I told her Jack had volunteered to help out this afternoon and she laughed. "The cavalry's coming over the hill," she said. "All the others are coming."

As the three of us sipped our coffee we strategized on how best to use our free labor pool. "I won't be back until about one," Esme said, "so just put whatever I need to do on my worktable."

"You got something after church?" I asked.

"I'm having lunch with Detective Carlson," she said, her look daring me to comment. "I told him I'd meet with him and see if there's anything useful we can contribute about Dorothy and that's what I'm doing. And that's *all* I'm doing."

Just at that moment a woman approached our table. It took me a moment to place Leticia Morgan, Denny Carlson's ex-wife. A man I figured must be her husband trailed behind her. He seemed cool as a cucumber even in his dark suit while the rest of us had beads of sweat popping out on our foreheads like bubble wrap.

I braced myself for whatever kind of altercation was coming, but Leticia Morgan introduced herself and her husband, friendly as can be, then dispatched hubby to get her a latte.

After he'd gone Leticia sat next to Esme, perching on the chair as if ready for flight. "I just wanted to meet you," she said, "and have a chance to tell you that even though Denny and I are divorced I still consider him a friend and one of the best men I know. It didn't work out for us, but I want him to be happy."

Not waiting for a reaction, she rose and headed for the door without a backward glance.

"Oh Lord," Esme said. "First you, now I'm gettin' it from her? What is wrong with this man that he needs this many people lobbying for him? His mother's even gettin' into the act."

"When did you meet his mother?" I asked. "Does she live around here?"

"No," Esme answered.

When she didn't elaborate Jack asked, "Where does she live?"

"She *doesn't*," Esme answered with a sigh.

"*Ooh*," Jack and I said in unison.

I decided to have Jack help me archive materials to clear workspace for the reinforcements. He smirked as he pulled on the cotton gloves I handed him. "You know, every time you make me wear these things I feel like a mime. Maybe you ought to give me a striped shirt and beret to go with them and I'll make like I'm trapped in an invisible box."

"Scoff all you want," I said. "Your oily fingers can do a lot of damage to these fragile photos."

"I washed my hands," he grumbled, "used soap and everything."

"Stop your griping and help me with this." I pointed to a stack of Harrison Pritchett's company papers. I quickly sorted through them to make sure no personal items had accidentally gotten mixed in and handed them off to Jack to seal into airtight bags. There was a near-zero probability these items would ever be needed again but it wasn't my call to cull. Dorothy had gone through only two small boxes of material before she decided she'd rather pay us to inventory and organize the whole lot than risk breaking a nail.

Business papers stowed away, I turned to the personal materials, carefully dividing a mound into smaller piles.

"What's this?" Jack asked, looking over my shoulder as I inserted vellum sheets between the pages of a commonplace book kept by Harrison Pritchett's mother, Laurena Bascom Pritchett. "Is that a baby book? It looks old."

"It's very old, from the 1860s. But not a baby book exactly. Commercial baby books weren't around until a couple of decades later. Scrapbooks either. People like Laurena made homemade books of friendship or remembrance from whatever materials they could lay their hands on. Somewhere around the turn of the century they started calling them memory books or scrapbooks and companies started producing blank albums."

"But isn't that baby measurements there?" he said, pointing to a page that had been constructed on the cover of a seed catalog.

"Yeah, it is. It wasn't that parents didn't write down things about their babies, they just didn't parse out their lives. They put everything together in the same book. A little bit diary, a little bit sketchbook, accounts for the farm or household and a place to save the ephemera of daily life. This little book will break your heart. Laurena's young husband, Lawton Pritchett, went away to the Civil War when their baby, Harrison, was an infant. He was killed and Laurena never remarried. She raised Harrison on her own."

"Wow, that's what really gets you when you start looking into your history," Jack said. "There are so many forks in the road where if a different decision had been made or if the timing had been a little off you wouldn't be here."

"Makes you feel lucky to be alive, doesn't it? Laurena Pritchett was writing all this about the baby for her husband," I said, pointing to a densely written paragraph, "and all the while Lawton was already dead. The word just hadn't reached her yet."

"You can read that?" Jack said, squinting at the passage written in scratchy handwriting with fading ink.

"I've gotten pretty good at reading these old scripts. Course, it helps that I can scan them and manipulate the size and contrast. This seems to be a log she was keeping for Lawton for when he returned so he wouldn't miss out on all baby Harrison's milestones. She tells how he's grown fat and happy, despite the deprivations of the war. Then here she writes that instead of placing a lock of hair from his first haircut she'd had to gather blond hairs from his baby brush to prove he wasn't totally bald."

"Is that what's supposed to be right there?" Jack asked, indicating a rectangular blank spot on a page otherwise covered with writing.

"Yeah," I said. "I could have sworn there was an envelope there when we first found the book, but it must have fallen off. Keep an eye out for it."

I sandwiched the book between two pieces of acid- and lignin-free chipboard and taped it with archival tape before handing it to Jack to vacuum seal.

"I'll bet half the people who do this kind of thing don't even know what lignin is," Jack said.

"Probably doesn't mean the same thing to an archivist

that it does to you botany people. For me it means impurities in paper pulp. That's bad."

"And for me it means something the plant needs to form woody tissue. That's good."

Winston and Marydale came in just then and placed two large bags on the floor inside the door. The bags undulated and wiggled until two topknots and four black eyes appeared in the openings. Ordinarily pets would be verboten in the workroom, but Gadget and Sprocket get special permission since they don't shed. Maybe they just don't have a chance to since they get brushed and petted so much. We make sure we keep them away from the artifacts and they're generally content to sleep in their little bag beds when they aren't running around in the backyard.

Winston bent down and scooped up a pup in each of his big hands, clutching them to his chest. "Oh, for Pete's sake," he said, tsking. "Marydale, you've gone and put bows in their hair? Man's gotta be confident in his manhood to tote around dogs looking like this." I watched through the window as he took them into the yard and placed them on the grass. They trotted off to explore with their little button noses twitching.

I'd made design templates for the pages and we set up an assembly line with Winston and Jack trimming and mounting, then Marydale adding embellishments and finally me working on journaling and labeling. There was no time for handwritten calligraphy at this point so I selected a nice heritage font and began transcribing on my laptop. I printed in brown ink on a faux parchment, then trimmed the journaling boxes to size and chalked the edges with an umber chalk to make them look aged. The labels I tore with a deckle-edged ruler and dipped the ragged edges into walnut ink so they'd stand out on the page.

"You know, my dad worked on this house," Winston said, holding up a photo of High Ground when it was under construction. "He was a cabinetmaker. He loved working that High Ground job. Talked about it for years. Nothing but the best materials and he always said Harrison Pritchett was a good man to work for."

"They broke with southern tradition, didn't they?" I said. "Everyone back then seemed to be building another Tara but Harrison and Sarah decided on a craftsman style. There are so many built-in drawers, shelves and cupboards. Did your dad build them all?"

"No, not all," Winston said. "From what my dad told me there were lots of workmen. Let me think now, he worked on that house when my sister was a baby. I wasn't even born yet. Must have been along about thirty-seven or thirty-eight."

"They broke ground for it in May of 1936 and Harrison and Sarah Pritchett moved in just before Christmas 1937," I answered, reading from my report. "According to what Harrison told the historical society it had always been his intention to build a house on that acreage from the time he moved here in 1895 but he had to wait until he had enough money to build a house worthy of the site."

"Well, he sure did that," Winston said, "though the one he vacated wasn't anything to sneeze at."

"That was the middle house," I said. "Bigger and definitely

better than the little cabin he and Sarah lived in when they first moved here."

"Is the middle house the one there on Alta Vista Drive?" Marydale asked. "The one Dorothy and Ingrid grew up in?"

"Yep," Winston said. "It's not nearly as grand as High Ground, but it's a nice house. Harrison and Sarah gave it to William and his wife, Leila, when High Ground was finished. My dad did some renovation work on that house, too, but he wasn't nearly as happy about working for Dorothy's father. Dad always said William Pritchett wasn't a man who'd do to ride the river with."

"Did you know Dorothy's mother, Leila?" I asked. "She's a shadowy figure. No one we interviewed had much to say about her."

"I remember her," Winston said, "but barely. I don't think I ever saw her but a half dozen times. She was a little woman. Pretty, but delicate looking. I don't know if she was shy or sickly or what, but she kept pretty much to herself."

"I always wondered if it was losing his wife that made William such a bitter man," Marydale said. "I don't think I ever saw him smile. I was half afraid of him when I was a kid."

"I was half afraid of him when I was a grown man," Winston said with a chuckle. "He used to come in the bakery and bark his order like some banana republic dictator. It was just his natural disposition."

We heard a "Woo-hoo" coming from the front hall, followed by the tinkling of Coco's bracelets. A couple of minutes later she came in the door, wiping her hands on a paper towel. "Okay, here I am, clean hands, good eyes and a willing spirit."

Marydale scooted down to give Coco room to work and Jack passed down a layout he'd finished.

"Sorry I'm late to the party," Coco said as she studied the pages. "I took my folks out to brunch at the Sunrise Café then I had to take them back to their condo. You can't believe how riled up their neighbors are getting. They're all convinced there's a gang of home invaders here in Morningside and that Dorothy was just their first victim. Daddy wanted to go out and get a gun, but Mom won't have one in the house, so yesterday he went out to the sporting goods store to buy a Louisville Slugger. And guess what, they'd sold out!"

"Crazy," I said, neglecting to add that both Esme and I already kept softball bats within handy reach behind our headboards.

"Oh, and I ran into Ingrid Garrison," Coco went on. "She was having lunch at the café with Jeremy and Cassidy. She said she might come by for a few minutes later this afternoon." Coco stopped talking and looked around the room. "Where's Esme?" she asked as if I might be hiding her, which would be quite a feat.

"She should be here any minute. She's having lunch with Detective Carlson."

"You've gotta be kidding me," Coco said. "Is this voluntary or is he still giving you two the third degree?"

"Oh, he's done with me," I said. "But he's still quite eager to talk with Esme." I raised an eyebrow and Coco's face broke into a wide grin.

"*Ooh*, I see. He must be a brave, brave man."

"Well, I think it would be wonderful if Esme went out with him," Marydale said, "socially, I mean. He seems like a good guy and, no offense, Sophreena, but she needs something in her life besides hovering over you like a mother hen."

"Pot callin' the kettle," said a voice from the doorway.

I was sure guilt was etched on all our faces as Esme swept into the room and hung up her bag.

"I won't argue with that, Esme," Marydale said. "But I don't have suitors knocking at my door."

"I met with the detective to see if there was anything we could do to help and that was all of it. Now since when did y'all start talking about my business behind my back?"

"Since never, Esme," Coco said. "Let's talk about your business in front of your face. Why wouldn't you go out with him? He's handsome and he seems nice. You might have some fun."

Esme turned to give me a look.

"I did not put her up to that," I said. "She's expressing an independent opinion."

"What about you two?" Esme said, putting her hand on her hip as she turned toward Winston and Jack. "You don't have opinions about Detective Carlson?"

Both men got a deer-in-the-headlights look. Finally, with a smirk twitching at the corners of his mouth, Winston said, "Well, now Esme, if pressed I'd have to say he's a pretty good-lookin' man." He turned to Jack, who faked giving the question consideration.

"A regular Adonis," Jack agreed with a grin.

Esme flapped a hand at them. "You know very well that is not what I meant. First off, the man has not asked me out. And secondly, as I've told you all, I'm satisfied with my life just the way it is. This was strictly about the case.

Sophreena, Spencer's decided to get ahead of things, I guess. He called and made arrangements to come in tomorrow to make a statement. Today was his wife's birthday and her family was all over at their house, so it wouldn't have looked too good for him to say he had to go off to be questioned by the police, I suppose."

"Did you find out anything about the investigation?" Marydale asked.

"A little," Esme said, serious now. "Joe Porter's got an alibi. He was in a meeting with one of his suppliers."

I was really happy about that bit of news and I knew the others were, too, judging by the smiles all around.

"And," Esme went on, "I learned they're running DNA off two coffee cups that were found on the floor near Dorothy's body. There was evidence of a struggle, which we would already have figured considering how she died. Course, they ordered those tests before they knew about Hank Spencer."

"If he admits he had coffee with Dorothy that will probably make the results a moot point," I said.

"Which is good," Esme said. "Detective Carlson says there's at least a month-long backlog at the state lab."

"Admitting he was there and had coffee with Dorothy makes it look really bad for Spencer," I said. "He himself says he was leaving as Linda was getting back from her errands. There simply wasn't time for anyone else to come in there and do the deed between the time he left and the time Linda found Dorothy's body. Not unseen or unheard."

"Yeah, you're talking a different story now," Jack said. "Keep that in mind in case you get a wild hair about going off to meet him again, will ya?"

I felt heat in my face and was working on a snarky reply, but Esme saved me from myself.

"I was with her, Jack," she said. "I wouldn't let anything happen to her."

"See? Mother hen," Marydale said.

The doorbell spared us Esme's comeback and I went to answer.

Cassidy looked like she'd lost her last friend. Ingrid gave me an apologetic look. "We're back—*again*," she said, mouthing the last word. "I hope it's okay we dropped in like this. We were at the park but when we passed your house Cassidy begged to stop in."

"It's fine," I assured her. And it was. If being a part of this project was a comfort to Cassidy it was well worth the minor inconvenience.

Once in the workroom Ingrid glanced over Marydale's shoulder at the pages she was working on. "Oh, look here, Cassidy, this picture was taken up at High Ground when it was my grandparents' house. They used to have a big party for the whole town every Fourth of July."

"Highlight of the summer," Winston said. "Food and fireworks, games and prizes. All that good stuff."

"I only got to go once in my whole life," Marydale said. "We usually went to my grandparents' house in Wilmington for the Fourth. Not that the beach wasn't fun, but I hated always missing the big party. Everybody would be talking about it for weeks afterward."

"Gigi, there's a pony," Cassidy said, tiptoeing to see the pages. "Who is that little girl riding it? Can we get a pony? I love ponies."

"I'm not sure about that," Ingrid said. "But maybe we can find a place for you to ride one. And you know I think the girl in that picture is me." She leaned over to study the photo closer. "Yes, that's me. And you know who that is standing right over there by the tree? That's Miss Vivian. And that's her grandmother holding her hand."

"Was she your friend?" Cassidy asked.

"Well, we were friends, sort of," Ingrid said, tilting her head to one side, "but not friends like you and Tiffany. Vivian didn't live in Morningside so I didn't see her very often. She'd come to our house to play with me sometimes but she was younger than me so I didn't much like having to play with her. You know how it is when Tiffany's little sister wants to play with you two."

"She likes baby games," Cassidy pronounced. "Tiffany and me like to play Xbox and her daddy's teaching us how to play Blackjack."

"Really," Ingrid said, a forced smile on her face. "I'll have to ask Tiffany's daddy about that."

Cassidy gasped as she caught sight of Gadget and Sprocket frisking in the yard. "Can I go play with the puppies?" she asked.

Ingrid looked a question at Marydale.

"Sure you can, sweetie," Marydale said. "And can you take that little water dish and the water bottle from that bag and give them a drink?"

Marydale knew there was a fountain on the patio the dogs loved to lap from, but I sensed her strategy was to give Cassidy a chance to take care of something for a change. With all the adults around her constantly taking her emotional temperature she had to be feeling smothered.

We all watched as she went out and put the dish onto the grass. She splashed water into it despite some enthusiastic interference from the dogs. They jumped up on her and licked at her fingers and face. We could hear her giggle and it sounded magical.

"Thank you for that," Ingrid said, her voice quavering, "she doesn't laugh much these days. She's scared. She asked me last night if somebody was going to come to our house and hurt her, or me or her daddy. She goes around with me every night and checks the locks. Frankly, I'm a bit afraid myself. Until we know why Dorothy was killed it's easy to let your imagination run away with you. And since I was out of the family fold so long I have no idea whether it could be tied up with family business or what."

"I doubt that," I said. "Your father sold the business in 1972. And anyway, Dorothy never worked in the company."

"I didn't mean literally in the business," Ingrid said. "I just meant somehow tied up with the Pritchett family. I'm trying to think of every possibility. Maybe it had something to do with Dorothy's work with the town council. I got an earful from some people about that when I first moved back here."

"There were hard feelings at the time," Winston said. "But now most people give Dorothy her due. This town would have died out if she hadn't pushed for changes. I hate to think it could have anything to do with that."

"So do I," Ingrid said. "Morningside is a wonderful place. People have been good to me since I've been back. And I'm proud of all Dorothy did to make the town what it's become." Her voice went to a whisper. "I never told her that."

Again the doorbell saved us all from an awkward moment. Esme answered this time and returned a moment later with Vivian hot on her heels.

"Ingrid," she said, ignoring the rest of us, "I've been calling you all afternoon."

Ingrid frowned and reached into her pocket for her phone. "Sorry, I turned it off at church and forgot to turn it back on."

"Jeremy told me where you were," Vivian said, strolling along the tables and examining the pages we were working on. She looked like an instructor checking the work of underachieving students. "I had some questions about the guest list for the memorial. There are a couple of names I think you should add."

"Guest list?" Ingrid said. "I thought it would just be open to anyone who wants to pay respects to Dorothy."

"Oh, Ingrid," Vivian said, looking at her as if she felt sorry for the poor ignorant woman, "that's just asking for trouble. You need to control the numbers so you don't run out of food or be overrun by people who are there out of some morbid curiosity or something. That would be so unseemly and you know that's the last thing Dorothy would've wanted."

"Still," Ingrid said firmly. "I wouldn't want to turn away anybody who wants to honor Dorothy. I'll talk with Joe about it, but I'm sure he'll feel the same way."

"Whatever you want," Vivian said, though she made it evident she felt that was the wrong decision. "I'll do my best to deal with whatever challenges you throw at me."

"I appreciate that, Vivian," Ingrid said. "Here, come look at this picture of us at the High Ground summer party."

Vivian seemed impatient, but she came over and I slipped the pages into a protective sleeve and handed them to her.

"I think this was the year Grandpa Harry died," Ingrid said, "so it must have been the summer of 1957. I would have been almost six, so that means you would have been what? Three?"

"Almost four," Vivian said. "That's me there in that one as well, the one with William Pritchett bending down to talk to me. I know you had your issues with him, Ingrid, but he was always very nice to me at these events. Over all the years he never failed to ask me how school was going and things like that. He seemed really interested in hearing about my life."

"Well, he sure didn't care to hear about mine," Ingrid said. "But yes, he could be nice—unless you dared cross him. Then you were dead to him. With William Pritchett it was one strike and you're out."

"I don't even remember you being at the Fourth parties," Vivian said, frowning. "I was there every year until I went off to college."

Ingrid sighed. "After our grandparents died and we moved into High Ground the big bash seemed less about fun and more about appearances. We had to be there, it was mandatory. And Father expected Dorothy and me to be perfect in front of the townspeople. Any little misstep and there was a price to pay. It was a test, and I frequently failed. I'd beg off claiming a stomachache and if that didn't work I'd go to the attic or the guest house and hide."

"Sad," Vivian said then looked around the room. "Well,

anyway, you know Sophreena and Esme are being paid to do this. You don't need to be over here helping out."

Ingrid smiled. "I think Cassidy and I have been more a hindrance than a help and Sophreena and Esme have been great to let us hang around. I'm learning things about my family I never knew."

"Dorothy always said family was everything," Vivian said, reaching over to pat Ingrid's arm. "Too bad you're learning that so late." She gave the rest of us a perfunctory nod. "Y'all carry on. I'll show myself out."

Cassidy came back inside with the dogs at her heels. "I think they're tired," she said.

"They probably are," Marydale said. "Honey, could you fix their little beds for them?"

Both pups immediately wound themselves into little balls and fell into an untroubled sleep. Cassidy retrieved her bag and curled up on the futon couch we use for guests. She took out her stuffed dog, a book and finally the puzzle box. She picked up the box and started to manipulate the moving parts and pry at the cracks with her fingernails.

I went back to working on my pages and when I looked over a few minutes later, Cassidy was fast asleep. Ingrid followed my eyes and saw the sleeping child.

"I need to get her home," she said. "She has enough trouble sleeping at night as it is." She gently shook Cassidy awake and helped the groggy child gather up her things.

We worked on for another half hour before Jack stood and stretched. "I need to get going, too," he said, glancing at his watch.

"Thanks for your help," I said.

He came over to my table and leaned down. "Do me a favor, Soph. If you get any other leads about Dorothy's case, just pass them on to the cops, okay?"

"Sure thing," I said, making a shooing motion. "Now, go, you're going to be late for your dinner date." I tried to force out a "Say hi to Julie," but my lips refused to make the words.

fifteen

I FOUND ESME AT THE KITCHEN TABLE THE NEXT MORNING looking downright frowsy. I looked equally bedraggled, but for me that's not rare. We'd worked late into the night and when I'd finally fallen into bed I couldn't get to sleep. Thoughts had chased one another around in my head as I lay there in the darkness.

I kept recalling the party photos of the Fourth of July celebration at Harrison and Sarah Pritchett's and contrasting that festive event with the sterile and rigid home life Ingrid Garrison had described with her father.

Dorothy had always spoken of her grandparents with warmth and deep affection. In contrast, though she'd never said a negative word about her father through all the months we'd worked with her, there had been code words: *exacting, high standards, unrelenting, assured.* At one point she'd said that a person would flout William Pritchett's advice at her peril and I'd found that pronoun telling, though I didn't know if she'd meant Ingrid or herself.

And I kept getting flashes of pitiful little Cassidy every

time I closed my eyes. I wondered what lasting effects Dorothy's murder would have on the child.

Then there was the Jack issue. I had to face the fact that I was just plain old garden variety jealous. But that was *my* issue. He'd done nothing wrong and he'd been nothing but a friend to me. Which was, I had to admit, *exactly* the problem.

"I know why I didn't sleep, what about you?" I asked Esme as I poured myself a tankard of coffee.

"Sarah Malone," Esme answered. "The poor woman is not going gentle into that good night. She's restless as the wind and apparently she enjoys my company."

"What are you getting?" I asked.

"Oh, paradoxes, Catch-22s, enigmas inside conundrums wrapped up in perplexities and tied with Gordian knots." She set down the newspaper and rubbed at her eyes. "I sense great joy and great pain coming from the same place. And I get a strong feeling that ring is at the crux of it all somehow, at least as a symbol."

"If the story Hank Spencer told us is true I can't think how Sarah Malone might have felt about being given a ring that her suitor won in a poker game. Doesn't that seem, I don't know, a little less than romantic?"

"It's a spectacular ring," Esme said. "And Harrison Pritchett put it on her finger after taking it from a woman who'd treated her shabbily. That payback had to feel a *little* good to Sarah. It's got kind of a knight-in-shining-armor feel to it, don't you think?"

"True," I said. "You know, Sarah never passed the ring on. Maybe she didn't much like her daughter-in-law either."

"No, that wasn't it," Esme said.

"Well, what do you suppose it was, then?"

"Don't know—yet," Esme said. "But it had nothing to do with her daughter-in-law. I think she liked her. Or at least she didn't dislike her."

"You know, everyone we interviewed who knew Harrison and Sarah described their marriage as happy, unusually so. No one had an ill word to say about them as individuals either. But their son, William? Nobody had a *good* word to say about him, unless you count Dorothy, which I don't because even her praise sounded forced. How could Harrison and Sarah Pritchett, two such good, caring people, have produced a family legacy like the one that filtered down to Dorothy and Ingrid?"

"Hard to know," Esme said. "Anyhow, Sarah's what kept me sleepless all night. What set you tossin' and turnin'?"

"Just this whole situation."

"So, not about Jack, then? And before you get all spluttery and deny it, remember who you're talkin' to."

I sighed. "Okay, I'm a little put out with him. And I know that's unreasonable. He's got a right to date whomever he pleases. I just don't think she's right for him, that's all."

"And you base this on what, exactly?"

"I met her," I said, enunciating each word. "And she isn't Jack's type."

"So you and Julie had a long heartfelt conversation and you got to know what kind of person she is? Her hopes and her dreams? Her beliefs and her ways?"

"Well, no. We only talked for a minute or two. But she's just—she's really pretty, okay? She can't possibly be a serious person and be that pretty."

"Um-hm," Esme murmured. "Well, I can tell you one thing, she's got good sources," she said, handing over the newspaper.

I scanned, fuming as I read. "She knows about Hank Spencer? She doesn't mention him by name; she calls him a distant relative, but that's who she means. Okay, first off, she got that wrong. Hank and Dorothy are not blood relations. Agnes Pritchett was related to Dorothy's grandmother, Sarah, but even that kinship was distant. Dorothy and Hank weren't related at all, not by blood. She got that *completely* wrong."

"So you said," Esme mumbled.

"Wow, she says here sources close to the investigation say robbery is thought to be the motive for the murder and that police are close to making an arrest."

"That's sure news to Detective Carlson," Esme said.

"Well, I think I can guess where she's getting her information," I said, slamming the newspaper down on the table.

"You know Jack didn't tell her any of this. Has he ever betrayed a confidence?"

"Maybe he didn't realize. She's trained to get information out of people. And did I mention she's extremely pretty, and flirty, and all sparkly?" I shuddered.

Esme shook her head. "Regardless, you know Jack didn't spill anything." She laughed softly. "Sophreena, Mama used to say, 'You can get glad the same way you got mad.' Jack was worried about you and maybe he got a little bossy, but you know it's only because he's concerned. Now, you can make up your mind to be mad at him and be miserable, or you can decide you're glad he cares."

"You're right," I said, blowing out a breath. "He's a good

friend. I should support his choices. I should be happy for him. I hope he'd be happy for me if I found someone."

"Um-hm," Esme said again. "'Nother thing Mama always said was 'Don't go crossing the creek to find water.'"

"What does *that* mean?"

"You'll figure it out," Esme said.

Esme took over trimming and mounting photos and I continued with labeling. I wasn't happy with the mechanical precision of the computer font. I love the authenticity of hand calligraphy, but that wasn't an option with the deadline looming. I was hoping Marydale would volunteer to help again. With her practiced eye for the details she could make a page beautiful without distracting from its documentary value.

"Vivian was not kidding when she said she went to that High Ground Fourth of July party every year," Esme said. "You can watch her grow up in these pictures."

"That must have been where she got her first glimpse into the world of the rich. She seems to covet that."

"Yes, and don't you wonder at that?" Esme said. "With her and Dorothy so close she had to see money and a prominent family didn't guarantee happiness. I don't get people who think money will solve all their problems and who want to get close to it, like little kids pressing their noses up against the candy store window."

"Esme, do you think Hank Spencer could be one of those people?"

"I don't know what to make of him. I agree he seems like a regular guy who's pretty content with his life—maybe a little cowed by his wife, but other than that. But what it boils down to is how could it have been anybody else?"

"But he seemed so shocked to hear Dorothy was dead. And he didn't appear to be hiding anything. Maybe I'm gullible, but I totally bought it."

"And maybe I'm too cynical," Esme said. "But what better way to throw everybody off than to 'fess up to what he knows will be discovered anyway? Look, no matter what either of us thinks of him, it's hard to argue with the timing. And anyway, it's out of our hands now."

I pulled over the next two-page layout and consulted my notes. "Ah, 1956. Dwight David Eisenhower's president, Elvis hits the charts for the first time with 'Heartbreak Hotel,' *My Fair Lady* opens on Broadway and the *King and I* and *Around the World in Eighty Days* are smash movie hits. Gas is around 22 cents a gallon, coffee 85 cents a pound and the average monthly rent $88. School kids get sugar cubes doused with Sabin oral polio vaccine, transistor radios hit the market, the *Andrea Doria* sinks, Grace Kelly marries Prince Rainier, Castro brings revolution to Cuba, and Rosa Parks sparks a bus boycott in Montgomery. What a time it was."

"You're gonna sprain your brain doing that one of these days," Esme mumbled.

"And in our little corner of the world the Fourth of July party at High Ground rolls around again," I mused. "Look at Harrison and Sarah. They were elderly when this picture was taken and they're still holding hands."

"Yeah, they're cute oldies," Esme said, "but I can*not* look at another picture of Sarah Malone Pritchett right now. I'm hoping she'll give me a break tonight and if I've been staring at her face all day it's just like putting out the welcome mat. Now, I'm going in to fix us some lunch."

"I need a break, too, and anyway I've got to run over to Keepsake Corner and get some more tape runner and photo corners."

"There's tape runner and tabs over in that drawer," Esme said, nodding toward the old dresser we'd converted into storage for supplies.

"It's all low tack," I said. "And there's no reason anyone will ever need to take anything out of these books, so we need high-tack tape for a permanent bond. This puts The End to the Pritchett family line."

I didn't think it was possible Marydale could fit more inventory into Keepsake Corner but when I arrived she was down on her knees assembling a display shelf that looked like it would just fit the niche between the checkout counter and the door. She'd jumped on the honeysuckle bandwagon and had tangles of silk honeysuckle vines framing the windows and more honeysuckle-themed papers, stationery, stickers and greeting cards than I would've thought existed stacked on the counter ready to be loaded onto the new shelf.

"What is it they say," she asked, grimacing as she twisted the screwdriver, "if you build it, they will come? Well, I'm building it."

"I hope you get swamped with customers," I said, as I stepped around her to gather my supplies. "I have selfish reasons for wanting you to succeed. You're my custom supplier."

"If I had a few more customers like you I'd be set," she said, blowing her bangs off her face as she set the screwdriver aside and struggled up off the floor. She stared at the shelf a moment and then over at the spot it was to occupy. "This sucker better fit," she said. "I measured three times."

I helped her lift the shelf and shoehorn it into position and we chatted as she filled it with honeysuckle swag.

"Did you hear the police asked Linda to come in again this morning?" she asked.

"No, why?"

"To answer more questions, I guess. I figured maybe they wanted to talk to her again before they questioned that Spencer guy. But Linda's husband, Ben, says this is the last time they'll talk to her without a lawyer. I sure hope it doesn't come to that; a lawyer's fee is about the last thing they need right now."

"So things really are bad for them financially?"

"Oh, they're not destitute," she said, "but they're struggling a bit. Aren't we all? And now with Dorothy gone I guess Linda will be without a job, depending on what happens to High Ground."

"I'm wondering about that," I mused. "Joe Porter says it won't go to him. Maybe Dorothy left it to Ingrid. Seems like that would be the natural thing."

"Maybe," Marydale said, arranging glass dome paperweights with honeysuckle blossoms captured inside into a pleasing cluster, "but natural wasn't really Dorothy's strong suit, was it? I guess everyone will know soon enough. Linda says Dorothy's lawyer asked to meet with the family tomorrow for the reading of the will. She's been asked to be there, too, so Dorothy must have left her some little bequest. I hope she did, for Linda's sake and because it would be one more thing that would pleasantly surprise me about Dorothy Porter."

"I know what you mean. Esme and I worked with the woman for months and yet we both feel we never really got to know her."

"Unfortunately Dorothy seemed to put a lot of people off. Several of the old-time merchants still have hard feelings over how she bulldozed them into upgrading their places instead of giving them time to defray the cost over time. And some of the old-timers are not happy about how the town has been improved, especially the ones up on Crescent Hill. They complain about Morningside becoming Disneyfied, and really don't like the tourists coming in. Howard Granger, Dorothy's next-door neighbor, has been *very* vocal about his feelings on the subject. And apparently Dorothy even got into a wrangle with her own pastor over some improvements to the church. Honestly, I think the only people who truly loved Dorothy without reservation were Cassidy and Vivian."

"We should all have such a friend," I said.

"We do, darlin'," Marydale said, patting my cheeks. "We've got each other."

As I walked back to my house I looked at Morningside with new eyes and thought about what Dorothy had done for the town. It was a pity I hadn't appreciated her contribution when I could have told her so. I admired all the wrought iron, the abundance of ornamental plants, the well-placed pocket parks, green spaces and classy storefronts. But it was more than appearance. I'd always thought Morningside was not only a pretty town but a good town. The people here looked after one another. There was the usual small-town gossip and bickering, but people were good at heart and cared about their neighbors. It made me ill to think Dorothy's killer could be among us.

Esme had lunch ready and we ate quickly then worked steadily for the next few hours. Ingrid called to say she had a meeting and wouldn't be bringing Cassidy over, which was just as well. She'd been right when she said they were more hindrance than help. Coco came by and helped out for an hour, then Winston showed up in the late afternoon to bring cinnamon buns with a lava of cream cheese frosting running down the sides. For energy, he said. For ecstasy, I said.

About five o'clock Esme stood up and stretched. "I hate to leave you working, Sophreena, but you know I've got that volunteers' meeting at church. I can't miss it 'cause I'm the committee chairperson. I shouldn't be gone long and I'll do some more when I get back tonight."

I told Esme it was no problem, but after she left I felt abandoned. I ate another cinnamon bun and called it dinner and went back at it, working on 1961, the year Dorothy graduated from the University of North Carolina in nearby Chapel Hill. Dorothy came away with a degree in American history, but I had a hunch she'd never had a real college experience. Her father had insisted she continue to live at High Ground throughout her college years.

After she graduated her job seemed to consist of running the household at High Ground and serving as hostess for her father's business and social gatherings. He sold the company in 1972 and spent the rest of his years traveling extensively while Dorothy stayed behind and looked after High Ground, filling her hours with gardening and lunching before eventually launching her campaign to resurrect Morningside.

In the pictures from that period the vivacious, funny girl Winston had described was nowhere to be seen. Dorothy looked somber and spinsterish.

Then another transformation occurred after Joe Porter came into her life. She bloomed. A smiling Dorothy looked out from pictures of that era. In the ones where she was looking at Joe she was positively beaming. I never noticed the woman had such a perfect set of teeth.

William Pritchett had not attended Dorothy's wedding. The way Dorothy had explained it he'd been stranded in Vienna at the time, no flights available, but I had a hunch he hadn't expended much energy on finding a way to be a part of the day.

Dorothy and Joe looked so gloriously happy in their wedding photo I couldn't bring myself to use a computer font to label it. This photo needed to be honored with a personal touch. As I went to the cabinet to get my calligraphy supplies I had an overwhelming urge to call Jack, then I remembered how awkwardly we'd left things. I wasn't sure how this was supposed to get fixed. We'd never had a real falling out before. He'd dated other people since we'd been friends and so had I. We'd even talked about the dates afterward, rating them, calculating whether a second date was in order. It had never been an issue in the past, so why was it now?

The doorbell rang and for a moment my spirits lifted, then I realized it couldn't be Jack. He'd have let himself in.

It was full dark out and I hadn't been expecting anyone so I turned on the porch light and slid over the stool so I could look out the peephole. Hank Spencer was on our front porch shifting from one foot to the other. I cursed myself. No pretending I wasn't home now, not after I'd switched on the light. What in the world did he want? For the first time ever I wished we had a safety chain on our door. I called out loudly, "I'll get it, Esme," so he wouldn't know I was here alone, then opened the door a crack.

"Miss McClure," Spencer said, "I'm sorry to bother you, but could I talk to you a few minutes? It's really important."

Jack's warnings echoed in my ears, but curiosity won out. I opened the door and motioned him inside, guiding him into the living room. I gestured for him to sit but I stayed on my feet. "What can I do for you, Mr. Spencer? And can I ask how you found out where I live?"

"It's Hank," he said, adjusting his position on the sofa, "just call me Hank. And probably the same way you found me. Google search? Look, I'm sorry. I should have called or something, I know. I'm really rattled right now. You must think I'm some kind of head case. Look at this, my hands are shaking." He held them out and they were, indeed, vibrating as if he were hooked up to an electrical current.

"I came in to talk with the police today about my visit with Mrs. Porter," he went on, talking fast, his voice raspy. "I wanted to get it all straightened out before they came looking for me. I figured I'd come over, tell them what I told you and be on my way. But they kept me there for four hours. Four hours! They must have asked me the same questions twenty times." He ran his hand through his blond hair as he'd done the day we'd talked with him. "I'm so stupid, I didn't even realize I was a serious suspect until halfway through it all."

"The police are just being thorough," I said. "They're questioning everyone."

"But this could ruin me," Spencer said, raking at his hair again. "Who is *ever* going to want to take a tour with me if they hear I've even for a minute been a suspect in a murder? I should never have gone to see that woman. I shouldn't have told her that stupid story about the ring. She got so *mad* about the whole thing, I was afraid she might attack me. I thought the whole episode was funny and I expected she would, too, how her ancestor had outwitted mine and come away with the prize. I mean, if anything I should have been the one to be upset by it, right? That ring *had* been in the Spencer family for generations."

He was up now and pacing in front of the sofa and I was getting increasingly uncomfortable.

"The police will find whoever killed Dorothy and this will all blow over soon, I'm sure," I said, making a gesture toward the front hall to signal it was time for him to go.

Spencer stopped pacing and looked at me, his face ashen and little beads of sweat forming on his upper lip. "It may be too late for me by then. And my wife is going to kill me 'cause I'm gonna have to hire a lawyer. That'll cost a bundle. She was already ticked off that I was spending so much time on the family history thing. She didn't get it. The cops don't either. That's why I came here. Maybe you could talk to them. They act like I was stalking Dorothy Porter or something. They don't seem to get the whole genealogy-as-a-hobby thing. But you could make them understand. Please, you've gotta help me."

Before I had a chance to reply he was across the room and had me by both shoulders. *"Please*, can't you talk to them?"

His eyes looked a little wild and he had me in a vise grip. I was starting to panic when a voice came from the doorway.

"Get your hands off her."

I turned to see Jack, his face granite and his fists clenched at his sides.

Spencer stepped back, a stricken look on his face. "God, I'm sorry. I'm *so* sorry."

"It's okay, Jack," I said. "This is Hank Spencer. He's upset, that's all. Everything's okay."

"Everything did not *look* okay," Jack said.

"I'll go now," Spencer said. "I'm sorry I bothered you. Maybe we can talk later."

"Or maybe not," Jack said.

I held up a hand. "Mr. Spencer—Hank—I will talk to Detective Carlson and try to make him understand, but that's all I can promise."

"Thanks," Spencer said, giving Jack a sidelong glance, "that's all I'm asking."

At the door he turned to give me one last look and mumbled another "sorry" before I closed the door, my own hand shaking now.

I couldn't look at Jack. "Don't say I told you so," I said, my voice muffled by the door. "I should never have let him in."

"I came by to apologize for yesterday," Jack said, turning me around and putting out his hand. "Truce?"

I reached to shake but he pulled me to him and put his arms around me, resting his chin on the top of my head. "What's gotten into us, Soph? No more fighting, okay?"

I waited for the brotherly *pat, pat, pat.*

But it never came.

sixteen

We'd gotten practically nothing done after Esme got home that night. Jack told her about my visit with Hank Spencer and she went ballistic. She'd wanted to call Detective Carlson immediately and I'd had to do some fast talking to get her calmed down.

This morning she was on it again. "I really think we should call Denny and tell him about Spencer showing up here last night. He could well be Dorothy's killer, Sophreena. And you let him in. You were here alone with him."

Denny? When had he jumped that hurdle? When I finally found my voice I was firm. "I am not calling the police on the man, Esme. He was just worked up last night, that's all. You remember what it was like when the police questioned us? Well, multiply that times ten. He got everything but the bright lights and rubber hoses."

"Maybe for good reason," Esme said. "Sophreena, I know you want him to be innocent. But from the way Jack told it the guy was unhinged."

"He was upset," I allowed. "And I wouldn't welcome any more unannounced visits from him. Seeing how he was last night made me wonder how he reacted when Dorothy threw him out of her house."

"No more visits, period," Esme said, the swish of the paper cutter emphasizing her words. "Unannounced, announced or booked in advance."

"Agreed," I said with a sigh.

About an hour later Vivian called wanting me to come up to High Ground to help her decide where and how the scrapbooks would be displayed. I considered telling her if she didn't stop bothering me there might not be any scrapbooks, but she was already wound a little tight about this event so I dutifully grabbed my bag and one of the scrapbooks and answered the summons.

The police had only this morning removed the yellow crime scene tape and released the house and there was a buzz of activity as everything got put where it belonged. It was the first time I'd been to High Ground since the day Dorothy died and it seemed surreal that the house stood seemingly permanent and unchanging yet Dorothy was gone.

Vivian had decided to have a carpenter build reading stands for each scrapbook. Even I thought this was over the top. She couldn't decide between easel-type stands for the long oak dining table or freestanding floor stands, and asked my opinion.

"Wow, Vivian, I'm not sure that's necessary. You know, after Dorothy's memorial these will be just like any other family albums."

"Oh, no, no. That was the original intent, but everything's changed now. The Pritchett family is a major part of the history of our community. I'm sure the town council will want them on public display. And as new facts come to light those will be incorporated until a complete history of the family is known."

This was the third time Vivian had insinuated we hadn't done our job. It was really starting to rankle.

"Vivian, do you know something about the Pritchett family that we missed? Something that should be included here?"

She gave me a wan smile. "Sorry if I offended, Sophreena. I wasn't questioning your abilities. I'm just saying I know you traced the family history way back, but now that Dorothy has passed that changes things. I'm sure people will want more on the Pritchetts of this and future generations."

"Vivian, these books are meant for the family. They'll probably just be put on a shelf here after the memorial. Here—or someplace. Nobody knows yet what's to become of this house, do they?"

"Not definitely," Vivian said, "but I'm sure it won't leave the family. Which reminds me," she said, studying her watch, "I've really got to run. Dorothy's lawyer has called a meeting with us today about her will."

I was glad for the opportunity to escape and get back to work. On my way out I passed the staircase that eventually led to the attic. Over the past months Esme and I had spent hours amidst the jumble of family treasures and cast-off belongings crowded into that hot, dusty space.

With no real intention I found myself mounting the

stairs. I knew them so well I could accurately predict which ones squeaked. Esme and I had hauled dozens of heavy boxes of photos, memorabilia and artifacts down out of that attic.

We'd done the first sort on tables set up in the gatehouse at High Ground. Dorothy would drop in daily to look over what we'd found but she left the grunt work to us. She, too, had been keen on Laurena Bascom Pritchett's Civil War–era memory book. That was one of the few items she'd taken to the big house for a closer look. But the only thing she'd asked about specifically—and *repeatedly*—was her grandmother's ring. She'd been fixated on it. It must have been devastating for her to hear Hank Spencer make it into the centerpiece of a joke.

I opened the door at the top of the attic stairs and gaped at what I saw. Esme and I had left everything tidy; now boxes were standing open, the contents strewn about, and everything was in general disarray. I closed the door and went back downstairs and out the back door to my car. Should I call someone to let them know about this? An untidy attic wasn't exactly something to raise alarms about given the more pressing concerns of this family right now. And anyway, who should I call? Still, it bothered me.

When I told Esme she was vexed. "We left that place clean and organized. Now somebody's gonna say we left a mess. I don't like that."

"I don't like it either," I said. "Maybe the police left it that way."

"Well," Esme said, "there's yet another thing we need to let Denny know about, I suppose. I'll call him a little later."

She nodded toward the pile of layouts she'd done while I was gone. "You've got a backlog there, you'd best get at it."

"What time period are we in now?"

"Still the sixties, so a lot of it is William Pritchett. You know that old saying, 'a face only a mother could love'? Well, I'm not so sure even she did."

"She still dropping stuff on you?"

"Off and on," Esme said. "She's a weary soul and she's wearing me out, too. I wish I could help her but I can't figure out the message. Seems like that's the way it goes. The longer secrets have been buried the more mud I have to shovel to finally uncover them."

"Do you think there is some Pritchett family secret?"

"I don't know if there's a deep, dark secret," Esme said, "but there were definitely things left unresolved. If there is it must have been Dorothy's lonely burden to bear. I can't imagine who she'd confide in since I don't think she quite trusted anyone, nor regarded anyone around here as her equal."

"How about you, Esme?" I asked, teasingly. "Do you regard me as your equal?"

"Sometimes," Esme said.

I felt my skin prickle. I'd meant it as a joke.

"Oh, don't go pouting," Esme said. "Sometimes you're my equal, sometimes you're not. Sometimes I'm *your* equal, and sometimes I'm not. That's why we're a good team. Now be a good teammate and get to work."

William Pritchett had amassed a monumental amount of material in his lifetime, but very little of it had anything to do with family. He'd kept a travelogue of his various trips that was interesting if you wanted facts about Madagascar or

Cyprus or other far-flung places, but useless in terms of the Pritchett family life. I'd already slogged through all that. But there was still a small stack of correspondence I needed to mine for whatever tidbits might be buried within.

Most of the material up through 1972 when the company was sold related to the business, and other documents were important enough to keep but not succinct enough for scrapbooking, such as William Pritchett's last will and testament. For the scrapbook I made a journal box stating when the will was executed and where it could be found in the family archives. Other things were simply too unpleasant to be included. While I believe in warts-and-all family histories it's not necessary to rub salt in wounds, or expose a family's less-than-finest attributes to public scrutiny.

It was generally understood within the community that William Pritchett had been an offish prig and his character was certainly well known to his remaining child, Ingrid, but I still balked at including the letter I'd just found.

It was dated October 3, 1972, a few days after the business was sold. William had rewritten his will and was getting his finances in order in preparation for an extended trip abroad. He'd written to his lawyer: *In regard to your inquiry about disbursements, the child in question has now reached the age of majority and my obligations are fulfilled. There will be no further monies transferred and no provisions made for the child to inherit any portion of my estate. The matter is ended.*

No wonder Ingrid was so bitter. Her father had cut her off finally and completely and seemingly without a single regret. The words were so cold they made me feel like reaching for

a sweater, even though temps had reached the ninety-degree
mark outside and the air-conditioner was laboring mightily.

I was happy when I was done with that and could turn
to reconstructing the Civil War commonplace book with the
copies we'd made. Laurena Bascom Pritchett, as was the custom of the day, had glued all sorts of things into her remembrance book. Newspaper and magazine clippings, buttons
and snippets of cloth from favorite clothing she'd worn out,
feathers, pressed flowers, colorful candy wrappers and ornate
soap boxes, calendar pages and a maple leaf that had once
probably been colorful, but was now only a powdery crust.
There were matchbooks, homemade cards and lots of used
postage stamps in addition to the autobiographical writing
sprinkled throughout the book in Laurena's straight up and
down handwriting.

We'd carefully taken the book apart and scanned the
pages that could be safely placed on the scanner bed and
copied the more vulnerable ones with a camera on a copy
stand. Then we'd put the book back together again.

I placed the reproduction pages in the original order and
made a front plate for the book documenting everything
known about its origins. This was my favorite piece in all of
the Pritchett family archives, even though it represented a
tragic story.

The sun slanted in our west-facing window and I knew
it must be near four o'clock. Sure enough the bell from the
church down the street tolled four gongs and our doorbell
dinged an echo.

Esme went to get it and I hoped for his own sake it wasn't

Hank Spencer again. Esme was tired and her mouth was set in a hard line. But then I heard her cheerful voice and knew it must be Cassidy.

When they came into the workroom I was surprised to see it was Jeremy who was with Cassidy, not Ingrid.

"Mom strongly suggested I come over and learn a few things about the Pritchetts before Dorothy's memorial," he said. "Would it be okay if I get a quick preview?"

"Sure," I said, wondering what had caused this change of heart.

"I had to go back to day camp today," Cassidy chattered to Esme. "Daddy and Gigi had adult business. We went bowling. I didn't even need the bumpers. I can do real bowling. Tiffany's not got the hang of it yet, that's what our counselor, Miss Mendy, says, but we're not supposed to laugh at Tiffany because what she really needs is *encouragement*."

"Miss Mendy is right," Esme said, "everybody needs encouragement. Maybe you could give us some right now. We've been working really hard and we're tired."

Jeremy had the same reaction as everyone else had when he looked around the room. "Quite an operation," he said. "No wonder you're tired."

I knew Jeremy had been in the meeting with the lawyers and I was dying to ask questions that were none of my business. He seemed in a good mood and I wondered if that was due to the terms of Dorothy's will.

"These don't look like Tiffany's mom's scrapbooks," Cassidy said, carefully turning the pages of one of the heritage books the way we'd taught her to. "Tiffany's mom doesn't write stuff down in hers. And she uses red and blue and yellow and all the rainbow colors and cut-out shapes and ribbons and lots and *lots* of stickers. I like stickers. These look old."

"That's the idea," I told her. "These people lived back in olden days, so we're trying to make them look old on purpose."

"You don't want them to be pretty?" she asked.

Jeremy put a hand on her shoulder. "They're pretty, Cass. Just a different kind of pretty."

She shrugged and walked over to watch Esme work.

"Sorry," Jeremy said. "We're big on honesty at our house, but unlike bowling she hasn't quite got the hang of tact yet."

"That's okay," I said. "Lots of grown-up scrapbookers feel the same way she does. Is there anything in particular you'd like to see?"

"I'll be honest with you," Jeremy said, "I really wouldn't *like* to see any of it, or at least that was true before today. I've never wanted anything to do with the Pritchett family after what they did to my mother. I suspect that's been pretty plain. I was dead set against it when Mom wanted to come back here. But she seemed to need the move and Cass and I needed her, so here we all are."

I didn't have the foggiest idea how to respond to that, so I simply slid the memory book I'd just finished across the table. "This is a commonplace book that was kept by your number fifteen, or in layman's terms, your great-great-grandmother, Laurena Bascom Pritchett."

"And which Mr. Pritchett did this poor woman have the misfortune to marry?" he asked with a sigh.

I'd gotten to know Laurena Bascom Pritchett in the course of reproducing her heartfelt little book and in some small way I felt I shared her sorrow. Jeremy's comment made me defensive.

"She married Lawton Morgan Pritchett and from all accounts she loved him very much. He went off to the Civil War and never came home again to get to see his son, Harrison, grow up. Harrison Pritchett, as you know, was your great-grandfather."

"Yes, that much I do know," Jeremy said, "but you shouldn't assume I know much else. Don't be afraid of insulting me. I've tried my hardest to avoid learning anything about the Pritchetts, though living here some of it soaks in through your pores. So this ancestor died in the Civil War? Were there other kids?"

"No, Harrison Pritchett was an only child. Laurena was only nineteen when he was born. Lawton Pritchett was twenty-four. Harrison wasn't quite three months old when Lawton went to war, and not quite a year old when Lawton died in the battle at Kelly's Ford along the Rappahannock River in Virginia."

"That's a terrible story," Jeremy said, "so why is it I'm glad to know it?"

"That's a pretty universal reaction," I said. "People like to know about their people."

Jeremy puckered his lips, considering. "I thought Dorothy did this as a vanity thing. You know, look at us, we're the big cheese family around here. But maybe I should have given her the benefit of the doubt."

"Sometimes people have complicated reasons for wanting

to trace their lineage, and maybe there was some vanity at play with Dorothy, but she told us numerous times she wanted it done for the family, and especially for Cassidy."

He returned to the book, leafing through pages with more concentration now. "So this woman, my great-whatever-grandmother, looks like she saved everything she came across."

"Yes, very typical for the day for women who kept a book. They saved personal mementos and objects of daily life that triggered a remembrance, were pleasing to the eye or caught their fancy in some way."

"What was supposed to go here?" he asked, stopping to examine the blank spot on the page Jack had asked about.

"It was a lock of your great-grandfather Harrison's hair in a little envelope. It's gotten lost. We're hoping it will turn up before we're finished."

"Would it have been one of those waxed paper envelopes? The kind they used to put stamps in at the post office?"

"Glassine. Yes. I'm pretty sure it was in the book when we found it, but it must have fallen out when Dorothy had it. She kept it overnight to look at it."

"I think I might know where it is," he said. "I saw something like that on Dorothy's desk. I meant to ask about it. I thought maybe it was my mother's from when she was a baby. She was a blond tyke."

"Thanks for telling me. I'll see if we can locate it and put it back in the original book," I said. "Would you like to see what this ancestor, Laurena Bascom Pritchett, looked like? She was a blonde, too."

"There are pictures?"

"There's a nice ambrotype of her as a young woman," I said, reaching across to turn the pages to the back of the scrapbook. "It was in a half case that was falling apart, but we managed to get a pretty good reproduction of it."

"Wow, she looks like my mother," he said. "Or I guess it would be my mother looks like her. Cassidy, look at this, this is Gigi's—" He looked a question at me.

"Her great-grandmother."

"Why was she great?" Cassidy asked, coming over to have a look.

I made a stab at explaining consanguinity links, but Cassidy's frown only deepened. I reached for an example. "It would be like if you'd known Gigi's mother," I said. "She would be your great-grandmother."

"No, that would be Auntie Dot," Cassidy said. "And she's dead now."

"Aunt Dot was Gigi's sister, not her mother," Jeremy said.

"No," Cassidy insisted, her mouth setting in a stubborn line. "Gigi told me, Auntie Dot was her only mother."

Jeremy started to correct her, but I pre-empted him. "You're right, Cassidy. She's told us that, too. Let's just say this woman is someone from your family who lived a long time ago. She's related to all of you."

Cassidy studied the picture. "Gigi looks sad like that sometimes," she said. "Why didn't this lady smile for her picture? You're supposed to smile nice."

"Back in those days a person had to sit still for a long time to have a picture taken. I mean really still, like they were frozen. It was hard to hold a smile that long so most people have serious expressions in their pictures."

Cassidy considered this for a moment. "I'm going to see how long I can smile," she said, pulling her mouth back until her whole face contorted. She held it as she took her bag and went to the futon.

"Thanks," Jeremy said. "I'm a fact guy. I forget sometimes there's different ways to interpret things. I guess Mom did think of Dorothy as a mother figure." He was silent for a few minutes, seemingly lost in thought. Finally he said, "I admit it, I was unfair to Dorothy in some ways. In my defense, she didn't make things easy. She was a hard woman to deal with, but Mom's told me a lot over the last week and now I realize I blamed Dorothy for things she had no hand in. And at the end of the day she did try to make it up to my mother." He glanced over to make sure Cassidy wasn't listening. "This will be all over town soon enough, so you might as well know. Dorothy left High Ground to the town of Morningside."

"Oh," I said, wondering how this made anything up to his mother. "And you're *pleased* about that?" I asked tentatively.

"Yes," he said, "I mean, who'd want to live in that old mausoleum? And the upkeep would make it unsustainable as a private home. The town can make good use of it. But she left my mother the house they grew up in and the gatehouse at High Ground."

"Oh, that gatehouse is beautiful," I said. "Esme and I did a lot of our work in there when we were going through all this stuff."

"Yeah," he said, "and apparently it's one of the few places around here that holds good memories for my mother. She used to play out there when she was a child."

I was hoping if I left a silence he'd volunteer more about Dorothy's will, but no such luck.

"Anyway," he said, his voice shaky, "I wish I could go back and tell Dorothy I'm sorry for some of the things I said to her."

I heard a huffing sound coming from the futon and turned to see Cassidy sitting cross-legged with the puzzle box in her lap. She was almost clawing at it now, near tears.

"Man, I wish Dorothy had never given her that thing," Jeremy said. "Or at least that she'd never told her that bit about her dreams coming true if she could open it. She's driving herself crazy and us along with her."

"Maybe she just needs to take a break. Maybe put it away for a while?"

"How I wish," he said. "She won't let us. Even sleeps with it and if I try to move it she wakes up and gets upset." He sighed and turned back to the scrapbook.

He flipped a few more pages and then watched me work on embellishing pages with borders, hand-drawn decorative elements and ornate metal photo corners.

"You two are really good at this," he said.

"Yes, we are," Esme said.

"Esme doesn't believe in modesty," I said.

"Not *false* modesty," Esme replied. "We're good at what we do. Nothing wrong with taking pride in your work."

"Nothing at all." Jeremy smiled. He looked like a totally different person when he smiled. "So, I don't suppose there's any photos of her husband," he said, pointing to the somber portrait of Laurena Bascom Pritchett.

"Yes. Turn to the next page, there's a reproduction from a tintype of him in uniform. He must have sent it to her since there's no evidence he ever saw her again once he left for the war. Tintypes were faster, cheaper and more durable than the glass ambrotypes, and some enterprising photographers built portable rigs and followed the military units to their camps to take affordable likenesses the men could send home to their families."

"I doubt affordable was an issue for him. He was a Pritchett," Jeremy said.

"You really *don't* know much about your family history, do you?" Esme said.

"What Esme means to say is that not all your Pritchett ancestors were wealthy. They did well, but the real money didn't come into the family until your great-grandfather Harrison built his successful company."

"But he had to have seed money from somewhere, right?" Jeremy said. "An inheritance probably."

"Can't tell you where he got the start-up money," Esme said, "but a grand inheritance was unlikely. We heard he was a bit of a gambler in his younger days. Maybe he had a winning streak."

"No kidding?" Jeremy grinned. "How'd you find that out?"

"It's unsubstantiated," I said, avoiding the question.

"Okay, but who'd you hear it from? Somebody who knew him back then?"

"We heard it from Hank Spencer," Esme said, ignoring my warning look.

"Spencer? As in the guy they're about to arrest for Dorothy's murder?" Jeremy said, his voice low as he spoke through clenched teeth.

"Did the police tell you that?" I asked, glancing over to make sure Cassidy was still absorbed in working the box.

"No, but we hear things," Jeremy said. "And I know you do, too."

I looked over at Esme and she gave me a what-can-I-say shrug.

I hadn't realized until that moment how desperately I wanted to believe Hank Spencer was as innocent as he seemed. I barely knew the man. And while all our interactions hadn't been the greatest, even on his worst behavior he'd seemed so guileless. Still, I had to face facts. The ring disappearing after his visit was a big problem and the timing seemed to seal his fate. There simply hadn't been time for anyone else to do it. The thought made me physically ill and I tilted my head back and closed my eyes to stave off a wave of nausea.

Suddenly there was a loud snap followed by a squeal. My eyes popped open to see both Esme and Jeremy moving toward Cassidy. The girl was holding up her hand and I thought she'd pinched her finger in the box mechanism.

"I did it! I did it!" she shouted, then squealed again, showing us the puzzle box with the secret drawer splayed open. "Now my dreams will come true. And look, Daddy, Auntie Dot gave me her pretty ring."

We all stood, mouths agape, staring at the ring Cassidy had slipped on her thumb.

Jeremy looked over at me, eyes wide, eyebrows migrated halfway up his forehead.

"Yeah," I said, "that's it. The Pritchett family ring."

"Lord. Have. Mercy," Esme whispered. She put her hand across her forehead and let out a big breath. "I'll go call Denny."

seventeen

"WHAT WAS THAT WOMAN THINKING?" DENTON CARLSON asked when we were sitting at our kitchen table an hour later. He'd talked with Jeremy and Cassidy then sent them on home. "Giving an expensive thing like that to a kid? And hidden in that gadget? They might've chucked that thing in the trash. It could be in the landfill by now."

"It wasn't the smartest move," Esme said, "but she did make sure Cassidy knew it was important to hold on to the box."

"But why the games?" Denton asked. "Why didn't she just give it to her?"

"You saw the note she put in there with it. She wanted to teach the girl a lesson about perseverance and responsibility," Esme said. "And she intended to be around to supervise the lesson. She'd meant the box to stay at High Ground. And she certainly wasn't planning on getting killed that night."

"Yes, but Esme," I said, "Dorothy was over the moon that we'd found that ring, then two hours later she's giving it away? That doesn't make sense."

"Maybe it does if you take into account what Hank Spencer told her about how it came into the family. I expect that might have changed her feelings about it. She had this whole myth built up about it being a generations-old family heirloom and then all of a sudden it was only an expensive gee-gaw her grandfather won in a poker game."

"Well, whatever, this changes everything as far as the investigation goes," Carlson said. "Now the only thing that seems to be missing from her home is that pearl necklace. And I might as well tell you we're almost certain that's what the killer used to strangle her, as you guessed, Esme. So I doubt it was stolen for its value but taken to prevent us from getting prints or other forensic evidence."

"So, Detective Carlson, does this mean Hank Spencer is no longer a suspect?" I asked.

"I'm not saying that," he answered. "And please, can't you just call me Denny? I've long ago breeched the professional barrier with you two."

"Okay, Denny," I said. "Why would Spencer still be suspect? Obviously, he didn't steal the ring."

"Maybe not, but that doesn't mean he didn't lose his temper," Denny said. "He admits they argued."

"She argued with pretty much everybody," Esme said. "But I sure wish I'd been able to see past that while she was still alive. Some of the things we've learned since make me believe underneath her bluster she was a nicer person than I gave her credit for. I'm not proud of it, but sometimes I make up my mind about people a little too quick."

"Yeah, you do," Denton mumbled as he got up from his

chair. "Okay, well, I'll let you get back to work. I know you're up against it."

Esme walked him to the door and then to my astonishment she walked him on out to his car, where they stood talking for a while. A whiplash of emotions overtook me. I was tickled pink and also alarmed. I felt as if this was meant to be, yet at the same time felt blind-sided. What if he took Esme away from me? I hadn't considered that possibility.

Denny had just driven off and Esme had headed back inside when Joe Porter came strolling up the walk, literally hat in hand. "I know I'm bothering you while you're trying to work," he said, "but I wanted to come speak to you while something was fresh on my mind. I'd like to speak to both of you if I could," he said, nodding to Esme.

"Well, then, come on back and we can talk while we work," I said.

Once we got into the workroom Joe looked around and pursed his lips. "So how's it going here at Pritchett central?" he asked.

"Things are coming together," I said, hoping he couldn't judge how much we had yet to go. "Would you like to look at any of the finished scrapbooks?"

"No, no, thank you." He pulled out a chair and sat, then frowned as if he couldn't remember why he'd come. I certainly couldn't help him with that.

Esme seemed to think she could. "What can we do for you?" she asked.

"Well, first off, I understand you had a little excitement over here earlier this afternoon," he said.

Esme and I glanced at each other.

"Cassidy called me," he said. "She was so excited she'd solved that box, not so much interested in the fact that Dorothy put that ring in there. Jeremy read me Dorothy's note. Dorothy gave her blessing to sell the thing to finance Cassidy's college education if need be. Now *that*," he said, punching the table with his finger, "that was *my* Dorothy! I hadn't seen her in a long while, but that was her."

"It was very generous," Esme said.

"Yes it was, but anyhow, that wasn't what I came to talk with you about," Joe said, sitting forward and resting his elbows on the table. "I'm sure you've heard we met with the lawyers about Dorothy's estate today."

"Jeremy told us a little," I said.

"I think Jeremy got a little shock," Joe said, smiling. "I think everybody did. The Pritchett fortune was, let's say, watered down. William Pritchett's world travels didn't come cheap. Dorothy didn't have much left in the way of assets and a good chunk of what she did have she left to the town for the upkeep on that big old house for the next couple of years."

"It'll be great for the town," Esme said.

"I believe it will," Joe said. "I hope they open it up for people to use for celebrations, weddings, maybe some classes of some kind. That'll be nice. But I'm getting off track again. What I wanted to say is that while Ingrid got the house she and Dorothy grew up in and the gatehouse at High Ground, she didn't get much in the way of ready cash—as I say, there wasn't much left to get. I don't want Dorothy's memorial or any expenses to do with this"—he nodded toward the table—"to be a hardship on Ingrid. If you need anything else for it you send me the bill."

"We're paid in full," I said. "I told you that when you gave me that check."

"I know," he said, "but as Vivian reminds me, things come up. I've told her the same thing about the memorial."

Esme made a sound I understood well. Apparently Joe did, too.

"I know," he said, laughing. "She's a dangerous woman to offer a blank check to, but it's for Dorothy and there's nobody who'd know better what Dorothy would have wanted. Vivian was her best friend. She'll do it up right and proper and I think it'll help her, too. Poor Vivian is taking this hard."

He got up from the table and slapped his hat against his thigh. "That's all I wanted to say. I know Dorothy would really be pleased with the job you're doing here."

"I like to think so," I said, "especially because Ingrid and Jeremy and Cassidy are interested in it now, too."

Joe nodded. "Maybe I'll even find something to admire about the Pritchetts. Though I wouldn't bank on it."

The other club members had agreed to forgo our usual Tuesday night meeting at Keepsake Corner to help Esme and me save this job and our sanity. Winston was first to arrive with a bagful of deliciousness in the form of fresh-baked rosemary olive oil bread. Marydale came after she closed the shop and I stole a few minutes to play with Gadget and Sprocket. Coco showed up an hour later and it was all hands on deck. Except for Jack, who was conspicuously absent.

This time our potluck was more for sustenance than so-cializing. We ate and cleared quickly and were soon hard at work again.

"I've got news and I can't wait to tell y'all about it," Winston said. "Can I tell you while we work? It's a good story."

"Let's hear it," Esme said.

"I told you about the guy who had the diaries," he said. "Well, he emailed them as promised and I've been reading nearly non-stop since yesterday. In case you've forgotten, the ancestor I was looking at was my twelve. And my question was whether he'd had children with one of his slaves. The answer appears to be yes and that slave woman, her name was Delsie, is actually my thirteen, not the woman whose name was put down in the old family Bible."

"Okay," I said, "now you've got to know what my next question's going to be."

"Yes, I do," Winston said with a laugh. "What is the weight of my evidence?"

"And is it—" I prompted.

"Consistent, connected and conclusive," the rest all re-cited in unison.

"I can tell you this is original material," Winston said. "A diary written by a woman who personally experienced and witnessed the situation she describes and who had no ax to grind. In fact, just the opposite, and you'll soon see what I mean."

"Enough with the lesson, Sophreena," Coco said. "Let him get on with the story."

"The woman who kept the diary was the legal wife of my twelve, Horace Lovett. Her name was Theodora Haskins

Lovett. But that marriage was a sham and she is not my biological ancestor. Theodora was a Quaker woman from a family of ardent abolitionists. It's not clear how she and Horace
got acquainted or how they came to their strange arrangement, but she became his beard wife while he had a secret
common-law marriage with Delsie. And I am happy to report
that this was an arrangement that both Horace and Delsie
entered into willingly, which isn't to say there's not plenty
about it that makes me wish things had been different. But
at least according to Theodora's diary the secret marriage between Delsie and Horace was a true love story. They had six
children together. Three were light complexioned and those
were raised, publicly and legally, as the children of Horace
and Theodora. Three were dark skinned and were raised by
Delsie. None of the children knew their true parentage until
all three—Horace, Delsie and Theodora—were dead. Theodora entrusted her diary to her family with the stipulation
that the story not be told until twenty-five years after the last
of the three had died."

"How in the world did that work?" Coco asked. "And why,
if he loved this Delsie so much, didn't he just marry her?"

"First off," Winston said, "it was a crime. There were anti-
miscegenation laws, as they were called back then. It was
illegal to marry outside your race in South Carolina and some
other states."

"Are you joking?" Coco asked.

"Not joking," Winston said. "People were prosecuted,
fined and jailed. But you asked how they managed to make it
work. Delsie had always worked in the house, not the fields,
and she had quarters attached to the house on the first floor

behind the kitchen. Theodora lived on the top floor and as far as everyone else knew so did Horace. The children weren't told for fear they wouldn't keep the secret. The consequences would have been dangerous for everyone."

"So does that mean one of the children raised by Theodora is your ancestor?" Marydale asked.

"Yes, Josiah Austin Lovett was the firstborn child of Horace and Delsie. He's my number eight, my great-grandfather. He was raised as the child of Horace and Theodora and died never knowing Delsie, the woman who'd looked after him as his nursemaid, was his natural mother."

"That is quite a story, Winston," Esme said. "And now that you know, how do you feel about it all?"

"Conflicted," Winston said. "It makes me sad that it had to be that way. But I feel relieved, too. I was afraid I'd find an ancestor who'd taken unfair advantage, or worse. I had a terrible dread of that. So this has put my mind at ease. Nobody wants to think they owe their existence to a situation like that."

The doorbell rang and Esme went to answer it.

"Do you know what became of the children who stayed with Delsie?" I asked.

"Yes, I'm happy to say all the children were well provided for. They all went to school and grew to adulthood and had families of their own and lived full lives, save one daughter who died in the 1918 flu epidemic.

"That's amazing," Coco said. "So, all along this man was hiding his children in plain sight."

Just at that moment Vivian came through the door. She was white as a sheet and I wondered if the sight of so much work still undone had scared her.

"What did you say?" she asked, staring at Coco with her mouth half open.

"Nothing," Coco said, frowning.

"No, you did," Vivian insisted. "Something about hiding something."

"This is our regular meeting night, so we're talking about our own family histories while we work," I said. "Is there something we can do for you, Vivian?"

"Actually, it was Winston I was looking for," she said, turning in his direction, a deep frown cutting lines across her forehead. "I thought I might find you here since Esme and Sophreena seem to have drafted everyone for miles around to help with their work. I was wondering if you'd mind delivering the baked goods for Dorothy's memorial yourself. It was nice of you to agree to make all those pastries, but I'm going to be spread very thin that day and I don't know when I'd pick them up."

"Don't worry, I'll bring them up, Vivian," Winston said. "Is there anything else I could help out with?"

"Well, since you asked," Vivian said, the words coming out fast, "could you come up to High Ground tomorrow to help with some of the outdoor preparations? One of the men I hired has a family emergency and he's left me in a lurch."

"I'll be there," Winston said.

"Good, then," Vivian said, glancing nervously up and down the tables.

"Everything will be ready," I said, pre-empting her question.

"Good, then," she said again. "I'll let myself out." She moved toward the door as if her legs were made of wood.

There was dead silence until we heard the door close.

"I'm worried about her," Marydale said.

"I think she's still in the denial stage of grief where everything seems unreal," Esme said. "Planning this memorial's the only thing holding her together right now."

eighteen

I'M ALLERGIC TO MORNING. MY EYES ARE ALWAYS ALL PUFFY
and I'm generally opposed to everything the world has to
offer for the first fifteen minutes after I'm forced to start the
day. Today I was especially tired, and cranky to boot. Jack
had finally shown up the night before, but not until after
nine when the others were getting ready to leave. He'd been
dressed up so he hadn't been working late. He didn't volunteer where he'd been and I couldn't ask since I didn't want
to know the answer. He seemed happy and said he was just
dropping by to say hello and that he needed to get home to
bed since he had a big project today.

Fine. By. Me.

And now Esme was insisting on our morning power walk,
which I would just as soon have skipped. As always I was
practically trotting alongside her as we hit the sidewalk. She
had a head of steam up about something this morning.

"You wanna talk about it?" I asked, trying to keep from
puffing.

"I can't understand why this has to come this hard," she

said. "I've been open. I've been willing. Why can't she just tell me flat out whatever it is she wants me to know like she did with the ring being in the puzzle box?"

"Sarah Malone?"

"Of course, Sarah Malone, who else are we talking about?" Esme said. "I've about had it with the woman. At first everything was clear, then it was like you said, bad poetry and now it's only images. And I don't have a clue what they mean. We didn't find any special quilts in the Pritchett family heirlooms, did we?"

"No, no family ones. Which is sort of unusual, especially for a southern family. But no quilts. Not that Dorothy knew of, anyway, and there weren't any in the attic. Why?"

"I keep getting this image of a quilt," Esme said. "A really pretty hand-pieced quilt in pastels, like a baby quilt. But as I'm admiring the pattern it gets turned onto the backside, which is plain old hopsacking."

"Are you sure this is coming from Sarah Malone?"

"Positive."

I knew better than to ask Esme how she could be so certain. She's tried a thousand times to explain to me how these things come to her, but I don't pretend to get it.

"Well," I said. "All I can tell you is I haven't run across any quilt that was significant to the family, not to Dorothy anyway."

When we got to Top o' the Morning I scanned the parking lot for Jack's Jeep, but it wasn't there. I was disappointed, then relieved, then disappointed again.

Esme was still agitated and when she yanked the coffee shop door open Denton Carlson was standing there, coffee cup in one hand, the other extended as if about to push. His partner, Detective Jeffers, was right behind him and when she caught sight of Esme and me she got a sullen look on her face.

"I'll be in the car, make it quick," she said to Denton, giving us a curt nod before she hurried across the street to a blue sedan.

"Who peed in her Wheaties?" Esme said, scowling after her.

"Never mind her," Denny said, motioning for us to follow him a few feet down the sidewalk for privacy. "This case is a career maker, or breaker. It's that last that's worrying her. And with that in mind I'm gonna trust you two with something we just learned. But this can't go any further right now, not even to your friends. The DNA results from those coffee cups came back this morning."

"What happened to the massive backlog?" I asked.

Denny shrugged. "Prominent family. Money. You know how that goes, things jump to the front of the line."

"What did it show?" Esme asked.

"Nothing in the system," Denny said. "But here's the thing. One sample is Dorothy's and the other is from a male—a *related* male."

"Jeremy?" I breathed.

"As far as I know he's her only living male relative, right?" Denny said. "You'd know. That's the reason I'm telling you about this."

I mentally ran through the family chart. "Yeah, I think so, but let me go back to the house and double-check. Maybe there are distant cousins or something."

I was almost positive that wasn't the case, but I desperately wanted there to be another explanation. Now that we'd gotten to know Jeremy Garrison better and had seen the way he was with Cassidy I realized I'd made the same mistake with him as with Dorothy. I'd operated on assumptions. He wasn't the brooding guy I'd pegged him for at first. He'd had good reasons for resenting the Pritchett family, but enough to kill Dorothy to exact revenge? I didn't think so.

"The thing is, Jeremy denies he was even in that room that day," Denny said.

"Why would he lie about that?" I asked. "He was in and out of that house all the time. He had free run of the place. And he was there that day. He picked up Cassidy."

"So why deny it if he had coffee with Dorothy in that sitting room? That's what I'd like to know," Denny said. "In fact we're about to go ask him that question and see if he'll give us a DNA sample so we can see if we get an exact match. Let me know if you turn up any long-lost male relatives," he added, glancing across at the cruiser where an impatient Jeffers was waiting behind the wheel. He gave Esme a quick smile that had nothing to do with the case then strode across to the car. He barely had a chance to close his door before Jeffers pulled away from the curb, tires squealing.

"Give it up, Sophreena," Esme said an hour later. "You've been bent over those charts for long enough. If there was anybody to find you'd have found them by now."

I slapped the notebook closed. "You're right. You know, when you look at the charts it's a miracle the Pritchett name

survived as long as it did, or that the family didn't die out altogether. Before Dorothy and Ingrid there were four generations with only one child."

"So, that leaves only Jeremy," Esme said, pursing her lips.
"That's troublesome, very troublesome, but I just can't accept
that this means what it appears to mean. First off, Cassidy
truly loved Dorothy and that had to count for something big
in his book, right? And he's not a hothead, in fact, just the
opposite—he's kind of aloof. Even when he's angry he's always in control. And from everything we've heard this was a
violent outburst, not something planned."

"But what if it wasn't? What if it was a coldly calculated
act? Joe Porter said Jeremy was shocked there weren't more
assets in Dorothy's estate. And I'm sure Jeremy and Ingrid
both figured Ingrid was going to benefit in some way from
Dorothy's will."

"Hard to think about," Esme said. "But I know I'm not
objective. I don't want anything bad to happen to Cassidy.
Let's just hope there's some rational explanation for that coffee cup having Jeremy's DNA. Right now we've got enough
to worry about, Sophreena. We only have one more day to get
all this finished."

We worked without interruption for the next three hours.
The pages got plainer as we went along, with fewer embellishments and less detail work, but I tend to be a minimalist
so that suited me fine. Plus, if Vivian was right and these
ended up in some community display, the cleaner pages
would be more appropriate—and more honest. These scrapbooks weren't works of love constructed by a family member;
they were produced by our hired hands. To me it was like

paying someone to pick out your wedding dress—or maybe your husband. I much preferred Laurena Pritchett's humble commonplace book. It was messy and had little to offer in the way of design or aesthetics, but it was heartfelt and reflected real lived experiences.

I stretched my arms high and worked my head from side to side. Esme stood and reached for the ceiling, nearly touching it with the tips of her fingers, then twisted and slung her arms around. Our eyes swept the room and then we looked at each other, wide smiles spreading across our faces.

"Mercy, mercy," Esme said, "I can see the end of this thing. I think we can finish this up tonight."

But the good cheer didn't last. A minute later we got a call from Linda Burnette.

"I'm up at High Ground," she said. "Winston took a spill off the ladder. He's hurt but he won't let us call an ambulance. I think he's broken something. Can you or Esme come and see if you can talk him into going to the hospital?"

Stiff muscles and fatigue were forgotten and Esme broke her own land speed record getting from our house to High Ground.

Linda, Vivian and a couple of other volunteers were gathered around Winston, who was sitting on the decking of the wide porch off the back of the house. He was clearly in pain but when he caught sight of us he started grousing.

"Oh, for pity's sake, don't tell me they called you. I'm fine. I just need to walk it off." He tried to scramble up, but his foot wouldn't hold and he fell back onto the planking with a thud.

I knelt beside him and folded up his pant leg. His ankle

was hugely swollen and turning purple. I untied his shoe and though I tried to slip it off gingerly he winced and made a grunting sound.

Esme sat on the steps and leveled a look on him, her dark eyes flashing. "Winston, you're going to the ER one way or the other. Now do you want me to call an ambulance, or do you want us to carry you to my car?"

Winston took one look at her and knew not to argue. "Fine, I'll go with you," he said.

While Esme pulled her SUV up close I went into the kitchen to round up something to make an icepack. As I was rummaging in the drawers looking for a big dishtowel I heard voices I recognized coming from the hallway.

"Quiet, Cassidy will hear you," Ingrid said.

"She's upstairs," Jeremy answered. "And besides, you don't think she's going to hear about this? The police questioning her father? It'll be all over town."

"They have no reason to suspect you of anything," Ingrid said. "None at all."

"You weren't there, Mother," Jeremy said. "I'm telling you, I'm a suspect. They kept me there for two hours; they took my DNA, for God's sake."

"They don't know anything," Ingrid said. "If they did they'd have made an arrest by now."

I realized—too late—that their voices were moving closer. Ingrid stopped short as she came into the kitchen and saw me standing there with the dishtowel I'd taken from the drawer flapping in the breeze from the open door.

"Sophreena!" she said. "I didn't realize anyone was in here. What are you doing?" She frowned as she saw the cluster of people out on the porch, trying to get Winston to his feet. "What's going on?"

I moved to the refrigerator and made a lot of noise getting the ice, hoping she wouldn't realize I'd overheard their exchange. I told her about Winston's injury and she asked if there was anything they could do.

"We've got it," I said. "I know you must have a lot to do to get ready for tomorrow."

"Vivian can handle things here," Jeremy said. "If you need help just let me know."

He seemed sincerely concerned and I wanted to believe that's the kind of person he was. But could I? There was something unsettling about what I'd just overheard.

When I got back outside Winston was getting situated, his leg stretched across the two seats in the back of the SUV. I put the makeshift ice bag over his ankle, causing him to flinch again. Within seconds Esme was behind the wheel and we were off to the ER.

We'd have left an ambulance in the dust.

"I do not understand that woman," Winston's daughter-in-law, Nancy, said as we sat in the ER waiting room while Winston's broken ankle was being put in a cast. "Patsy's still at her sister's. I called her and told her what happened, but she doesn't want to come home. She says he can manage fine and it would be too expensive to change her ticket. I mean, I hate to be a walking cliché and complain about my mother-in-law, but she is such a cold fish!"

Nancy, a petite, vivacious brunette, was a kindergarten

teacher. She was married to Winston's oldest son, Foster, and they had two rambunctious pre-teen boys. Winston loved Nancy like a daughter. He'd been reluctant to let me call her, but once it became clear the injury couldn't be brushed off he'd had no choice.

"He could come to our house," I said. "We have a guest room on the ground floor."

"No, he'll want to go home; he'll insist," Nancy said. "Foster's out of town on business, but he'll get the first flight home and the boys and I will stay at the house with Daddy Win tonight. He'll hate being fussed over, but he'll just have to get over it."

"That's really sweet of you," Esme said.

"He's a sweet man," Nancy said. "He brings out the good in everybody." She curled her lip. "Well, almost everybody."

Winston came out a few minutes later, struggling to work the crutches.

"Daddy Win," Nancy said, rushing to give him a hug. "How in the world did this happen?"

"I'd like to know that myself," he said. "I was helping hang baskets of ferns around the porch up at High Ground. I checked the ladder, I know I did. Vivian even came over and held it for me. Linda was handing the ferns up and we were talkin', sort of remembering this and that about Dorothy, and everything was going along smooth. Then somehow the ladder slipped and I went keister-over-teakettle."

"Thank goodness it's just an ankle and not a knock on the head," Nancy said, tiptoeing to kiss him on the cheek. "Now come on, let's get you home. The boys want to set up a crutch racing course in your backyard."

"God help us," Winston said, but he was grinning.

As I watched them make their way to Nancy's car I felt sad. When I'd first met Winston I'd assumed what I heard about Patsy Lovett was exaggerated. But then I got to know her and she really was a God-awful harpy. How did a lovely man like him get hitched up with someone like that? I thought of how Joe Porter had described a vibrant and fun Dorothy, a woman neither Esme nor I could imagine based on our experience with the imperious matron Dorothy had become. People change. Or more troubling still, people aren't always what they seem.

After another two hours of steady work Esme and I had finished all the scrapbooks and packed up everything to cart it up to High Ground the next day. Complete. *Fini*. Done.

I should have been elated. So why did everything feel so *undone*?

I called Jack to tell him about Winston and heard dishes clanging and restaurant noises in the background. "Does he need anything?" Jack asked. "Is there anything I can do?"

I told him I thought Nancy had everything covered and began telling him how the accident had happened but he cut me off.

"Hey, Soph, this isn't the best time to talk. Can I call you back?"

Sure, he could.

But he hadn't.

Esme accepted a supper invitation from Denny and I didn't even have the energy to tease her about it. She continued to claim she was only doing it to stay close to the investigation, but I don't think she expected me to believe her, especially since she came down the stairs looking gorgeous and she allowed Denny to pick her up at our house and drive her to the restaurant instead of meeting him there. This was definitely a date. She tried to get me to come along with them, but I had no interest in being a third wheel. I told her I was looking forward to vegging out and watching a movie.

I was happy for her. Really, I was. But the house seemed big and empty after she left. I couldn't find a movie that held my interest. I was restless and it felt like I should be doing something, but for the life of me I couldn't figure out what.

I wandered out to the kitchen to fix myself some supper, more for something to do than because I was hungry. I was staring at the meager contents of the fridge when the doorbell rang. It was a promising sound. Maybe Jack had decided to come by instead of calling me back. But no, he wouldn't ring the bell—would he? We weren't on such friendly terms right now, so maybe he would.

It wasn't Jack; it was Ingrid and Cassidy and both of them were obviously out of sorts.

"You left this up at the house and I thought you might need it to finish up the family history." Ingrid held out a small notebook before I'd even had a chance to say hello.

I took the notebook and looked at the cover. "No, it's not mine," I said.

"Oh," Ingrid said, frowning. "I saw that list and I assumed it was yours or Esme's."

"List?"

"On the first page," Ingrid said, grabbing at Cassidy's hands as the girl flapped them back and forth against Ingrid's hip, twisting from side to side and making whiny noises.

I opened the notebook and glanced at the page. The list read: *birth certificates, handwriting samples, bank statements, letters.* I handed it back to Ingrid. "I can see why you thought it was mine, but no, I've never seen it before and it's not Esme's."

"Strange," she said, putting the notebook back in her bag. "I just assumed . . . maybe it was Dorothy's, though it doesn't look like her handwriting. Oh, well, wasted trip. As you can see I need to get Cassidy home to bed. She's had a long day and she's tired."

"I'm not tired," Cassidy said. "I'm sad."

This seemed to me a gross understatement. The poor child looked absolutely desolate.

Ingrid gave me an exhausted, pained smile then guided Cassidy along to the car.

I closed the door and leaned against it, mentally and physically exhausted. Hadn't this turned out to be a peach of a week? My client had been murdered. I'd been the subject of horrid gossip. My wonderful little town had been turned inside out. Jack and I were on the outs. Winston was hurt. Two guys I'd come to like were suspects in Dorothy's murder. I was starting to be suspicious of everyone who crossed my path. Esme might be slipping away from me and I was powerless to ease the suffering of a grief-stricken six-year-old.

I didn't need food or a movie. I needed to be doing something. I went into the workroom, where I felt I had some control. The timeline of Dorothy's last day was still bothering me.

Genealogists depend on all kinds of charts and graphs to help keep track of family lineage, historical events and cultural phenomena and to make sense of how they all intersect. Timelines are my personal favorite.

I grabbed a handful of old dot-matrix printer paper from the three boxes I hoard for just this purpose, unfolded ten sheets along the length of the worktable and reinforced the perforations with tape. I drew a line across the bottom of all ten sheets and crosshatched at intervals to represent the hours from noon until seven. I labeled this line *Me & Esme.* Then I repeated the process in parallel three more times, one for Jeremy, one for Hank Spencer and one for Linda Burnette.

The coroner had established Dorothy's time of death at 5:30 p.m., give or take an hour. A pretty big fudge factor, but I guess it's an iffier proposition than they make it out to be on the TV crime shows. I drew a box that took in that interim across all the lines.

On our line I made a red tick for the time stamped on the receipt we'd gotten from the big box store, then marked another one for the plant nursery. I moved up and made a blue tick at that point on Jeremy's line since I knew he was still at the nursery when we checked out.

And so it went. For the next two hours I strained to remember and scribbled feverishly, ticking in every time marker I could think of based on what I'd seen or heard, putting a question mark by those that were unverified, or to put it in layman's terms, wild guesses. I went at it like a woman possessed. I was so absorbed I didn't even hear Esme come in until she was standing over my shoulder.

"What in heaven's name? Sophreena, what are you doing, darlin'? We are done with this business. It is signed, sealed and about to be delivered."

"This is something else," I said.

"Yes, I see that," Esme said, leaning over the table and looking closer at my complicated color-coded schematic. "Oh, Sophy-girl," she said, then let out a long sigh.

I'd been expecting her to scold me, to yell at me to let it go. That would have gotten me riled up, given me something to fight against. But her tenderness undid me.

I burst into tears.

And this is what I love most about Esme: Though she encourages me to be strong, when I've reached my limit she knows. Without a word she gathered me in her arms. "Open up the waterworks," she soothed. "Let all the bad out."

And I did. I blubbered, I wailed, then I blubbered some more and Esme patted and crooned. A half hour later I was spent and it was all I could do to get up the stairs and climb into my bed.

nineteen

TRADITIONALLY ESME AND I SPEND THE DAY AFTER WE FINISH A job organizing the workroom and checking inventory before we begin a new project. We had two smaller jobs coming up within the next month. One was for a recent widower who, having been reminded of his mortality, was having his family line documented for his children. The other was for a large extended southern family with half a dozen amateur genealogists in its midst. They'd taken up a collection at a family reunion to have us construct a chart that resolved the conflicting family trees the amateurs had put together.

Today the state of the workroom wasn't on my radar. I was consumed once again by the wonky timeline. I studied and muttered, marked and studied some more. I simply couldn't make it work.

"I need to talk to Hank Spencer," I said.

Esme, who was trying to clean around me, harrumphed, "Good luck with that. Denny says he's lawyered up."

"You sound like a cop."

"Maybe I did pick up a little of the lingo last night." She

laughed. "But, Sophreena, I think he's a good cop. He really wants to find the person who did this because he really means that protect and defend thing."

"Good, but can he do it?" I asked. "So far it seems like they're getting nowhere."

"Yeah, that ring showing up means no robbery, so that opens things up for a whole new theory of the crime. And with the DNA results from that cup coming back like they did . . ."

"I know, I know," I said. "And I keep going back to that conversation I overheard between Ingrid and Jeremy. She said, 'They have no reason to suspect you,' she didn't say, *You didn't do anything wrong.* Could it possibly be the two of them plotted against Dorothy? That all their grief and regret is just for show? That thought just disgusts me."

"I agree, but let's face facts. Jeremy had a lot of anger stored up. And Ingrid and Dorothy had issues—big issues. How many times did we hear them fighting during the last six months?"

"Tons of low-decibel fussing and a few epic throwdowns," I allowed. "But harsh words are one thing; cold-blooded murder's something else. And Ingrid has an airtight alibi."

"Which only means she didn't actually kill Dorothy," Esme pointed out. "Doesn't mean she wasn't in on some plan. But let's not go down that road, Sophreena. It's too awful to think about."

"If Jeremy would just nail down where he was during this little window here," I said, rubbing my pencil eraser along his timeline, "he'd be in the clear. It's the only time he can't account for his whereabouts."

Esme came over to look at the chart again. "And unfortunately it falls right into the window for Dorothy's time of death." She reached over and started folding up the timeline. "You're obsessing, Sophreena. Now put this away. We've fulfilled our obligation to Dorothy."

I decided Vivian must have been a general in another life as I watched her coordinating the operation at High Ground. The actual memorial service would begin at noon tomorrow and with Vivian at the helm I had no doubt it would start precisely on time. The caterers were doing as much as they could ahead of time and a small army of gardeners was trimming, raking and fluffing a backyard already meticulously manicured. The programs Vivian had designed were delivered and the florist's van pulled up and began carting in a plant extravaganza, the floral arrangements to follow in the morning.

Vivian had ignored my advice to skip the bookstands, but at least she'd cut back. There were four beautiful oak pieces standing at wait in the dining room. Some carpenters must have been burning the midnight oil, too. Esme and I set books on each stand and placed the rest on the dining room table at appropriate intervals, then Esme went off to find Vivian to get her stamp of approval.

I wandered out to the kitchen where a woman was at the sink moving dishes from one side to the other. She was dressed in black slacks and a crisp white shirt and her hair was up in a chic French twist. I assumed it was the caterer but when she turned I was surprised to see it was Linda.

"Wow," I said, "you're all gussied up for a work day."

"Not my idea," Linda said, looking meaningfully out to where Vivian was barking orders at the gardeners from the porch. "I mean I would have dressed up for tomorrow, of course, but these are going to be ruined before this day is over. I have real work to do. She thinks it would show a lack of respect for Dorothy for me to come in jeans, though Dorothy never had any complaints about it."

"Vivian's priorities may be skewed, but it looks like she's got things well in hand here."

Linda nodded. "She does. Don't mind me. Vivian's doing a great job and I know this is just her way. It's just hard to be back here without Dorothy."

She threw a dishtowel onto the counter and knocked off a notebook that had been balanced on the edge. "Oh, for heaven's sake. Again?" she grumbled, reaching down to pick it up. "I wish she'd find somewhere else to put this thing."

I glanced at the offending book.

Linda saw my frown. "Sorry, like I said, I'm grumpy. It's Vivian's sketchbook. She leaves it there all the time and it's in my way." She rested her back against the counter, wiping her hands on a paper towel. "But I'm trying to make it clear she's in charge for now. I don't know if you heard but it looks like I'll have a job, for a while at least. Dorothy donated the house to the town and she put in some kind of clause that I be kept on as manager of the place for at least a year at full-time salary. Vivian is finding that a hard pill to swallow."

"That's fantastic," I said. "Listen, Linda, would you mind

if I asked you a couple more questions about the day Dorothy died? I know this isn't exactly the time or place, but I think it might be important."

"But I've already told you everything I remember," she said.

"I know," I said, "but something is bugging me about the timing. Could you close your eyes and describe to me exactly what you did that day, let's say from the time you first agreed to go to the store for Dorothy?"

"I'm willing, and I'm overdue for a break," she said. "But we've got to get out of here to talk. Vivian will have a conniption if she thinks I'm slacking. We could go out on the patio."

I looked to the backyard where the leaf blowers and lawn mowers were going full force. "How about we try the front porch?"

Linda nodded, and after pouring us each a glass of iced tea she led the way. We settled into a couple of wicker chairs and I gave her a couple of moments to relax.

"This may be nothing," I said, my pen poised over a yellow legal pad, "but bear with me. Close your eyes and tell me every single detail you can think of. You never know what little thing might be important."

I could see she thought this a complete waste of time, but she closed her eyes and began. "Dorothy was on another of her diets and wanted cottage cheese and fruit for supper. But we were out of cottage cheese and the fruit we had was sad looking. She asked if I'd mind going to the store before I went home. I told her I had some other errands to run and I could swing back by to bring her the groceries on my way home. I asked if she'd be okay eating a little later and she said that would be fine."

"So do you have any idea what time it was when you left?"

Linda frowned. "Not really. We had this conversation quite a bit earlier in the day. I still had a few chores to do. I made up a pastry tray and put out the coffee service. I set the Mr. Coffee so all Dorothy had to do was push the button when whoever it was she was meeting with arrived."

"And she didn't say who this person was?"

"No. She was always having meetings in the evening about garden club or town business or whatever, so it wasn't anything out of the ordinary for me to set up the coffee and put out pastries or snacks before I went home. It was a regular routine."

"Okay, so you left for the store," I prompted again, eager to speed her along before Vivian caught us loitering.

"I had a couple of other errands to do," Linda said. "I went by the drugstore to pick up Dorothy's prescription—"

"Did you get a receipt?" I interrupted.

"I'm sure it was stapled to the bag. I don't even know where the prescription is now. Maybe the police took it."

"And the receipts from the grocery store?" I asked.

"No idea. Normally I keep up with them. Dorothy keeps—kept," she corrected, "an envelope of petty cash in the kitchen drawer that I used for little things. I'd put the receipts and the change back in the envelope after an errand and I was religious about it. But that day I hadn't gotten around to that before I found—" She stopped talking and I saw a shudder run through her body before she went on. "And I don't even know what happened to the groceries I bought for Ben and me. I suppose Ben did something with them. The receipt would have been in the bag."

"I'm sorry, Linda," I said. "I know this is hard. Let's just back up a little. When you pulled up in the driveway there were no cars here and you didn't notice anyone around?"

"No one. I figured her meeting must have been a short one."

"So, you took the grocery bags from the car, and . . . ?"

"Grocery bag," she corrected. "It was just the one bag. "I brought it into the kitchen," she said slowly, reliving the memory. "I set it on the counter, and of course, knocked off Vivian's sketchbook as per usual." She shook her head and chuffed before going on. "I puttered around in the kitchen for a few minutes. I put the mugs Jeremy and Dorothy and I had used earlier into the dishwasher then peeled some fruit and—"

"The *mugs* you used?" I asked. "Coffee mugs?"

"Yes. When Jeremy came to pick up Cassidy, Dorothy and I were having a cup of coffee in the kitchen. Well, actually, Dorothy was having tea; I was having coffee. Jeremy had a cup while he waited for Cassidy to gather up her things."

"And you put those cups into the dishwasher?" I asked.

"Mugs, yes," she said, frowning.

"When you set up the coffee tray for Dorothy's meeting, did you use mugs for that?"

"Oh, no, she always used the good dishes for her meetings. Fancy little coffee cups, you know, the useless ones? You can barely get a finger through the handle. Bone china with gold rims that have to be hand washed. I'm not a fan," she said, wrinkling her nose.

"So, it's not likely that Jeremy would have had yet another cup of coffee with Dorothy an hour later," I said, thinking aloud.

"Well, no, that's not quite right," Linda said, frowning. "Jeremy drinks more coffee than any human being I know."

"But surely she wouldn't have needed a meeting with him that night if she'd just seen him. Why wouldn't she just cover whatever it was when he came to get Cassidy?"

"Dorothy didn't operate off-the-cuff like that," Linda said. "If she had an issue to discuss it got her full attention and she liked there to be some rules of order and ceremony about it. She held that people had clearer understandings about things when they were paying full attention."

"Well, that's true enough," I mused. "Esme and I got that treatment while we were working for her. We'd see her daily out in the gatehouse and chat about the artifacts and she'd still call me to come up here to give weekly reports."

"That's how she operated," Linda said. "I'm sorry, Sophreena, I've really got to get back in there. I wish I could have been more help."

"No, this has been good," I said, reassuringly.

In truth I was nowhere closer to solving my timeline problem, and instead of staying fixed in place every time-marker I tried to nail down kept moving like a slider on a scale, tipping the balance as it shifted one way or the other.

I was studying my notes when a voice from somewhere behind me made me jump. "You hiding from Vivian?"

I turned to see Jeremy coming around the corner of the house, his hands jammed into the pockets of his chinos.

"Not hiding," I said. "Just staying out of the way." I

wondered if his appearance was as casual as he made out or if he'd been lurking around the corner eavesdropping on my conversation with Linda.

"Me, too," he said, trudging up onto the porch and settling down in the chair beside me, stretching out his legs and crossing them at the ankles. "Mom insisted I take another day off work to help, but honestly Vivian seems to be running the show. I feel useless, no, worse than useless. What's that old saying about a screen door on a submarine? I think me being here is making people uncomfortable."

"Why do you say that?"

He gave me a look and I was embarrassed at how fake the question sounded now that it was hanging in the air.

"Okay," I said, "so I've heard things."

"Everybody in town has heard things," he said glumly. "That's what happens when the police haul you in for questioning. People can't even look me in the eye."

"That's a little dramatic, isn't it? The police didn't exactly throw you in the back of a paddy wagon in shackles. They just asked you to clear up some things, right?"

"Oh, yeah," he said, sarcastically. "Just clear up a few minor matters and oh, by the way, give us your DNA."

I decided I might as well be as blunt as he was. "You're sure you didn't go back to Dorothy's that night after you took Cassidy to your mother's?"

He laughed mirthlessly. "You sound just like the cops. That's what they kept asking."

"And what did you tell them?" I pressed.

"That I think I'd know if I'd gone back to Dorothy's, that I *didn't* and that I'm not sure exactly where I was at any given second for the rest of that afternoon. I dropped Cassidy off with Mom and then I was just, you know, out and about."

"Any receipts from anywhere? Run into anybody? Make or get any phone calls?"

"Don't think so," he said. "Didn't buy anything. Didn't see anybody I know. No phone calls, not until later. I was just enjoying some time alone. I went to the lake for a short hike and to take some pictures. Photography's a hobby of mine. I left my phone in the car. I was afraid I'd drop it in the water again. I wanted to get a sunset shot so I was still there when the sun went down. I was on the way back from there when Mom caught up with me to tell me what had happened to Dorothy."

"Well, that's great," I said, perking up. "I assume the photos are digital. There would be a time stamp. Did you show the police those?"

"No, I didn't," he said, coughing and adjusting his position in the chair. "I don't have them. I deleted them. None of them were any good."

"You deleted them all?"

"Yeah. They weren't worth saving."

"Well, that's a shame," I said.

Now Jeremy was the one who wouldn't meet *my* eyes.

twenty

WHEN WE GOT HOME I WAITED UNTIL ESME HAD GONE UPSTAIRS then darted into the workroom to call Hank Spencer. I had to try.

"I can't talk to you," he croaked after I'd identified myself. "The last time I talked to you I got into all kinds of hot water. I had to hire a lawyer, and let me tell you that just went over great with my wife. His fees are astronomical. I may have to sell a kidney on the black market. He'd have a canary if he knew I was talking to you for even this long."

"I understand," I said. "But I—"

"But nothing," he said and hung up with a *clunk* so emphatic I had to hold the phone away from my ear.

"Told you not to call him," Esme said as she came into the room, not even bothering to look in my direction. How could a woman who wears a size ten shoe pad about silent as a cat?

"He wouldn't talk to me anyway," I said, chewing at the inside of my cheek as I started doodling on the timeline again.

"That's just as well, Sophreena. As you may recall the last

time you had a discussion with him he was about to come unglued. You need to stay away from that man. Far away."

"Yeah, well, looks like I don't have any choice. I thought you were going up to take a nap."

"I thought so, too," Esme said, rubbing her temples. "But she has other ideas." She rolled her eyes toward the ceiling. "I swear if she shows me the back side of that quilt one more time I'm going to lose my religion."

"Still no idea what it means?"

"Not a clue," she said with a sigh as she began putting the background papers we hadn't used for the scrapbooks back into the proper bins.

I went to the computer and searched for the time of sunset on the day Dorothy died. I made a hash mark at 8:33 p.m. and wrote *Sunset, Jeremy taking photos at lake?*

"Who deletes all the pictures they take of something?" I asked, thinking aloud. "I can see getting rid of the ones that aren't so good, but wouldn't you save the best two or three? I mean, why not? With digital all it's costing is a bit of storage space."

"Maybe there weren't any pictures in the first place," Esme said. "You said he sounded dodgy about it."

"But why lie? Why come up with that as an alibi when he knows he can't produce the evidence? And even if he could that would only prove his camera was at the lake; anybody could have taken the pictures. *Unless* he was actually in the pictures. Too bad he didn't get a long-arm shot."

"Long-arm shot?"

"You know, the pictures everybody has on their camera or phone where you take it yourself by holding the camera as far away as you can. That'll be as iconic a photo style for our generation as a man holding his suit coat lapel was in olden days."

"Sophreena, regardless of all that, there is no getting around the DNA on that coffee cup and the fact that Jeremy is Dorothy's only living male relative."

"But that's the other thing. He'd just been there. He'd just had coffee with Dorothy and Linda. What could have been so important it would have brought him back to the house to see Dorothy again an hour later?"

"I have no idea," Esme said. "Did you ask him?"

"He swears he didn't come back."

"Well," Esme said with a sigh. "DNA says otherwise."

I was relieved when the phone rang an hour later, forcing me to get up from my chair. The timeline was getting me nowhere unless utter frustration counted as a destination, but I couldn't quit it on my own.

Marydale, sounding unusually chipper, told me she'd just been closing up shop when she got into a conversation with a woman she thought might be a potential client for Esme and me. She wondered if I could pop over for a moment.

I know Marydale well and I heard the hidden message. She had a live one on the line and if I came now I had a chance of reeling her in.

I allowed as how I'd be happy to scamper right over. I was glad I hadn't gotten around to changing back into my at-home work clothes. I went up to my room and spent about thirty seconds tidying up my hair. I kicked off my flip-flops and slid my feet into my Mary Jane flats, then thought better of it. If this was as big a fish as Marydale's subtext indicated, best to look professional. I put back on the modest pumps I'd worn up to High Ground in the morning. They only have a two-inch heel, but for me this is ultra chic. I slicked on a little lip gloss and made sure my glasses were clean and with that my primping was done. As I say, I'm a minimalist.

Esme gave me a nod of approval when I came down and wished me well. There was never any question about whether she'd go along. She absolutely despises client meetings, and particularly the ones where I make our pitch. "Here are your keys," she said, dangling my key ring. "You left them on the kitchen counter again."

As organized as I am in other aspects of my life, my keys are mislaid on a regular basis and sometimes the hunt for them has me running late.

"I'll walk. I'll get there quicker if I don't have to park."

Esme looked down. "In those?"

"They're perfectly comfortable," I sniffed, taking an obvious gander at her four-inch spikes. She hadn't even bothered to kick them off when we came in from High Ground.

"I'm used to wearing them, you're not," she said.

"I'll be fine. Wish me luck."

We did our ritual touching of palms, a sort of two-handed high five, making it a high ten I suppose, and I was out the door.

Most of our clients are retirement age or older. They're the ones with both the interest and the means to hire our services, so I was surprised when Marydale introduced me to a woman who looked to be about my age.

Eve Cotes, I learned in the next few minutes, was the great-niece of a legendary former senator from our fair state, Talmadge Lunsford. She'd been sent in his stead for the memorial service for Dorothy. "Uncle Tal would have come himself, but he's just not able to travel these days," she said. "I never knew Mrs. Porter, but he had lots of nice things to say about her service to the community. It's a terrible thing, the way she died."

"Eve and I got to talking just as I was closing up," Marydale said, "and I was telling her about how you and Esme had done the heritage scrapbooks for Dorothy. She might be interested in having the same done for her uncle. Let's go to the back so we can talk."

I gave my usual sales pitch with my heart threatening to pound its way out of my chest. I wanted this job so much I was actually salivating. I was afraid I was going to drool on the potential client.

"That sounds like just what we had in mind," Eve said when I'd finished my tap dance. "Some of us in the family have been nagging Uncle Tal for years to hire a ghost writer, but he's completely opposed to writing a book. However, he is a big family history buff and I think I might get him to go for this. Let me talk to the rest of the family and to Uncle Tal and I'll get back to you."

I told her I'd look forward to her call, resisting the urge to break out into a chorus of "Ain't Too Proud to Beg."

She looked at her watch. "Oh, for pity's sake, I've lost track of the time. I'm late for a date. And a first date at that. Guess I'll be making a great first impression." She ducked out the back door and double-timed it to her car.

"She seems really nice," Marydale mused as we stood in the doorway and waved goodbye.

"Yeah. I don't buy that she has any trouble getting dates, or making a good impression. She's too pretty and too personable."

"So are you," Marydale said dryly. "And when's the last time you went out on a date?"

"I date," I said defensively. "I'm just—particular."

"Picky particular, or particularly interested in one guy?" she asked, arching an eyebrow at me.

"Not you, too," I groaned. "You and Esme should form a club. Jack and I are friends, period."

"Who said anything about Jack?" Marydale said, feigning puzzlement. Or at least I thought she was faking. If she wasn't I'd just given away too much information.

"I've really gotta go," I said. "I'll see you tomorrow at the memorial."

"It's dark out, Sophreena. Let me drive you home."

"Don't be ridiculous, Marydale. It's only a few blocks."

"I know, but with all that's been going on, I worry," Marydale said. "You shouldn't be out walking alone at night."

"I'll be fine," I said. "We can't let what happened to Dorothy keep us holed up in our houses."

"All the same," Marydale said hesitantly, "call me on my cell when you get home, will you?"

"Sure thing," I said, glad I'd diverted her from the Jack issue.

Of course, just because I'd distracted her didn't mean I wasn't dwelling on it myself. As I started for home I mentally weighed and measured. How *did* I feel about Jack? I missed him. That was a given. But how much I missed him was startling, especially since I still saw him regularly. It just wasn't the same now. And if Jack got serious about someone we wouldn't be hanging out anymore like we did now. I was really disheartened at the thought. I didn't have to explain myself to Jack; he totally got me. And I did sort of like it that when I was being stupid he called me on it and expected me to do the same for him. Plus he was fun to be around. He was smart and we both found the same things funny. And he had that terrific smile . . .

Suddenly I was aware of footfalls matching mine. I slowed, and so did they. I stopped and turned, but there was no one there, at least not in the circle of sidewalk the streetlamp illuminated. Outside that circle there were dark, lumpy shapes everywhere, any of which could've instantly sprung to life.

I gave myself a stern talking to for letting other people's paranoia get to me, but I stayed alert as I passed by a large hedgerow old Miss Etheleen Morganton had planted to separate her property from what she complained was the bustling business district of downtown Morningside. If I'd been willing to allow my imagination full rein I could have made out the shape of a man lurking in the shadows, but I made him go away by forcing myself to keep a tight hold on reality—and my messenger bag—and march on.

I picked up my pace and I could have sworn I heard the footsteps again. I tried to resist the impulse to turn around, but after a few more steps I couldn't stand it any longer. I whipped around, sucking in a breath for the loudest scream I could produce.

Empty sidewalk.

This time I laughed out loud. I was losing it. Me, the level-headed, practical one. If I was getting this jumpy what must this be doing to the drama queens?

I turned and ran smack into the chest of a man who'd planted himself in the middle of the sidewalk, his feet wide apart and his arms outstretched.

I squawked and jumped back but he didn't move. He waved his arms around and started repeating *it's okay* over and over like the words were rounds from a Tommy gun.

My heart was pounding and there was a terrible buzzing in my ears as blood rushed to my head. I couldn't decide whether to try to run past him or turn and flee toward Keepsake Corner. Marydale would be gone and everything else was closed, so neither option seemed like a good plan. Plus, I'd worn these stupid shoes and I wasn't exactly fleet of foot.

I found myself assuming a defensive karate-style stance, even though I've never had one minute of self-defense instruction. Suddenly that seemed like a severe deficiency in my education.

"Don't freak," the man said, and I recognized the voice. Hank Spencer. "I didn't want to keep following after you; I was afraid you'd think I was stalking you and you'd be scared."

"And you thought jumping out in front of me would be better?" I squeaked.

"Guess I wasn't thinking at all," he said, stepping up to where I could see him. "Look. I changed my mind about talking to you. I went to your house, but your partner or friend or whatever she is wouldn't tell me where you were. I don't think she likes me. And frankly, she scares the bejesus out of me." He walked over and sat down heavily on the river rock wall that bordered the sidewalk. "I wanted to tell you I'm really sorry about coming off the spool like that the other night and for being a jerk and hanging up on you earlier. I'm not like that. Really, I'm not. Usually I'm a pretty mellow guy."

"Evidence notwithstanding?" I said.

"I guess," he said. "It's just, lately I'm having some stuff going on in my life. My business is down and my wife is scared about that so she takes it out on me. And yeah, I know, times are tough all over. I wasn't too worried until this business hit me. I can't believe I've gotten myself into this mess. I met Dorothy Porter *one* time, to talk about something I do as a *hobby*. Next thing I know I gotta hire a lawyer—with money we don't have. And people are looking at me like I'm a stone-cold killer."

"How did you know where to find me?" I asked, looking around and wondering if I should still make a run for it.

"What?" he said, as if I'd snapped him out of some profound meditation. "Oh, no mystery there," he said. "I saw you when I was driving by. I parked down the street and hustled to catch up with you. I figured better here than going back to your house and facing that Esme woman."

I relaxed a little but stayed where I was. I decided I enjoyed being out of easy reach. "The reason I called you earlier," I said, "I wanted to ask you some more questions about that day. Something doesn't fit, but I can't seem to figure out what."

"That's why I came," he said. "I really am sorry about being such a tool earlier, but this lawyer has put the fear of

God in me about talking to the police. Course, he didn't say anything about talking to a genealogist. The way I figure it is if you can sort out all those begets and begots you're the one I want trying to make sense of this so I can get out from under."

I had him go over everything he'd seen and done at Dorothy's that afternoon. I pressed for information that might help with the timeline, but again he couldn't tell me much that was helpful. "I was totally messed up after she got so upset," he said. "Looking back on it now, I should have known better. I mean, half the people on my trips are into family history because they take pride in their distinguished ancestors. I should have kept that in my mind when I went to see Mrs. Porter."

"Dorothy could be a little stuffy sometimes," I said.

"Now you tell me," Hank said. "She was trembling and crying and she acted like I'd told her the story to make fun of her or something, which wasn't the case at all."

"And you didn't say anything to indicate you wanted the ring back?" I asked.

"Back? What do you mean, back?"

"Well, it was the Spencer family ring. It was in your family for generations."

"Well, yeah, but *was* is the operative word there, right? And that was ages ago. Plus my ancestor was the one stupid enough to lose the thing in a poker game, and it was never in my direct line anyhow, so even if it had still been in the Spencer family I'd have no right to it. I never said anything about putting any claim on the ring. It was just the story that upset her. And I feel bad about that, I do. I hate thinking the last minutes of the woman's life were unhappy and that I was the cause of it. But other than that unintended cruelty, I never hurt her. I swear it."

I relented and went over to perch on the rock wall with Spencer, though a few feet away. "Look," I said, "you had no way of knowing she'd react like that. A lot of people enjoy having a little spice in the family stew. An outlaw or a rakish ne'er-do-well. And you're gonna think I'm obsessing, which I am, but can we go over the timeline just one more time? And this time can you close your eyes and tell me absolutely everything you can remember about that day?"

He shrugged and seemed to resign himself to the exercise. He started in with the familiar narrative again, but this time he added a few details he'd left out before as I asked some guiding questions. Yes, he'd had coffee with her, yes in the fancy cups, but someone else was coming over after him.

"How do you know that?" I asked.

Hank opened his eyes, looking a little dazed. "Because she said so," he said. "When she *invited* me to leave she said I had to get out because she was expecting someone shortly and she wanted me and my scurrilous tales gone by then. Is that the word, *scurrilous*? What does that even mean? She was nattering on about how she had to make this person realize some hard truths and how she'd spent half her life defending and upholding the Pritchett family name. Yadda, yadda. She was rantin' like she was off her meds or something."

"You never mentioned this before."

"I forgot. Honestly, I forgot she said all that. I was so shocked when she wigged out everything went out of my head. I didn't remember 'til just now. Wow, that closing your eyes thing really works, huh?"

"Yeah, it *works*," I said with a sigh. "Unfortunately in this case it informs without enlightening."

twenty-one

THE FRIDAY OF DOROTHY'S MEMORIAL DAWNED CLEAR AND cooler, as if she'd arranged pleasant weather for the comfort of her guests. But I was filled with dread at the prospect of going up to High Ground.

It made me ill to even consider that Cassidy could lose her father, but every snippet of evidence that bubbled up seemed to be pointing directly at Jeremy. And he wasn't helping himself by being evasive, if not outright lying. Why did he feel the need to do that if he hadn't done anything wrong?

And what Hank Spencer had supposedly remembered last night didn't help matters. I'd heard Dorothy use that phrase, "hard truths," with Jeremy many times.

When I came downstairs I found Esme sitting at the kitchen table, hand across her forehead, staring down into her coffee cup.

"Another rough night?" I asked.

She nodded, almost imperceptibly. "Sometimes I truly wish those who've passed on would stop looking back over their shoulders, or their wings or whatever they've got now.

I feel like stamping all messages from Sarah Malone RETURN TO SENDER. Every time I close my eyes here comes that quilt."

"Must be something important to Sarah, but maybe we'll never know what it means."

"Oh, I'll eventually know. She's got no intention of leaving me alone until I figure it out. And one thing that comes through loud and clear is she's frustrated I'm being so thick-headed. So now she's not only haunting me, she's trash talkin', too."

I recognized several dignitaries sprinkled in with the regular Morningsiders at High Ground. As Esme and I threaded our way through the crowd I overheard remnants of conversation here and there, most glowing tributes to Dorothy for her public service.

Joe Porter was standing near the entrance to the kitchen talking with a group of men. I nodded to him as I went by and he reached out and pulled me aside.

"Sophreena, I want you to meet Rick Medlin," he said. "He's one of my managers. He tells me he thinks maybe he owes you an apology."

I looked up at the man expectantly, but didn't have a clue what this was all about.

"I was rude when you came to see Joe the other day," the man said, and only then did I look beyond the suit and recognize the guy as the wrench-wielding mechanic. "The reporters had been swarming the place trying to get to Joe and I was getting sick of it," he said. "Just before you came there'd been this tall, blond woman snooping around. She was way too pushy and I guess I took my frustration out on the next person to come along. I'm sorry about that."

"No problem," I assured him, thinking the reporter must have been Julie.

I liked Rick Medlin.

Esme had gone on out to the lawn where most of the regular folks were assembled. I'd seen Marydale and Coco out there clucking over Winston. I started out to join them, but then caught sight of Jack chatting with Julie and decided I couldn't deal with that today.

I went into the dining room to check on the scrapbooks and found Jeremy and Ingrid both leafing through the pages. We made a little stilted conversation, then I excused myself and got out of the room.

I'd gotten halfway down the hall before remembering I should have asked Ingrid about where she wanted the boxes of archives put. I was eager to get them out of our workroom and even more eager to turn over responsibility for them to someone else.

As I got to the doorway I overheard Ingrid and Jeremy in what sounded like an argument. I could only make out snatches of the conversation since they were both whispering furtively. "Careful what you say . . . told her too much already . . . your life we're talking about . . . your future . . . not much longer . . . sick of the lies . . . Cassidy's future . . . we've come this far . . . not much longer . . . the consequences . . ."

I crept away on my tippy toes, thinking I might be sick. I walked out to the kitchen where the drone of murmured voices and the clinking of glasses and silverware drifted in from the formal rooms.

"Sophreena? You okay?" a voice asked.

I was looking to the outside, searching for Esme. "Yes, Vivian, I'm fine," I lied.

"Vivian? That's about the tenth time I've gotten that today."

I turned for a closer look. "Linda, I'm sorry. I just glanced . . ."

"It's the suit," Linda said, pulling on the lapels of her stylish black business jacket. "I had to go out and buy it since I didn't have anything decent to wear. Dorothy's lawyer, Mr. Conover, is going to make an announcement later about High Ground being left to the town and he's going to introduce me as the manager, so I have to look respectable."

"You look very professional," I said.

"I must. People keep mistaking me for Vivian, which is okay by me; she's a pretty woman. But I don't think she's too thrilled with the comparison."

"She should be flattered," I said, which earned a smile from Linda, perhaps her first of the day. "Listen, have you seen Esme? I can't seem to find her."

Linda jerked her head toward the living room. "Last time I saw her she was in there with Cassidy."

I worked my way through a throng of adults who were juggling food plates and talking in low, respectful voices until I got to the front part of the living room where a window seat was nestled in the large bay window. Esme was sitting with Cassidy, who was cross-legged on the window seat with the puzzle box on her lap. She still kept it with her, even though she'd solved the puzzle. She seemed to find comfort in it.

She was busying herself by putting some small object into the hidden compartment, closing the box up, manipulating the pieces to reveal the object, taking it out, then doing the whole thing over again.

"Hi, Cassidy," I said.

She turned her sad eyes up to me and I felt heartsick. "Hi, Miss Sophreena," she murmured, then went back to her business.

I wanted to tell Esme what I'd overheard between Jeremy and Ingrid, but I couldn't very well do that in front of Cassidy. So I sat in a chair nearby and tried to give Esme eye signals that I needed to talk. But she was focused on Cassidy.

"That sure was nice of your Aunt Dot to give you her special ring," Esme said.

"Daddy took the ring and put it at the bank in a safe box so no one can steal it," Cassidy said, working the latches and sliders quickly now that she'd gotten the hang of it. "He says if I *absolutely* need to sell it for money to go to college that would be okay but we should try to keep it in our family if we can."

"I think either way would make your Aunt Dot happy," Esme said.

Cassidy shrugged, not much cheered.

I could see I wasn't going to get Esme aside anytime soon so I went off in search of Vivian. I found her ushering a group through the house, giving a running commentary on the architecture and history of the home as if she were the lady of the manor, or perhaps a well-trained docent. She seemed keyed up, even for Vivian.

I told her I had a quick question and she gave me a scowl. I had to resist the impulse to feel my face to see if the look she'd drilled me with had left a mark. She was reluctant to leave her audience but she excused herself and took my elbow, guiding me into the kitchen where Linda was supervising the caterers. "What is it, Sophreena?" Vivian asked, looking back to make sure her little group wasn't about to escape.

"I was just wondering if you wanted me to make an announcement about the scrapbooks in case people don't know they're out there."

She looked at me like I'd crawled from beneath a rock. "I cannot believe you are suggesting you use this occasion to promote your business. This is Dorothy's memorial, for heaven's sake, not a trade fair."

"Vivian," I protested, keeping my voice low. "I meant no disrespect to Dorothy, just the opposite. I know how much pride she took in her family and I wanted to make sure everyone had a chance to see that. That's all I intended."

Vivian's shoulders relaxed but only slightly. She fingered the single strand of pearls at her neck and struggled to speak. "Fine, but I'll make the announcement. Family meant everything to Dorothy. She and I were like family. She was the sister I never had and I was the sister she never had." She sniffled and wiped at her nose with an embroidered hanky.

I didn't think now was the time to point out that Dorothy actually had a sister so I just murmured, "I know, I know," and patted Vivian on the shoulder.

That small bit of kindness seemed to undo her. She turned and instead of returning to her group she hurried out onto the lawn. I watched as she walked all the way over to the edge of the property and stood by herself with her back to the crowd.

"Don't take it personally," Linda said. "She's been on edge all week. I mean even more than usual. I'm afraid she's due for a meltdown."

I watched as Vivian stood mopping at her face and staring off into the valley below. It occurred to me that had Vivian had her way there would be a row of port-a-potties along that area of the lawn. I couldn't imagine what could have been going through her head when she proposed that to Dorothy. Maybe she was trying to illustrate how Harrison Pritchett had risen from humble beginnings. But surely she must have known that would hit a sour note with Dorothy, who liked to pretend she was descended from gentility all the way back to some manor house in England, even when presented with evidence to the contrary.

Linda returned to her work and I spotted Vivian's sketchbook still sitting on the end of the counter. Something was still ticking in the back of my mind and I wanted to see what Vivian had proposed that had caused such an argument between her and Dorothy.

"You think Vivian would mind if I look at her sketches?" I asked.

Linda shrugged. "She can't expect much privacy if she's going to leave that thing sitting around here—in the way, *all* the time."

I opened the front cover where Vivian had written her

name, Vivian Pearce Evans, in a flowing script I would have been proud to use on a scrapbook page. The sketches were very good and even the one with the port-a-johns had a certain rustic charm. Off to the side on one page Vivian had scribbled an agenda for the originally planned Founders' Day open house. It looked familiar but I knew I'd never seen it before. It read: *welcome/cocktails on the lawn, heavy hors d'oeuvres in the living room, short family history presented by Dorothy, tour of High Ground, introduction of newest Pritchett family member.* Beside the last item Vivian had drawn a schoolgirlish heart followed by a row of exclamation points. I closed the book and sighed.

So sad. As it had turned out, instead of being introduced, Cassidy—the newest member of the Pritchett family—was being virtually ignored while Jeremy and Ingrid talked with people and attended to their bereavement duties. Esme was still sitting with Cassidy in the window seat and I went back in to join them.

I still wanted to get Esme aside to tell her what I'd overheard between Jeremy and Ingrid, but I'd lost the sense of urgency after I'd thought it over. Their words had raised goose bumps on my arms but it wasn't like they'd actually said anything incriminating.

"You still like the box, huh?" I asked Cassidy absently. "Even though you already solved it and you'll get your secret wish?"

"That's not what Auntie Dot said. Not a wish, your *dream*. That's different. And Daddy says we don't keep secrets. Him and Gigi and me tell each other everything. Except Sherry, that's a secret."

Cassidy looked up, her mouth flying open. "Oh no, I'm not supposed to say that. Daddy will be mad at me."

I put my finger across my lips. "We won't tell," I whispered.

I wanted desperately to find out the exact nature of the secret we were agreeing to harbor, but I didn't want to cause Cassidy any more anxiety.

"Okay, so you solved the box and that means you'll get your dream, right? Do you want to share what that would be?"

"I told you. I want to be a doctor and have a husband and two boy babies and two girl babies and live in a good house. I haven't decided about the purple on the house yet, maybe it will be yellow."

She slid the last piece of the puzzle box into place and took out the object again, but this time she pinched it between her fingers and held it up so the light from the window struck it. A bead. The luster made the bead appear illuminated from within and I almost gasped.

Esme had seen it, too, and we exchanged looks.

"Cassidy, where'd you get that bead?" Esme asked casually.

"Found it," Cassidy said, quickly pinching up the bead and depositing it back in the hidey-hole.

"Oh? Where'd you find it?" I asked.

"I didn't steal it," Cassidy said, pulling her feet up under her and turning away from us to face the window.

"Nobody's saying you stole it," Esme said. "We think it's pretty, that's all."

Cassidy turned her face toward us, looking as if she might

cry. "Is taking something without permission the same as stealing?"

"That depends, I guess," Esme said softly. "Let's see if we can figure that out. Where did you find the bead? Here in the house somewhere?"

"Nuh-uh, in the car," Cassidy said. "It was stuck in the crack part of the safety buckle. So it was already lost and I just found it. Finders keepers, right?"

"Sure," I said. "So you found it in the seat belt buckle of your dad's car? That's a strange place for it, isn't it?"

"Not Daddy's car," Cassidy said, as if I were slow witted, "Miss Vivian's car. Is hers a car or a truck? It's like in-between, I guess. I helped her bring in lots of bags from her car this morning. That's when I found the bead. I didn't think she wanted it anymore."

"Probably not," Esme said, her eyes locked on mine.

My brain was firing so rapidly it gave me a headache. It was like Cassidy's puzzle box. As one thing slid out of the way another thing was revealed and when that was lifted, another thing had to be pushed aside to find out more. I searched the room for Denny Carlson. I spotted him by the fireplace talking with the mayor and headed straight for him, parting the crowd with my arms as if I were swimming in a people-pool. I cut right into their conversation and Mayor Hudgins, a courtly older gentleman I'd known all my life, gave me a where-are-your-manners-young-lady look, which I totally ignored. I pulled Denny along through the crowd and onto the unoccupied front porch. While I was still catching my breath Esme came out, shutting the door behind her.

"Okay," I said, "just listen. I don't know what any of this

means and I'm still trying to put it all together." I launched into a series of seemingly unconnected information and to Denny's credit he listened raptly though I knew I sounded totally manic.

"First off, Vivian is wearing a string of pearls. One string. Second, Vivian's birth name is Pearce. Not rare, but not common with that spelling. I've seen that name in the Pritchett family papers somewhere, I just can't think where." I banged my head with the flat of my palm a couple of times hoping it would dislodge the information and dispense it like a vending machine, but no such luck. "Third," I went on, "Jeremy's got a secret, but I don't think it has anything to do with Dorothy's murder. Fourth, Vivian and Linda both drive dark-colored SUVs. And they both have dark hair and similar builds. I think maybe it was Vivian that Hank Spencer saw taking bags out of an SUV that afternoon. That alters the timeline. Vivian and Dorothy had argued the night before about the decorations for the open house and Dorothy had sent Vivian back to the drawing board—I mean literally. She sent her back to do new sketches. But Linda remembers Vivian's sketchbook being in the kitchen when she came back from her errands that next evening—the evening when it happened."

"Maybe she used a different sketchbook?" Denny offered.

Esme held up a hand. "Let her go," she said, "Sophreena's on a roll. We'll sort out the details later."

I prattled on a while longer, recalling some of the weird exchanges I'd had with Vivian over the past week. "Something is off here," I said. "I'm not accusing Vivian of anything, but something's just not right."

"Even if I agree," Denny said, "that's not enough to warrant questioning her here and now."

"I'll talk to her then," I said.

"No," he answered. "You can't do that."

"Why not? I'm not the police."

"But you'd be acting as an agent of the police if I asked you to do it, and that could taint the case."

"So, you're telling me *not* to talk to her?" I asked.

"Yes, that's exactly what I'm telling you," Denny said.

"Perfect," I said, making for the door.

twenty-two

from her audience. She was not pleased and tried to blow me off, but I leaned in close and whispered, "Vivian, I *know*. And I have the evidence."

I knew squat, of course. I had tons of questions and few answers, but I figured this would get her attention.

She stared right into my eyes and I thought she was going to tell me—nicely, in deference to the dignitaries present— to bug off. But then a strange smile spread across her face. She excused herself and hustled me off to Dorothy's private study at the back of the house. I felt like I was being hauled into the principal's office.

When she'd closed the door she wheeled on me. "Okay, tell me. Tell me what you've found."

That was the exact moment when I realized I'd acted in haste. Both Denny and Esme had tried to stop me, but I'd ignored them. I was still working my mental puzzle box and I hadn't gotten to the secret compartment that would reveal all just yet. I tried a stall.

"I know about *you*," I said. "I finally found the evidence."

And there was that odd smile again. "You did?" she said, sounding more amazed than scared. "Maybe I underestimated you. What did you find? Is it solid?"

"Solid enough," I said, all bravado. "It'll hold up."

"In court?" Vivian asked.

"Definitely," I said. "If that's where it ends up."

"Oh, I don't think it will," she said. "What would be the point? You know, when Dorothy decided to hire you and Esme I was elated. You two had such good reputations. And Dorothy was convinced that would be the best way to do it. Or so she said. Now I think maybe it was a test."

"A test?" I repeated, hoping my hair didn't catch fire from the friction in my brain.

"Yes. After all, if you two couldn't turn up the evidence when you were actually researching the family, what were the odds that anyone else would stumble across it?"

"Very slim, I suppose," I said, still playing for time. Things were clicking into place: Vivian urging us repeatedly to be thorough in our research, her insistence that I, *of all people*, should have understood her relationship with Dorothy, her odd reaction when she'd overheard us talking about Winston's ancestor hiding his children in plain sight.

"Wow," I said softly as things began to mesh.

Vivian didn't hear. She was pacing now, her blue eyes glinting like ice crystals in winter sunshine. "I'll admit I despaired," she said, with a hiccup of a laugh. "I mean, I really, really despaired when you didn't find anything in all that time you were doing the research. That's when Dorothy insisted we go scientific about it. But in a way that was your doing, too."

"Was it? How so?" I asked, figuring if I could keep shooting Vivian open-ended questions she'd paint me the whole picture.

"Dorothy got the idea when you showed her that Civil War scrapbook you found. The one Harrison Pritchett's mother kept. When she saw the envelope with the baby's hair in it she insisted that was how we needed to do it. She'd read somewhere that if you had hair with the root on it you could get DNA. Course, now we know that didn't work. Or maybe the lab wasn't any good. But, no matter, you've come through finally. I've tried to dig out the information myself. I searched through every inch of the attic trying to find something you two might have missed, but I had no luck at all."

That explained the disheveled state of High Ground's attic. And now I realized why the list in Vivian's sketchbook had looked familiar. It was the same handwriting as the list from the small notebook Ingrid has assumed was mine. The one that read: *birth certificates, handwriting samples, bank statements, letters*. The tidbits were adding up and finally the secret compartment sprang open.

"So what's the evidence you found? Come on, tell me," Vivian said, bouncing on the balls of her spike-heeled shoes.

"I will, I'll get to that," I lied. "But first let me ask you, how long did your mother work for William Pritchett?"

Vivian fluttered her hands together. "You did find it!" she said, clapping like an excited kid. "Okay, well, obviously long enough for the two of them to fall in love," she said, her voice taking on a dreamy tone. "I mean I know it was wrong, William was a married man, but only technically. His wife was feeble and wasn't able to meet his needs. And anyway, the heart wants what it wants. And his heart wanted my mother."

"Did she want *him*?" I asked.

"Well, I certainly can't see why she wouldn't have," Vivian said. "He was the most prominent man in town. He was a Pritchett. But my grandmother said my mother was her own worst enemy sometimes. I wouldn't know about that, I never knew her."

"Is your mother deceased?"

"Yes, she drowned in a swimming accident the summer after I was born. My grandmother raised me. My mother was a beautiful woman. Did you find pictures of her?"

"No, no pictures," I said.

All I'd actually seen of Helen Pearce was her name in an account book for High Ground. She'd been the country girl William Pritchett had hired to take care of the house and little Ingrid. The one who hadn't lasted long on the job. Apparently Vivian's mother had been either convinced or coerced into taking care of other things for William Pritchett as well.

"Did you always know William was your father?" I asked.

"Oh heavens, no," Vivian said. "I would *never* have been able to keep that secret. I mean, I always sort of wondered why my grandmother would take me over to High Ground every month or so. But when I asked she'd just say we were going to pay our respects and to visit her friend Mr. Pritchett. He would talk with me and ask about school and everything then send me off to play with Ingrid. I had no idea why he took an interest in me. And he supported me financially. I never knew at the time, but my grandmother got an envelope of cash every month for my expenses right up until I went off to college. He cared for me."

Not enough to publicly acknowledge you as his daughter, I thought. And an envelope of cash sounded more like hush money. Then I remembered the letter I'd found in William Pritchett's papers, the one instructing his lawyer that "the child in question" had reached the age of majority and there'd be no more disbursements. He hadn't been referring to Ingrid, it was Vivian he was dropping. Sheesh, William Pritchett had shed *two* daughters. Daddy dearest.

"So when did you know?" I asked.

"Not until last year when my grandmother took ill. She told me the whole story right before she died. Dorothy and I were both ecstatic. We'd been such good friends for so long and then to find out we were actually sisters was just thrilling for *both* of us."

I had serious doubts about that. I could not imagine Dorothy being happy about such a claim. No matter how it was framed it was not a pretty story. In Dorothy's world this would have been ruinous. A huge blot on the hallowed Pritchett name. Tacky, indeed.

"And that's when Dorothy decided to hire Esme and me?" I asked.

"Yes," Vivian said. "She said we couldn't just come out with it with no proof. She said Ingrid might raise a stink, saying we were up to something about the estate, or people might think we were making it all up for publicity or something. I was never clear on her reasoning, but she was very insistent it had to come from someone else."

"Like Esme and me," I said.

"Yes, I'm sure she thought you two would find the proof. Strange that you didn't. I mean if you're so good at what you do you'd think you would've found out something before now."

Not if William Pritchett covered his tracks, I thought, but did not say aloud. And not if we hadn't been specifically asked to look into it, which Dorothy definitely had *not* asked us to do.

"It's tricky," I said. "It wouldn't be likely we'd stumble across something like this in public records, Vivian. It required a more focused search."

"That's why I think it was a test. A test you failed before," she said, wagging a finger at me, "but you've redeemed yourself. Now I just can't stand it anymore, Sophreena. You've got to tell me what you've found. Is it good enough for me to go ahead with the announcement today? That was the original plan, to make an announcement at the open house."

"To introduce *you* as the newest member of the Pritchett family," I said, remembering the list in Vivian's sketchbooks and that last entry with the heart drawn beside it. Vivian, not Cassidy, as the newest Pritchett.

"Yes, yes," Vivian said. "Do you want to be there with me? I wouldn't mind. You've earned it. Where do you think we should do it? I think out on the lawn. Say in maybe half an hour?" She consulted her watch. "I'd like to do it while most of the guests are still here."

Maybe I'm slow, but only then did I realize Vivian had gone all the way to Crazy Town. She began pacing, wringing her hands. Her eyes had a feverish glint and her smile was demented.

I looked up to see Esme and Denny outside the window on the wraparound porch just out of Vivian's line of sight. Esme gestured to ask if I wanted them to come in. I mouthed a no and slipped my phone from my jacket pocket. I switched on the recording function and while Vivian had her back turned I nudged it behind a framed photo on Dorothy's desk where I hoped it could pick up both our voices.

"The lawn would be perfect," I said. "But we'd better get our ducks in a row before we go out there. We don't want anything to be contested, right?"

"Contested?" Vivian said, stopping in her tracks. "You said you had proof. Proof that would hold up in court."

"Yes, but you know how people can be. This needs to be irrefutable."

"You sound just like Dorothy," Vivian said. "That's why she decided DNA was the way to go. She said nobody could argue with DNA. Well, I can certainly argue with it."

"Let me make sure I'm clear on everything," I said. "Dorothy had your DNA tested against her grandfather Harrison Pritchett's using his baby hair from that Civil War–era scrapbook? Why didn't she just have her own DNA tested with yours?"

"She got it into her head that it had to come from a male ancestor. That's not true, is it? But she said since we had different mothers that wouldn't be solid proof. And she didn't have anything of her father's—of *our* father's—they could test. Then you two showed her that memory book and the light bulb went off." She lifted her arms and waggled her hands above her head and laughed crazily.

"And your DNA didn't indicate kinship?"

"Well, are you surprised?" Vivian said as if I were the class dunce. "I mean, that poor little twist of hair was more than a century old. Honestly, I don't know what Dorothy was thinking." Suddenly Vivian's smile was gone and she turned on me, her eyes narrowed. "Why are you asking about all that?"

"Just nailing everything down," I said, deciding I'd best switch tactics if I wanted to keep her talking. "Those are beautiful pearls, Vivian. I meant to tell you that earlier."

Her hand flew to her neck and she caressed the beads, the faraway look returning. "They're the Pritchett family pearls. I'm so glad I wore them today. I almost didn't. As I said, I was despairing. But now it's so appropriate."

"When did you get them?" I asked, cheerfully.

"Dorothy left them to me in her will. She left me several of our Pritchett family heirloom pieces."

Vivian's voice had changed. She sounded exactly like Dorothy.

"I thought Dorothy's pearl necklace had three strands," I said.

"Well, yes, but that really didn't suit me. It was a little old-fashioned," she said, wrinkling her nose. "I prefer this tasteful single strand."

I looked up to see both Esme and Denny gesturing urgently, and held up a wait-a-minute finger while pretending to adjust my hairpins.

"Vivian, when did Dorothy tell you about the DNA results?" I asked, trying to keep her talking.

"I don't quite remember," Vivian said, frowning. "I was a little mad at her about it. I mean, it would've been obvious to anyone the results meant nothing, but she acted like it was the be-all and end-all. Final answer!" She laughed then trailed off with a hum.

"Was Dorothy pleased with your sketches for the open house?" I asked, hoping the non sequitur would keep her talking.

Vivian looked off into the mid-distance and smiled. "She *loved* them," she said. "We had a few creative differences about it in the beginning, but she loved what I came up with in the end."

"When did you show that second set of drawings to her?" I asked. "Did you bring them over that night? Linda remembers seeing your sketchbook here."

"Linda needs to learn that I can put my sketchbook anywhere I please in this house," Vivian said, her voice tight, then the blissed-out smile returned. "Dorothy was really happy with my plans for the party. She said being an event planner was my true calling. She said I was the best event planner around."

Vivian fell silent and crooked her head to one side, a confused look on her face. "No, wait, that's not exactly what she said." She narrowed her eyes then went on haltingly. "She said I should be *satisfied* with being the best event planner around." Her frown deepened and she rubbed her temples. "That's not the same thing at all. She said I should never have bought into my grandmother's delusions about me being a Pritchett." Vivian repeated the word as if it were foreign to her. She turned toward me, but I didn't think she was seeing me anymore. "Delusions," she repeated again. "That's what Dorothy said. Well, my grandmother was the best woman who ever lived and she was *not* deluded."

She sat down hard in Dorothy's office chair. "Dorothy said I simply wasn't Pritchett *material*. Oh, she *claimed* she was sorry the results had come back negative." Vivian was crying now, oblivious to the tears running off her chin. But there were no histrionics; she was dead calm. "But she wasn't sorry. Dorothy wasn't sorry at all. She was gloating."

I stayed perfectly still, afraid any noise or movement might break the spell.

"I loved Dorothy," Vivian went on, her voice hollow and eerie. She got up and walked toward the window. "But she could be so mean sometimes."

I flapped my hands, so fast I must have looked like a hummingbird, to signal Esme and Denny to move out of sight as Vivian walked so close to the window her nose was almost touching the pane. She stared out, lost in another time and place.

"I loved Dorothy like a sister, and she loved me, too. I know she did," she said. "But we had our disagreements. Sisters do that. I mean, look at Dorothy and Ingrid; they fought all the time. And they were full sisters, not just half. Dorothy could be difficult. Well, you know that. Everybody knows that."

Several strands of hair had worked loose from her carefully coiffed chignon and mascara streaks had run down each cheek, giving her the look of a harlequin waking from a fretful sleep.

"Dorothy didn't mean half the things she said," she went on. "But a person shouldn't say things they don't mean. She said I had to face the hard truth that I wasn't a Pritchett. She said if you and Esme didn't find proof no one else would ever be able to find anything that would uphold my grandmother's claim. And she said if I ever said anything publicly she'd bring out the DNA evidence to prove I wasn't a Pritchett and I'd be a laughingstock. She said she didn't want to see me go through that. She *pitied* me. Well, I didn't want her pity. I wanted her to be quiet. She wouldn't let me think. I begged her to just be *quiet*. I grabbed at her and got hold of the pearls and pulled, and twisted. She tried to slap me and I pulled harder and harder. We struggled and the pearls broke. All but this last strand," she said, fingering the pearls at her neck. "It was strong, like me. The rest scattered. I had to find them all. I had to pick them up one by one. But these pearls, they held. Aren't they beautiful? These are the Pritchett pearls. They've been in my family for generations. *My* family. I have every right to them because I *am* a Pritchett. I won't give them back." She looked around the room wild-eyed as if someone was coming to take them from her.

"Vivian," I said, softly. "What happened to Dorothy when you grabbed at her and got hold of the pearls?"

She turned toward me, her eyes big as proverbial saucers, her cheeks ruddy. "She was quiet," Vivian whispered. "Dorothy was finally, for once in her life, without an opinion. She was quiet. Poor Dorothy. I think maybe I killed her."

I motioned for Denny and Esme to come on the double, hoping against hope my phone battery had held out.

twenty-three

"IF I WASN'T STUCK IN THIS CAST I'D GET UP AND DANCE," Winston said, tapping the arm of his lawn chair along to the music of a bluegrass band, his baroquely illustrated cast propped up on the picnic basket.

"So we're saved from that spectacle," Esme said. "You just enjoy the music and I'll enjoy this éclair you brought." She popped the last gooey bite into her mouth.

We'd staked out our picnic spot on the town square early in the morning while other good citizens of Morningside were still in church. We'd found a spot where a row of fir trees on one side and the fountain on the other gave us some privacy.

"This has been the best Honeysuckle Festival ever," Coco said. "And boy, were we all due for some fun. I know it's only been a couple of days but I'm still in shock about Vivian. Do you think she really didn't remember killing Dorothy? Was that an act or had she actually blocked it out?"

"I don't know what to think," I said. "It seemed genuine to me, but as Esme reminds me constantly, I can be gullible."

"I hear she's going for a mentally ill defense," Marydale said.

"In North Carolina it's not guilty by reason of insanity," Esme said. "Pretty strict standard." She passed a container of finger sandwiches to Jack, who helped himself to three.

"Well, listen to you," Coco said, "you'd think you've been hanging out with a member of law enforcement or something."

"Y'all are the ones who ragged on me to get out and have fun," Esme said.

"It's strange about Vivian and Dorothy," Marydale mused. "I think they really did care about each other. But it was a peculiar relationship all along. And adding in Vivian's discovery that she'd been the child kept hidden all her life, denied the Pritchett name and any part in the life Dorothy had? Well, if Vivian really did just snap I feel sorry for her."

"I'm not so generous," Winston said. "The more I think on it the more sure I am she was the cause of me falling off that ladder. I *know* that ladder was steady before she decided to come over and hold it for me. Me and Linda were talking and Linda was getting a little emotional, telling me some things about the night she found Dorothy. I think Vivian was afraid of what she might say. I'm not saying she meant for me to get hurt, but I think she wanted to get us off that subject any way she could."

"In that case I withdraw my sympathy," Marydale said.

"All this tragedy," Coco said. "All because of the Pritchett name. Vivian wanting it so bad and Dorothy thinking she had to protect it."

"The irony is *neither* of them was a Pritchett," Esme said, which caused all heads to whip around in her direction —except for mine. Esme and I had spent some time with Vivian's Aunt Anita the afternoon after she was arrested. And we'd spent hours that night combing through every piece of information we had. With that, plus the information Esme had gleaned from *elsewhere,* we'd finally put it all together. And what a tangled web it was.

"You know I told y'all Sarah Malone kept visiting me and flipping that baby quilt over again and again," Esme said. "I finally figured out what she was trying to tell me. Like they used to say back in the day, a baby was born on the wrong side of the blanket. An illegitimate child."

"She was trying to tell you about Vivian," Coco said.

"No, she was trying to tell me about her own son, William Pritchett, Dorothy and Ingrid's father," Esme said. "And Vivian's father, too, as it turns out."

Frowns all around as everyone ticked through what they could remember of the Pritchett family history. I jumped in to ease their strain. "Remember that Sarah Malone was a girl from the tidewater area who was sent to the big city of Richmond to live with the Spencer family? Not as a guest as Dorothy liked to tell it, but as a nanny to the two Spencer children. And remember that Agnes Spencer did not treat Sarah well and was resentful of the attention Sarah got from men? One of those men, presumably, was Agnes' husband, Raeford. We believe in one way or the other, either through seduction or force, Sarah became pregnant with his child."

"Force," Esme said.

"We don't know that for sure," I said. "We don't know any of this for sure, and there's obviously no documentation."

"Force, and I *am* sure," Esme said. "Got it straight from the woman in question."

"Okay," I said, "let's just say we couldn't prove it in *this* world."

Esme nodded. "Go on with your story."

"Anyway, Sarah was being wooed by Harrison Pritchett and it seems she returned his affections. It was a short courtship. They eloped and moved here to what was to become Morningside very shortly afterward. We think she was pregnant with Raeford Spencer's child."

"Do you think Harrison Pritchett knew?"

"He absolutely knew," Esme said.

"We *think* he knew," I corrected.

Esme huffed. "I know he knew," she said, lifting her chin.

"We believe he loved Sarah fiercely and wanted to rescue her from the situation she was in. He was her Sir Galahad. We know Harrison's friendship with Raeford Spencer ended at about that time. They quarreled bitterly and we think it was about Sarah. Agnes Spencer made reference to that in her diary, but you have to read between the lines. I don't think she knew about Sarah being pregnant, but she knew something had happened. She wasn't at all sorry to see Sarah go."

"So, let me get this straight," Jack said. "William Pritchett wasn't really a Pritchett?"

"If our theory is correct, then no, he wasn't a Pritchett by blood," I said, "though Harrison raised him as his own. And since Harrison and Sarah had no children, that Pritchett bloodline ended with Harrison."

"Ah," Coco said. "So Harrison Pritchett's hair from the

baby book didn't match up with Vivian's because William wasn't his blood son."

"Correct. And Dorothy's wouldn't have either," I said. "Though if she'd chosen to run the test with her own hair against Vivian's that *would* have shown they were related— and maybe Dorothy would still be alive."

"That's assuming Dorothy ever intended to tell her the truth if it came back a match," Winston said. "Or that she even had the hair tested in the first place. Do you think maybe she was just bluffing?"

"No, I found the test report in her desk," I said. "Jeremy had seen the envelope with the baby hair in her study and Denny and I went looking for it after the excitement was over. When Linda overheard them arguing the night before she thought it was about hairstyles, but it was actually about the test results from the hair. Vivian was afraid it wasn't going to come back in time for the Founders' Day event, but Dorothy'd already had it in her possession for days. She must have been trying to figure out how to tell Vivian and she'd arranged one of her formal sit-down meetings to break the news."

"Oh, oh, oh," Jack said, scrambling to a sitting position from where he'd been lounging on the picnic blanket. "I got it. Okay, so those coffee cups they tested for DNA. It *was* from a male relative of Dorothy's. Hank Spencer. They'd be related, right?"

"They'd be related," I said. "They shared a common male ancestor."

"So this happened two generations in a row?" Marydale asked. "The head of the household and the nanny? That's just revolting."

"History repeats," I said with a shrug. "But this shame isn't on the Pritchetts. By all accounts Harrison Pritchett was a principled man. And according to Vivian's aunt, when Harrison and Sarah figured out what was going on with William they were the ones who insisted he support Vivian financially and that he look out for her welfare. They weren't willing to go so far as to publicly ruin him, or themselves by extension, but the aunt says Harrison made some sort of arrangement that insured William would live up to his obligations to the girl or else he'd forfeit part of the estate to her and her grandmother."

"I can only imagine how conflicted Sarah must have felt," Marydale said, "knowing her son had done to someone else the same thing that had been done to her."

"The circumstances weren't quite the same," I said, "though it's still a sordid story. Vivian's aunt was very frank with us. She says Vivian's mother went into the job with the Pritchetts looking for a way to make it her meal ticket. She's convinced Helen Pearce set out to seduce William Pritchett from the start. But afterward it didn't go as she'd planned. The aunt thinks Helen suffered from postpartum depression, plus the disappointment of having her big plan derailed when William made it clear he wasn't going to do the honorable thing after Dorothy and Ingrid's mother died. She doesn't believe the drowning was an accident. She thinks Vivian's mother meant to end her life. It's all just so scrambled up and tragic."

"Much as I hate all this," Marydale said, "for Cassidy's sake I'm relieved Jeremy had no part in it. He was looking pretty sketchy there for a while what with that DNA stuff and him being so evasive about everything."

"Jeremy *is* harboring a secret," I said. "I'll tell you, but you are all hereby sworn to keep mum for a little while. You know he's a manager at the bank, but what you probably don't know is that the bank has a very strict anti-fraternization policy. Management and those in subordinate positions are not to date."

"It's a no-no," Esme stage-whispered.

"Anyway, there's a woman named Sherry in my yoga class and a couple of weeks ago I overheard her telling a friend that she was seeing someone seriously, but that she couldn't say who just yet. Her friend asked if she was involved with a married guy but Sherry swore that wasn't it. Did I mention Sherry works at the bank as a teller?"

Heads began to nod.

"He was with Sherry that day," I said. "They really were out taking sunset photos at the lake. But Jeremy wants to keep his job so he couldn't very well say anything or show the pictures since she was in them. Sherry's going to quit her job and go back to school as soon as she gets enough money saved, then they can be together out in the open, but until then we're all guardians of the big secret." I grabbed an apple from the bowl in the middle of the blanket. "Now, no more about Dorothy or the case. Today's for fun. Can we please talk about good stuff?"

"I got something," Jack said. "I landed a new client. I've been wining and dining the guy for a couple of weeks now. He's building a new condo complex on the west side of the golf course and he's given us the contract for all the land-scaping."

"That's fantastic," Coco said, giving him a high five.

"Yeah, that's who I was with when you called the other night, Soph. Sorry I never got back to you. He wanted to drive out to the site and discuss some things and I got caught up and forgot to call you back."

"That's okay," I said. An employment opportunity I could easily forgive.

"Esme, I think somebody's looking for you," Coco said, pointing to the middle of the square.

We all looked over to see Denny scanning the crowd. He spotted us and nodded his head in greeting.

"He's only got a couple of hours off duty," Esme said, getting up from her chair. "I think we'll go stroll around the festival for a bit."

As I watched them walk away, laughing together about something, I told myself if this got serious I wouldn't be los-ing Esme, I'd be gaining a cop.

"We should go check out the crafts booths, too," Jack said, getting up off the blanket and offering me a hand. "Any-body else game?"

"I've gotta go get my parents and bring them in to enjoy the festivities for a little while," Coco said. "I'll get up with y'all later."

"I'm game, but I don't think this thing is," Winston said, tapping his cast with a spoon. "Y'all go on, I'll be fine right here."

"I'll keep you company," Marydale said. "Roxie's watching

the shop for a couple of hours. I was there at six this morning getting everything ready and I'm tuckered. I'll enjoy just chillin' here with Win and the pups. You two go on."

As we walked across the square I got lots of stares. I knew the word was out and this time I was being hailed as a hero, the one who'd gotten Vivian to confess and solved the case. I didn't deserve that any more than I'd deserved the suspicious looks I'd gotten just after Dorothy died. I tried Esme's advice and looked straight ahead, ignoring it all, knowing it would blow over in a few days.

The last couple of weeks had been awful but I'd learned some valuable lessons. One of which was what can befall a friendship when one person wants what they can't have from it. I was going to have to find a way to accept Jack and Julie's relationship if I wanted to keep his friendship, and I needed to start now. As sincerely as I could manage I asked, "What's Julie up to today?"

"Working, I suppose," Jack said. "This is a hot story, she'll be all over it."

"That's good, I guess. But it's too bad you two probably won't be able to see each other very often for a while. Between your new job and her being caught up in this story, that doesn't leave much time for dating."

"Dating?" Jack said. "You think Julie and me are dating?"

"Well? Aren't you?"

"No, we're not," Jack said. "I took her out a couple of times to get information for you and Esme," he said. "And she was in town a lot covering the story, so we kept running into each other, but we're not dating. She'd drive me nuts. I love her as a friend, but she's really high maintenance. I'm not saying anything I wouldn't say to her face; she knows she's a handful. That's what makes her a good reporter, I guess. But we're just old college friends."

"Friends like us," I said, almost giddy with relief.

"No, Soph, not friends like us," Jack said. "Nobody's friends like us." He looped his arm around my shoulders and gave me that smile I like so much.

Coco was right. Best Honeysuckle Festival *ever*.